BY WENDY HEARD

YOU
CAN
TRUST
ME

YOU CAN TRUST ME

A NOVEL

WENDY HEARD

BANTAM
New York

You Can Trust Me is a work of fiction. Names, characters, places, and incidents are either the products of the author's imagination or are used fictitiously. Any resemblance to actual persons, living or dead, events, or locales is entirely coincidental.

Published in the United States by Bantam Books, an imprint of Random House, a division of Penguin Random House LLC, New York.

Bantam Books is a registered trademark and the B colophon is a trademark of Penguin Random House LLC.

Library of Congress Cataloging-in-Publication Data
Names: Heard, Wendy, author.
Title: You can trust me: a novel / Wendy Heard.
Description: New York: Bantam Dell, 2023.
Identifiers: LCCN 2022058260 (print) | LCCN 2022058261 (ebook) | ISBN 9780593599310 (hardcover) | ISBN 9780593599327 (ebook)
Subjects: LCSH: California—Fiction. | LCGFT: Novels.
Classification: LCC PS3608.E258 Y68 2023 (print) | LCC PS3608.E258 (ebook) | DDC 813/.6—dc23/eng/20221209
LC record available at https://lccn.loc.gov/2022058260
LC ebook record available at https://lccn.loc.gov/2022058261

Printed in the United States of America on acid-free paper

randomhousebooks.com

2 4 6 8 9 7 5 3 1

First Edition

Book design by Alexis Capitini

For everyone who was born restless.
May you find joy (since you will never find peace).

I could not help it:
the restlessness was in my nature.
—CHARLOTTE BRONTË, *JANE EYRE*

YOU CAN TRUST ME

SUMMER

SAN FRANCISCO

I learned to pick a pocket when I was about eight.

I was panhandling with my mother and two of her interchange-ably bohemian friends at the Embarcadero in San Francisco. While they sat cross-legged beside a handprinted sign that read, "The light in me honors the light in you," my job was to scope out the tourists and approach likely donors with a sad little wave. "I'm sorry, excuse me, I was just wondering if you could spare any change for my mother and me," I'd say in a trembling, timid voice, like this was the first time I'd done this, like we were embarrassed to be reduced to panhandling.

I approached this one woman, a middle-aged white lady with her husband in tow, thinking she looked like someone's grandma and would probably be a good mark. Adult me would warn kid me—this type of woman is not to be approached.

"I'm so sorry, but could you spare any change for my mom and me?" I asked, smiling sheepishly and presenting my collection tin.

She stopped walking and stared down at me, lips pinching together. "Where is your mother?"

Thinking she wanted proof that I wasn't alone, I pointed back to where my mom was in Buddha pose by her namaste sign, eyes closed, lips curved upward in a faint smile. She was meditating, focusing on manifesting what we needed today, which was two hundred dollars. Her friends languished beside her, sharing a joint and calling out "Peace" to the passersby.

The fake grandma took me by the arm, marched me through the throngs of tourists, and presented me to my mother. "Excuse me. Is this your daughter?"

Her hazel eyes flew open and flicked between me and the lady holding my arm. "She is," my mom replied, ever calm.

"How dare you have her begging for your drug money! What is wrong with you? I should call the police."

I felt my stomach drop out of my gut and onto the floor. The police were our biggest fear. My mom's friends exchanged a worried glance, but she just cocked her head and studied the woman.

"We're truly sorry to have upset you," my mom said. "She offered to help. I thought it was a nice gesture, and I felt badly discouraging it." She could be like this: well spoken, reminding me that she'd gone to school, something she didn't make me do. "The world is your school," she always told me, but the world wasn't going to teach me to read, so I stole books and learned from them on my own.

The woman glowered down at her. "She should be taken away from you. You can't raise a child like this."

Panicked and angry, I wrenched my arm out of her grip. In the twisting motion, I noticed the twenty-dollar bill sticking partway out of the back pocket of her khaki pants, folded into a store receipt.

My mother stood, the soft cotton of her long skirt billowing around her ankles. She was a lovely woman, her honey-colored hair wavy to her waist, her light tank top silky around her loose breasts. "May I pray for you?" she asked. "We're going through a hard time, but it seems like you may be going through something as well."

The woman's face was shocked, hurt, and then something totally unexpected—tears sprang to her eyes and her face flushed bright red.

"You may *not*," she hissed. She turned her back and stormed off.

With no adults looking, my hand snaked over, pinched the twenty, and as she walked away, it slipped out of her pocket and into my hand.

And so I learned my first lesson about pickpocketing: The target must be distracted, and the friction of the item leaving their pocket must blend in with the friction they feel from movement. Pickpocketing requires empathy, knowing how it feels to be in someone's body, even the micro things like how their pants fit around the hips, how their purse slings across the chest.

My mom didn't notice. She was sitting back down, arranging her skirt.

I palmed the twenty. I could hide it, buy things with it, save it for the inevitable rainy day when our van broke down in the middle of nowhere and my mom decided to suddenly realize that the universe does not in fact provide things like mechanics.

I shoved it deep into my pocket. It was mine.

CHAPTER ONE

SUMMER

LOS ANGELES
TUESDAY, JUNE 6

The line for this abominable Hollywood nightclub is ten miles long. Twentysomethings crowd together, passing vape pens back and forth as bouncers survey the queue and beckon the prettiest people to the front. *Good.* For my purposes, the bigger the crowd and the more exclusive the venue, the better.

I bypass the line and give the bouncer a pretty smile. He looks me up and down and unclips the red velvet rope. It's not just my ass that's getting me inside; the last time I was here, I slipped him a Benjamin. Sometimes you have to spend money to make money. "Have a nice time," he says.

"Thanks." I stroll through the darkened hallway, pay the cover charge, and present my ID to a woman behind a little glass window. Music thumps from within like a heartbeat.

My phone buzzes in my purse while my wrist is getting stamped. It's Leo. *Going in. Wish me luck!* The words are followed by a money bag emoji and a photo of the stairwell leading to the rooftop hotel bar we cased out together. She's downtown tonight, a handful of traffic-clogged miles away from me.

I reply, *You got this.* I think she's nervous. I've tried reassuring her; we all have unlucky streaks. She'll feel better when she has cash in hand, a feeling I relate to on a soul-deep level. Money is security. Money is doctor appointments, gas in the tank, food—and we're running low.

I take my ID back—I'm moonlighting as someone named Claire tonight—and stow it in my bra. My car key is a hard little lump beside the license. I never keep my key in my purse. You can't tell what might happen to the things you're carrying.

I pull the nightclub door open. Warm, steamy air blasts into my face along with an assault of "Smack That" by Akon. I cringe, remembering the theme tonight is early aughts. The club smells like booze, cologne, and sweat. I stroll through the room, getting oriented. On the left are bottle service tables, a series of booths partitioned off with velvet ropes. Ahead is the double-sided bar with bartenders working frantically, arms flashing. Cocktail waitresses dart back and forth, graceful little hummingbirds sipping from flowers.

On the right is the packed dance floor, a bearded DJ presiding over it like a cult leader. My eyes follow the walls out of habit, locating the restrooms and the door that leads to the back room and service exit. I bypass dancers and tuck myself into a corner to take stock. The crowd is mostly early twenties and stupid rich, which is of course why I chose this club. I was tipped off by some UCLA students, and I can see in a single glance that tonight will be worth my time.

A smile creeps across my face. I didn't realize how much I've been worrying about our little dry spell until now. All my energy had been used to reassure Leo.

I take fifteen minutes to select my people. It helps to nickname them—an old memory trick a veteran salesman taught me—so I work up a mental list that includes Yacht Chad (spiky blond hair, expensive boat shoes, drunk); Tennis Chad (looks like Yacht Chad but with brown hair); Fitness Amber, who's trying to twerk while drinking her weight in Long Islands; and Med Student Jen, who's going to be really bummed when she realizes she lost her ID but who looks enough like me to be my younger sister.

I move to a corner near the bar and stroll back and forth until I catch one of the cocktail waitresses logging in to the point-of-sale terminal. Heidi, employee number 120801. Perfect.

The DJ pivots to "Milkshake" with a vengeance. The crowd cheers drunkenly, and the college girls turn around so the boys can grind up on their L.A.-toned butts.

I slip along the perimeter of the club and let myself into the ladies' room. Inside, someone is vomiting in the handicapped stall. I lock myself into the smaller stall and pull off my black dress. Underneath, I'm wearing a crop top with a deep V-neck and a pair of butt-cheek-baring booty shorts. Two bras have my cleavage welling up to an almost comic degree. It's overkill; my chest is big enough. I can hear Leo's voice in my head, teasing me about it. But the more my boobs bust out of my shirt, the less anyone will look at my face. Speaking of which, I slide on a pair of nonprescription glasses, which will be another thing people notice instead of my features.

I pull my long hair into a tight bun to hide its length, which is distinctive—it falls thick and wavy to my waist. Anyone remembering me from tonight will recall four things: big butt, big boobs, glasses, brown hair in a bun.

I tie a small black apron around my hips and tuck a server's black folio into the front pocket. Finished with my look, I stuff my dress into my purse, which I hide among the toilet paper rolls under the sink, and freshen my lipstick in the mirror while the girl in the handicapped stall enters a fresh round of puking.

"You all right in there?" I call.

She gurgles something that sounds like "Go away," then coughs. Okay then.

I exit the bathroom and am back on the dance floor. We're onto Eminem now. Man, it's packed in here. There must be a thousand people in this confined space. This is going to be an amazing haul,

I can feel it. I let the anticipation flood my bones, and I find myself bouncing on the balls of my feet. A lifetime of this and it still gives me the same rush it ever did.

I have a rule: thirty minutes from this moment. In and out. It's enough time to get a good haul without being a fixture long enough to be memorable. I spot Heidi the cocktail waitress on the far side of the bar, looking harangued. She loads a bunch of drinks onto her tray and hurries off into the crowd.

It's time.

Smile.

I show some teeth, stick my chest out, and enter the crowd. A pair of guys hollers at me within three seconds. I snap my smile onto them, and they tell me they want two Sex on the Beaches. One of them tries to dance with me, and I laugh like it's hilarious. He gets too close, an arm around me, and starts dry humping me in the most ungainly way imaginable. I slide a hand behind him, remove his wallet with two quick fingers, flip it open with a thumb, pull the cash out, and slide it back into his pocket. The whole gesture takes three seconds. It's my trademark.

"Do you really want to order those drinks?" I'm yelling up at him, making sure my boobs are bouncing hypnotically. "Or are you just being funny?"

His words are slurred. "If I'm funny, will you go home with me? I wanna see you naked."

"A tempting offer." I slide the cash into my folio. It's just a few bills, but every night has to start somewhere. "Gotta get back to work, though. Have fun tonight! Be safe!" I slip away and continue toward the POS at the side of the bar. While the bartender's back is turned and Heidi is taking orders on the other side of the club, I type in 120801 and click on the mixed drinks screen. I know this software well. This is not my first rodeo.

I order some rounds of shots. While the bartender makes them, I navigate through the crowd, taking drink orders I don't have to write down and searching for my Chads, my Amber, my Jen. Yacht Chad is making out with an unfortunate brunette against a wall, and I help myself to the stack of cash he's been flaunting, returning his money clip with a few twenties still inside. He'll think he just overspent.

While the DJ revisits the magic of "Smack That"—I'm never listening to this song again—I wait for Heidi and the bartender to be distracted, grab a tray, and load up the shots I ordered. I take them through the crowd, selling them, collecting tips and cash from wallets one-handed. I'm better with my tray than Heidi is. *I should do this professionally,* I joke to myself.

Med Student Jen is in the corner trying to have an actual conversation with a woman who's way too drunk to track anything she says. Poor Jen. I strike up a friendly, screamed-above-the-music conversation. We make fun of the song, roll our eyes about the stupid guys here, and I gift them two Cokes I "happen" to have on my tray. Jen is relieved to be drinking something non-alcoholic, and her conversation partner is too drunk to tell if it's Coke or battery acid. During all this, I get my hand into Jen's purse, remove her wallet, hide it behind my back while I get out the license, and then replace it in her purse with her none the wiser. The ID is the most valuable thing I'll get tonight. I've been needing a new one badly. *Sorry sorry sorry,* I think to Jen as I walk away. It won't cost her anything but a trip to the DMV, but I still feel bad. The Robin Hood thing is only fun when you're stealing from rich assholes, not when you're stealing from a nice college student.

Oh, well. I needed an ID, and now I have one. I didn't create the world. I just live in it.

Fifteen minutes later, I'm almost ready to wrap. Tennis Chad's wallet is a great find and includes an American Express black card, and I get no less than seven credit cards from Fitness Amber. This is why it's important to study people before getting started; you can't always size someone up with a single glance. You have to watch them move through a crowd, analyze their wardrobe, their mannerisms.

My folio is fat with cash from wallets and drink orders (*sorry, Heidi, you're going to get in trouble when the books don't balance to-*

night), and I'm making my way back to the restroom when I see him. *Oh, shit.*

A uniformed officer is moving through the club alongside a plainclothes cop who is immediately recognizable as law enforcement for twenty different reasons. As I watch, frozen in horror, the plainclothes officer taps the shoulders of a pair of girls and leans down to speak with them. They pull IDs out of their purses and show them to him. He nods and moves on, beckoning to a group of college guys. They listen for a moment, then pull their wallets out.

He's doing spot checks, carding people.

I have no less than ten stolen credit cards, a thousand dollars, and a stolen driver's license in my server's folio, not to mention the fake ID in my bra.

The fear comes with an image of future Leo, waiting outside the downtown hotel for a ride that will never come, followed immediately by another image: Leo when I met her, homeless, scrawny, uncared for.

I back up, bumping into someone. "Hey," a male voice protests.

The uniformed officer lifts his eyes like he can feel my stare. Our eyes lock.

I flip the switch on a smile and ease back into the crowd. Once I'm hidden behind people, I spin and push through bodies, desperate to get out as quick as I can. "Hate cops hate cops hate cops," I find myself whispering. Suddenly, the guy who'd dance-humped me when I first came out of the bathroom is in front of me again. His face stretches into a rubbery grin. "You never got my Sex on the Beach."

"Not now." I try to push past him.

This pisses him off. "I said, you owe me a drink."

I survey the people around us. Drunk jock—no help to me. More drunk jocks—shit.

Think.

I reach forward and pinch the butt of the jock right in front of him. The guy spins, his face going Neanderthal. "What the fuck?" He steps forward, ready to fight.

"It wasn't me," Sex on the Beach guy protests, but I cry out in full girl-victim voice, "It was him! I saw him do it!"

The jock wheels on him, and the two go head-to-head, yelling and pushing each other into surrounding clubgoers. I risk a glance back at the cop, who's now focused on the fight and is on his way to break it up.

I zip away like a snake, fast as water, heading for the back door. This is exactly why I scout out all the exits in advance. On my way, I grab my purse out of the bathroom, and then I'm through a door marked Employees Only, in a white-tiled hallway, and two seconds later I'm in the alley behind the club. I hurry for the street, untying my apron as I go. I feel like they're chasing me, closing in on me. I won't be okay until I'm back in the safety of my truck, speeding away toward Leo as fast as the roads will allow.

CHAPTER TWO

LEO

TUESDAY, JUNE 6

I clutched the banister on my way up the hotel staircase, my knuckles white against the black wood. These sandal heels were pretty, but they should be a human rights violation. I got out my phone and texted Summer a photo of the stairwell ahead of me. *Going in. Wish me luck!* I added a money bag emoji for luck.

Her reply came quickly. *You got this.*

She was right. My last few attempts hadn't worked out, but tonight was going to be different. I took a deep breath. I needed to focus on the positive. It was a Tuesday night, and my heart was pounding adventure into my veins. Each time I did this, it was like visiting a new country. What would I discover? Where would the night take me?

I slipped my phone into my small, delicate purse, threw my shoulders back, and summoned my persona for the evening. Sweet, a bit innocent, a little shy. It had been ten years since I took theater in high school, but I still liked to imagine the characters I was playing. The one I used most often when working with rich men was the girl I was pretty sure all of them wanted: a young ingenue overwhelmed by the glamour an older, wealthy man could provide. As I envisioned her, I felt my facial expression soften, my eyes widen. Summer would approve. "Control his attention," she always told me. "Find out what he wants, then decide when he gets it."

I clipped up the stairs and through the arched doorway out onto the rooftop hotel deck. A bouncer stood at the entrance, a watchful look on his face. Behind him, the glass-surrounded area was classy and dark, the neon city sparkling below. Firepits dotted the space, and a pair of bars with dignified-looking, white-shirted bartenders had walls of bottles towering behind them.

I approached the bouncer. "Good evening," I murmured.

He raised his eyebrows. "Joining someone?" He was already opening the rope for me. That was L.A. They didn't care if you had a right to be anywhere as long as you looked like you did.

"Yes. My friend will be right behind me in a moment."

"Enjoy." His eyes lingered on my legs, and I moved past him with a *you're dismissed* attitude I thought appropriate to the setting.

My eyes roved, landing on a gathering of men seated on a sectional sofa near a large firepit. A beefy man in all black stood at the periphery of the group, searching the room with suspicious eyes— hired security. Seated, a group of Asian men in crisp suits listened with great intensity to a white man in his late forties with dark hair going gray at the temples, dressed down in an old Radiohead T-shirt and ripped jeans.

This was my mark: Michael Forrester, billionaire tech start-up guy, entrepreneur, UN climate ambassador, global philanthropist, blah, blah, blah. His accomplishments were boring, but his assets gave me seven billion reasons to find him fake-fascinating.

I let my eyes move past him. I could all but hear Summer in my ear, coaching me, cracking jokes as she did. We had different strengths. She did volume, clearing a room of cash in minutes. I played the long game, catching a big fish and keeping him on the line for a while before the release. Sometimes I made more than she did, but not usually. I was determined to change that with Michael Forrester. I'd never snagged a billionaire before. It was a new milestone.

But the main reason tonight had to be different was that we were broke. I had forgotten about some unpaid bills from way back in Fresno, and creditors had started stalking me. In the end, Summer had helped me pay them off and taught me about prepaying for everything. The guilt was eating me alive. It was hard enough for her to feed herself, but she'd taken me in, and I knew I'd been a burden.

But that was over now. In the spirit of manifesting, I took a deep breath and thought, *I am* going *to snag us this billionaire. I am* going *to pay her back. Our luck is turning around.*

I approached the bar, needing a drink in hand to dissuade all the scrubs from offering me liquor. Sure enough, I was no sooner at the bar than a young man with gelled hair and a cheap watch swooped in. "What are you drinking?"

I waved him off. "I'm good. Thanks."

He frowned and backed off with a muttered, "Bitch." I ignored this and signaled the sole female bartender.

"What can I get you?" she asked.

"Can you give me cold water in a martini glass with a twist?" I pulled a twenty out of my purse and slid it across the bar to her.

"Absolutely." She shook the water with ice in a martini shaker and handed it to me with a wink.

I approached the firepit where Michael Forrester was deep in conversation, right hand outstretched. It was cold; I didn't have to pretend. The black slip dress kept me as warm as a bathing suit, and the torture shoes left my feet basically naked. The moment I got close enough to warm up, the bouncer stepped toward me. "You need to do that somewhere else," he commanded.

I raised my eyebrows. "Um . . . no?"

He looked like he was enjoying pretending to be a real cop. "Miss, you need to move on."

I glanced back and forth between him and Michael Forrester's group. "Are you serious right now?"

He palmed my upper arm and tried to guide me away. "Let's go."

"Get your hands off me," I protested. "What is the matter with you?"

Forrester jumped up and put a hand on the bouncer's shoulder. "Hey, man, chill out. She's just cold." His voice was melodic, and I realized he was more handsome than I'd registered from his photos online, with beautiful, long-lashed blue eyes. His dark hair was attractively messy, giving him the look of an aging musician.

"Thank you," I said. "What's up with this guy? Does he work for you or something?"

"Not anymore." He gave the man a commanding flick of the hand. "Go home. Tell the agency to send someone else, someone who doesn't manhandle young women trying to warm up by a fire."

"I'm just doing my job," the bouncer protested.

"Out." His voice was so authoritative, I shivered.

The bouncer stormed away. Mentally, I gloated. I wished Summer could have seen this.

Forrester turned his eyes on me and smiled. "I'm so sorry. Would you like to go ahead and warm up now?" He made a sweeping gesture toward the fire and stepped backward, allowing me space.

"Thanks," I said shyly, making a show of being embarrassed by the attention. "I'm waiting for my friend and just thought I'd stand somewhere warm. I'm freezing." I waved a hand at my bare legs, my pedicured feet strapped into the delicate heels.

He followed my gesture with appreciative eyes. "By all means, feel free to wait here." He sat down on the couch and returned his attention to the businessmen, who were watching this exchange with impatience.

I sipped the fake martini. An older man in a beautifully tailored suit walked by me, eyes raking down my body, and I gave him a little smile. If I struck out with Forrester, I'd try him next. No way in hell was I leaving this bar without the lead I needed.

The businessmen and Forrester stood up. They all started shaking hands, and they moved away from the fire toward the entrance. *Shit*. They were leaving.

Had I failed?

I sank into the couch Michael had vacated and let my eyes rest on the tongues of flame.

Maybe I'd lost my touch. Maybe I didn't have what it took to live the life I'd signed up for. Despair gripped my gut. I needed to get my emotions under control. That's one of the first lessons I'd learned from Summer: Stay in the driver's seat, always.

The sentiment never rang true to me. It felt like a fool's errand. The universe piloted the ship, and we were all passengers. She dealt the cards, we played the game, and the house always won.

"Your friend didn't show up yet?"

I didn't have to fake the delighted smile that spread across my face. Michael Forrester was back, and clearly, he was back for *me*. "No, she flaked on me. Did I take your spot?"

"Not at all." He sat beside me and lifted his hands to the fire. "L.A. is funny. It's so hot during the day but the nights feel freezing. This temperature wouldn't bother me at all at home."

"And where is home?"

"Palo Alto."

"Ahhhh," I said. "You're a tech guy?" Like I hadn't memorized everything the internet had to offer on him.

He laughed. "Yeah, it all makes sense now, right? Why I'm dressed like a homeless person surrounded by Chinese investors?"

"No, it's not like that," I protested, but he nudged my shoulder in a friendly way.

"It's fine. I know what I am." He grinned, good-natured. He was *really* cute. He leaned closer. "Confession time. I think I recognize you. Are you an Instagram model?"

As though his liking my post wasn't exactly how he'd caught

my eye, I replied, "No. Just a regular person who takes way too many selfies."

"You're as beautiful as any model I've ever met."

The line was too smooth. I almost laughed at it. I raised my drink to my lips, but he reached out, took the hand that held it, and brought it to his nose.

"I knew it!" he cried. "Water. Why?"

I'd never had a man notice this, and I didn't have a ready answer. I went with the truth. "I don't drink. But if I don't have a glass in hand, a million men will try to sponsor me."

"And you don't want a sponsor?" The air between us felt suddenly hot.

I met his eyes. They were very blue. He was waiting with bated breath. I had him. He was a fish on the hook.

"I'm not saying I don't want to meet people. I just don't want to meet *them*." I waved a hand toward the bar.

He clearly liked this answer. "What's your name?"

When he smiled, I felt things. I remembered the businessmen, so captivated by him, and I understood. He could talk about any boring thing all night and I'd be interested. "Leo. Short for Leoneli."

His eyebrows shot up. "That's an unusual name."

I shrugged, having heard that a million times. "What's your name?"

"Michael."

"It's nice to meet you." I offered him a hand, and he took it, not shaking it but holding it for a long moment, thumb running softly across the knuckles. It gave me chills.

"Where are you from, Leo?" he asked, looking up from my hand into my eyes.

"A suburb of Fresno. It's not exciting, I know. Lots of cows, lots of open space. A river, though, which was cool."

He looked intrigued. "You're a country girl?"

"A little bit."

"What are you doing here?"

"Just meeting a friend for a drink. Same thing everyone else is doing here."

"No, I mean, what are you doing in L.A.? Are you looking to break into the industry?"

I laughed. "No way. Absolutely not."

"Well then, why?" He wasn't going to let it go. From his expression, I had the feeling he got answers to every question he asked.

"Why not L.A.? Why not anywhere?" I found myself grinning unrestrained, my too-wide smile that showed my crooked canine tooth. It was difficult not to be myself with him; he seemed so interested in me. Some men liked the idea of a spontaneous, bohemian girl as long as she didn't challenge them in the wrong ways. It was that manic pixie dream girl thing they purported to like until she had opinions or desires that conflicted with their own.

But that was fine. I wasn't in this douchey hotel bar to find true love. I was here to bring home the bacon. I was glad to be a sanitized dream girl if it paid the bills.

He sat back in the cushions and looked up at the sky. "Why not anywhere indeed," he murmured. "Do you know how much of my time I spend in, like, three different places? And then an assortment of hotels around the world where I never see the city I'm visiting. Tokyo looks like Hong Kong looks like Paris when you're in the same curated spaces."

I relaxed into the cushions and looked at the sky with him. There were no stars downtown, but two beams of light crisscrossed above us, then moved on, then came back together.

"Where are the three places you spend most of your time?" I asked.

Instead of answering, he turned to me, head resting on his hand. "I'm assuming you like to travel?"

"I just don't like being in one place too long, that's all."

He leaned in like I'd said the most interesting thing in the world. The tension between us was thick. I could reach out and touch it if I wanted.

This was my moment.

I pulled my phone out of my purse and checked the time. "I should go. It's getting late." I set my glass on the table and stood, making sure he got a good long look at my legs.

"You're leaving just like that?"

I tossed him a careless wave. "Have a good night, Michael. It was nice meeting you." I turned and left, and I could feel his eyes on me the whole way to the door.

CHAPTER THREE

SUMMER

TUESDAY, JUNE 6

I pull up to the curb by the hotel valet. Before the red-vested man can approach to see if he should park my Land Cruiser, Leo hurries out of the glass doors, saying something to him as she passes. He looks blindsided by her, which is a common reaction. It's fair; she is stunning tonight, all lean, tanned legs, brown hair brushing her collarbone, and smoky, billionaire-catching eyes. She lets herself into the passenger's seat and pulls the door shut behind her.

"How'd it go?" I ask.

She's glowing, face flushed. "Like shooting fish in a barrel."

"You all set for Round Two?"

"Yes, ma'am. And how was the club?"

I make a face as I pull into downtown traffic. "I'm getting too old for this shit."

She laughs her loud laugh, with her crooked canine tooth, and the polished veneer slips a little, the Fresno peeking through. "What's wrong, you tired of the Chads?"

"So tired. Ugh." I groan as yet another asshole in a BMW cuts me off on the one-way street I'm crawling down toward the 110 freeway. "I hate L.A.," I grumble.

"You are such a grinch tonight."

"I told you, I'm getting old." I'm only half joking. I think I'm about thirty-two—thanks to my nontraditional upbringing I have no clue when my actual birthday is—which makes me roughly six years older than Leo. I'm going to age out of my club thievery at some point, and then I'll have to figure out something else.

I contemplate this as I get on the freeway and head south. We sleep near the beach whenever possible. Leo chatters while I drive, telling me about her encounter with Michael Forrester.

"He's so much hotter in person," she's saying. "He's got this aging rock star thing going on. His *eyes!*"

"Maybe you should marry him," I suggest, grinning wickedly. "Have some babies, get alimony. Play the long game."

She cracks up. "Maybe *you* should have some babies."

I snort. "Sure. I'll raise them in my truck."

"It worked for you."

I point a finger at her. "I was raised in a van. Get it straight."

She puts her hands up in mock surrender. "Oh, I'm sorry." She starts unstrapping her shoes. "These heels are torture devices."

"But they worked."

"You should have seen this guy, staring at my legs." She cackles. "I'm going to slay him tomorrow in my bikini."

"He won't know what hit him." We're going to "run into" him on the beach in front of his hotel. From reading his interviews, Leo learned he goes jogging every evening, and when he's in L.A., he does his run on the beach in front of the hotel he always stays at.

Leo gets a napkin out of the glove compartment, pulls down the mirror, and starts removing her lipstick. "What was your haul?"

"Haven't looked yet. I almost got busted. There were cops checking IDs."

"Damn! But you made it out. That's what matters."

"Yeah, I left through the back." I reach down by my feet and retrieve the server apron. I toss it onto her lap. "Get a count for me, will you?"

She pulls out the folio. Organizing bills and credit cards, she murmurs numbers to herself. "You got an ID," she says happily. She knows I needed one. She holds it up. "Good one. She looks a bit like you. Younger, but no one will notice."

"Yeah, it'll work for clubs and stuff." I always keep a couple of identities going, one for the car in case I get pulled over, which is the expensive one because it needs to stand up to police scrutiny, and one or two stolen licenses I use for getting into clubs and bars. I have to rotate out the stolen ones pretty often; I'm worried about getting caught with them if the owner reports them missing.

I don't have an identity of my own, not a birth certificate, nothing. I was born in the back of a van and spent my childhood drifting from campsite to campsite with my mother. I thought I knew my date of birth because my mother had my astrological chart done a few times over the years, but when I was a teenager, I realized the charts all said different things. When I asked her about it, she confessed to not remembering. I don't have a last name. I don't even know my mom's last name, and I have no clue as to the identity of my father. As far as the world is concerned, I don't exist.

"Your cash haul is twelve hundred forty-nine dollars," Leo says. "And it looks like we're going grocery shopping tomorrow." She fans herself with the stolen credit cards.

I'm proud. This is my favorite feeling: money in my pocket, gas tank full, open road in front of me. "And we should pick up a couple of new outfits. We've been wearing the same three dresses for ages."

"Nice." She returns everything to the folio and leans back, propping her bare feet on the dashboard. Outside the windshield, the freeway glides by, headlights and taillights flames against the darkened road. "Malibu?" she suggests.

"Perfect."

We drive in silence, speeding along freeways to the Pacific Coast Highway, and then north with the ocean on our left. It's a

magnificent sight and one I never get tired of, the foamy break-
ers crashing against the deserted sand. I've spent a lifetime wearing a groove up and down the coast of California. It feels like I'm
already ashes scattered along the 655-mile PCH.

At the quiet northern end of Malibu, I do a U-turn and pull
onto the shoulder. It's a popular beach parking spot, and a few RVs
and vans are scattered along this stretch of road, one with lights
on, the rest dark for the night. I put the truck in park and take off
my seatbelt. "Want tea?"

"For sure."

We climb into the back, which is our little bedroom. Leo pulls
a plastic bin out from a corner, and I slide the camp stove out from
my side of the mattress. Outside, we flip the back hatch down and
set the stove up. Leo grabs a gallon jug of water from the truck,
and we boil some in our little teapot, then pour it into our favorite
mugs. We lay a blanket on the back hatch and perch on it to drink
our tea in comfortable, sisterly quiet. I shiver, but it's a pleasant
kind of cold, the kind that reminds me I'm outside, not stuck in-
doors, caged and contained.

The dark Pacific Ocean sails away to the horizon, glimmering
in the moonlight. The sound of cars flying by on the highway in-
termingles with the exhalation of waves, and I find myself taking
a huge, cleansing breath.

"We should go put our feet in the water before we go to bed,"
I tell Leo.

She's messing around on her phone, flipping through Instagram
while she absentmindedly sips her tea. "Ugh, look at this." She
turns the screen in my direction.

The photo is of a modelesque young woman posing in a bikini
on a rocky cliff. "What am I looking at?"

"This is my friend Anastasia. She's in Italy right now. You and
I would absolutely kill it over there. We'd have those guys wrapped
around our little fingers."

I take a moment to reply, frowning down at the phone. "Leo,
you know I can't leave the country."

"Sure you can. You just need to get your guy to do you a fake passport."

"And if it gets flagged in customs? I could go to jail." The idea of imprisonment makes my heart pound faster. I've never even lived in a house. I would lose my mind in prison.

"Then let's get you legitimized, find a lawyer to help. You can't be the only one in this situation. People are born in rural areas all the time without birth certificates."

"Leo, no." Shocked, I look straight into her face, trying to determine if she's serious. The phone lights up her features, turning her into a blue-faced apparition.

"Why not?" she challenges.

I don't know where to start. "I've spent my entire life doing petty crimes. Who knows what my fingerprints are on."

She sets the phone down, and her face goes shadowy. The wind picks up, whipping our hair around. "You're not a bank robber, Summer. You're a pickpocket. What could your fingerprints be on?"

"I've stolen other things, too," I remind her.

"But, like, shoplifting. You're not a murderer."

I search for other reasons. There are so many. "What about future crimes? If I have an identity, they can catch me."

"So don't commit violent crimes," she argues. "No one collects fingerprints from the scene of a pickpocketing."

My voice is rising in pitch and volume. "If I tell the authorities my situation, they won't believe me. I don't have anyone to vouch for my identity. For a thousand reasons, *no*."

She looks away from me, out at the ocean. "You're such a chicken."

I feel slapped by the words. "I'm a chicken who's kept herself alive for thirty years." *And who's helped* you, I want to add but don't.

She sinks into moody wordlessness, reading my mind, glaring out at the ocean, tea abandoned by her side. My insides ache. We've been traveling together for five years. She had a sister growing up, but I never had anyone who stayed this long.

Leo murmurs, "I'm bored, Summer."

"Bored?"

"We're in a rut. Get money, spend money, hide money, repeat; 101 freeway, Pacific Coast Highway, then go visit the woods. Arcata, San Francisco, Santa Barbara, L.A. Over and over again. You won't even go to Oregon. It's not that I don't appreciate you. I do. You've done so much for me. And I'm hoping with this Michael thing I'll be able to pay you back. I can't keep feeling like I'm constantly in your debt."

The words are like frostbite—they burn, they sting. "I don't know what you mean," I reply, so scared I almost can't think straight. Is she sick of traveling with me? Does she want to leave me? I'd be alone again. I can't stand it. I'm going to scream.

She says, "How long can you live like this? Aren't you claustrophobic?"

How can I explain it to her—California is my own body, its freeways and roads my arteries and veins. I'm no more claustrophobic in California than I am inside my own skin.

I gather my thoughts, turn toward her, and touch her on the arm. "This is my whole life, Leo. This is what it's always been."

"But it isn't what it has to be."

"It's all I have." My voice is low, a growl. "Some of us weren't raised in the suburbs—"

She yanks her arm away from me. "Don't even start." We sit in stiff tension for a full minute, and then she adopts a softer tone. "I know you're afraid."

"I'm not afraid," I protest. "I just don't want to settle down. I don't want four walls. I don't want hotels, apartments, a life on the grid. I thought you felt the same way."

"You *have* four walls." She knocks on the side of the Land Cruiser. "Your walls just travel with you. You're not that different from all those people out there." She gestures at the houses on the hills whose golden eyes observe the Pacific from afar.

"You can still go to Europe," I tell her, my voice tightly controlled. "After a few weeks with Michael Forrester, you'll be flush.

Why don't you fly to Italy and hang out with your friend for a couple of weeks?"

She nods, distant, sad. "Fine. I will."

Will you come back to me afterward? I want to ask. *Or will that be it?*

I know the answer. She's going to leave me. And I'll be alone. Again.

CHAPTER FOUR

SUMMER

SAN FRANCISCO
FIVE YEARS AGO

I was sitting across from a private detective named Mauricio, and he was showing me photographs of dead women.

"What about this one?" he asked, sliding an eight-by-ten across his black lacquer desk.

I examined it. The woman was the right age, in her late forties, fair-skinned with light hair. The morgue had a sheet draped across her chest, and her gaunt face was pinched in death, cheeks hollow. She had clearly been homeless; her skin was splotchy, hair a matted wreck, scarred hands dark with dirt, fingernails black.

"Not her," I managed through roiling nausea.

He studied me with apprehensive brown eyes. "You okay?"

"Fine. Show me the rest."

He pulled another photo out of the manila envelope. "This woman was found near Sacramento."

Her hair was too dark, her build too stocky. I barely glanced at it. "No. Next."

And so we continued. For three months, Mauricio had been

doing research for me all over California, searching for Jane Does from the last decade, looking for photographs, clues, anything that might match my mother's description. She had left fifteen years ago, when I was seventeen, and I'd been searching for her for the last two. That's how long it had taken me to stop being angry and start being worried.

At last, I was sufficiently traumatized and he was satisfied. We both sat back in our chairs.

"Do you want me to keep looking?" he asked. "At this point, I feel pretty confident that we'd have found her if she . . ." He trailed off.

"If she had ended up in a morgue in California," I supplied.

"Exactly."

I looked out the window. His tiny flat, which served as both living and working space, was in Lower Nob Hill, with a view. It was early evening, and the streetlights were blinking on.

"This was always a magical city to me," I told him. "I felt that anyone could belong here. No one was too weird, too different."

"I can understand that."

I couldn't breathe. I kept seeing those women I'd just looked at, dead and still, locked in the darkness inside a morgue drawer.

I was on the street moments later, having left Mauricio calling after me with concern. Was he worried about me or nervous I wouldn't keep employing him? He already had thousands of my dollars. And for what? Every lead he'd chased had led nowhere. My mom was either still alive or dead somewhere outside California. The possibilities were endless: Oregon, Nevada, Arizona. She could be buried in some forest, at the bottom of the ocean, or out in the desert.

I'd never find her. Not for the first time and not for the last, the lonely reality settled down on me, and I almost ran, trying to escape it. She had left me on purpose, and she'd told me she never intended to see me again. She wanted to be set free, and here I was trying to catch and cage her like a wild parrot. I had to let her go,

I had told myself a hundred times, but then I always ended up back here, handing Mauricio another thousand dollars.

Blind to the other pedestrians, I turned on Leavenworth and followed the dirty sidewalk, lit by garish signs. I came to a cluster of people stopping foot traffic and tried to circumvent them, but too many were coming in the opposite direction and I was stuck. What was the holdup? I looked over the shoulder of the guy in front of me. A young woman was sitting on the sidewalk, her back to a storefront, holding out a jar filled with change. In front of her was a sign, handwritten on a piece of torn cardboard: "Help people who can't help themselves." A few people had stopped to put dollars in her jar.

"Thank you," she said to each of them, dimpling a pretty smile. The tangle of people cleared, but the guy in front of me stayed put, looking down at her. "You want money?" he asked.

I had room to move past him now, but I waited. I didn't like the look of him: too preppy to be in the Tenderloin, probably here for sex work or drugs.

She smiled up at him. She was beautiful, with olive skin and messy brown dreadlocks. She was emaciated, obviously a long way from a place with regular meals. "Thank you," she told the guy. "Anything helps."

He took his wallet out of his back pocket. Holding it, he put his other hand on his belt and massaged his crotch. "I can think of a few ways you could earn some money." Sex work it was, then, apparently.

Her eyebrows came together in an expression that was half frown, half amusement. "So, what, you want me to, like, suck your dick right here on the sidewalk?"

I chuckled to myself. I liked her.

He glowered down at her. "We could go in the alley."

She glanced down at his crotch. "Do you include a finder's fee?"

I laughed out loud this time. She met my eyes and grinned. She had one crooked tooth, and it made her look a little reckless, the imperfection setting off the delicacy of her other features.

The guy shoved his wallet into his pocket and huffed off. In the instant before he vanished into the crowd, I pinched the edge of that same wallet and lifted it weightlessly out.

She made a shocked, amused sound. "Damn, girl. You're good at that."

I squatted down beside her and opened the wallet. There was a good amount of cash. I'd figured there would be, since he'd come to the Tenderloin looking for something. I took a twenty for myself and gave her the rest. "Finder's fee," I told her, tucking the twenty into my bra strap.

She accepted the wallet and extracted the cash. "You think I can use these credit cards, or will I get caught?"

I considered her for a minute, and then I sat down beside her, my back to the store window. "Here's what I think. I think you should go home to wherever you came from. You have parents who are worried about you? You have family? I think you should go back to them and try to get your shit together."

She gave me a sad, closed-mouth smile. "No one's waiting for me. My sister died in a car accident a few years ago, and my parents sort of . . . lost it. There's nothing to go home to."

"Ah." We sat in companionable silence. A few quarters clinked into her jar. *No strays,* I reminded myself. *Absolutely not.*

But the images of the dead women had softened me. I was alone, too. Maybe I was a stray as much as she was.

"Do you want me to teach you how I do the pickpocketing trick?" I asked her.

"Really?" She lifted her eyebrows. They were very expressive, striking and dark like her thick-lashed eyes.

I was doing this, apparently. "You look hungry. Want to get some food?"

She nodded eagerly.

Without coordinating it, we gripped each other's hands and got to our feet, pulling each other up. "I'm Leo," she said, keeping my hand and shaking it.

"Summer," I replied.

CHAPTER FIVE

SUMMER

LOS ANGELES
WEDNESDAY, JUNE 7

I wake up slowly, with the luxurious soreness from a night on my feet. I stretch and open my eyes. Leo is still asleep, facing away from me on her side, shoulders rising and falling gently in the quiet darkness inside the Land Cruiser.

I lie thinking about the day ahead, eyes roaming around the little nest I've made in here. Years ago, I removed the back row of seats and curtained the rear space off from the front, creating a little room. I'd finished it with vinyl flooring and constructed drawers and cabinets along the passenger's side, leaving space for a full-size mattress. We keep it nice and neat like a tiny hotel room. The drawers and cabinets house everything we own, which isn't much. We travel light through this world.

I think about that, snuggling in and propping my head on my hands. The ceiling is covered in midnight-blue cloth with crystal beads sewn on in the shapes of constellations. Leo did that. She likes to be outdoors, and this space feels claustrophobic to her sometimes. We go camping a lot, which gives her a chance to sleep outside.

I look at the fake stars, and fondness wells up inside me, tainted with worry as I remember our conversation last night. When I met Leo, she was a twenty-one-year-old runaway, having spent years in shelters and on friends' couches. She could never get her act together enough to organize a life. Like me, she couldn't tolerate sitting still, settling down. Unlike me, she couldn't envision a different way to live. I'd filled that hole for her, and she'd come into my life at a time when I'd been alone on the road for almost a decade.

She stirs and rolls onto her back. She stretches, arching her back, arms reaching above her head, and then she releases, looking at me.

"What time is it?" Her voice is thick with sleep.

"Dunno."

She sits up. "I had a dream about Michael. Do I have daddy issues or what, because he's *hot*."

She's like this: passed out one moment, wide-awake and chattering the next. I squint up at her, not totally alert yet. "You'll have fun tonight, then."

"Hell yeah." She runs her hands through her tangled hair. "And then it will be cards with no spending limits, diamond earrings, fancy hotel rooms, and . . . and . . ."

"You can steal photos off his phone and sell them to the paparazzi," I remind her.

"Right. Of course." She squirms out of the blankets and pulls the curtain back, then crawls onto the passenger's seat and starts rolling down the window. She can't tolerate being in here with the windows shut. The ocean air smells salty, and the waves and cars sound like whispers.

"Hey," I begin, clearing my throat nervously. "Are we . . . cool?"

She casts a look at me over her shoulder. "Of course. What do you mean?"

"I feel like we had a tense moment last night."

Leo climbs over the center console and sits beside me on the mattress. "Look. I know you. I understand all your little fears and quirks. I just want you to think outside the box. Stretch your imagination. I feel like you limit yourself."

I want to frown but don't let myself. I don't want to be in a fight with her.

She hugs me, and I hug her back. "Love you," she says, giving me an extra squeeze.

"Same," I reply, stiff, still not acclimated to physical affection. I never received it growing up and am generally bad at it.

She shoves me, laughing. "God, no wonder you never have a man." We're good again, our argument behind us.

We go through my folio, separating cash from cards, and I tuck the stolen driver's license into an inside pocket of my purse. We always split our earnings in three: some for me, some for Leo, and some for a rainy day. The rainy-day fund is in a gallon-size Ziploc bag under the mattress, which I distribute to a number of different hiding spots around California. I like to think of myself as a pirate with caches of booty hidden around the state. The thought of them plucks a note of concern. Our reserves are low. We really need Leo's billionaire to come through.

We pass the morning going to the gym, where Leo sprints like a gazelle on the treadmill and I huff up a mountain on the Stair-Master. After showering, we go shopping with our stolen credit cards for necessities that have worn out and for outfits we can wear in upscale settings. We buy a few Visa gift cards, always while wearing hats and sunglasses to protect against security cameras. We pick up a new screwdriver set and a fresh spare tire and, finally, a bag of nonperishable groceries. We finish by wiping the credit cards clean of fingerprints and depositing them separately into various public trash cans.

By four o'clock, we're tromping across the hot sand toward Michael's hotel, a three-story waterfront palace in Santa Monica famously frequented by celebrities. The beach is crowded, and the sounds of children screaming from the roller coasters on the pier drift along the roar of the waves, an eerie soundtrack to the idyllic day.

"I love your new sunglasses," Leo says, grinning at me.

I'm in high spirits. Nothing makes me happier than having earned enough to live for a little while. "I like yours, too."

She does a happy spin and gets her phone out. "Come here. Selfie time." She gets a cute photo in which I'm giving pouty lips and she's grinning happily, and she uploads it to Instagram. She reads the caption as she types it in. "Santa Monica dreaming on a beautiful Wednesday."

"Along with one million of our closest friends," I add, glaring at the crowded beach. This is one of the many things I hate about Los Angeles: Everything that seems like a good idea to you has also occurred to everyone else.

We find a spot near the hotel, strip down to our bikinis, and flop onto our towels. Our eyes meet through the sunglasses, and I can see my own voluptuous reflection in hers. She stretches out a leg. "Hot," she says.

"Hot," I agree.

We spray ourselves with sunscreen and relax. This is the moment I chase, after the work is done, after I've been on the road and running, when I get to pause and enjoy the world spinning around me for a minute. The ocean smells salty, the air is warm, and the breeze laces cool little fingers through my hair.

"Leoneli?" a voice asks. Michael Forrester is standing above us, wearing running shorts and a tank top.

Leo sits halfway up, resting on her elbows. "No way. Is that really you?" She sounds totally shocked. She's a hell of an actress.

He kneels by her side. "We met last night, right?"

She sits all the way up. "No *way*! How——"

"I was just working out," he explains. "I thought I recognized you but was also positive I was wrong and whoever this poor girl was would call the cops on me."

I sit up, too, examining him. He is handsome in person, but I wouldn't call him hot. Leo clearly thinks he is, though, from the look on her face.

He glances at me. "So sorry to be rude. I'm Michael." He extends his arm across Leo to shake, and I accept it. His eyes do not move down to my breasts, which is a point in his favor.

"Summer," I reply.

"A pleasure to meet you." He returns his attention to Leo. "Mind if I sit? It seems too lucky to run into you and not visit for a bit."

"Of course! Come share my towel." She scoots over to make room for him. "Are you staying nearby?"

"Yes, right there." He points to his hotel. "And where are you from? Are you local?" he asks me.

"I'm in the Bay Area," I reply smoothly. When I'm in NorCal, I say I live in L.A. When I'm in SoCal, I say I live in the Bay Area.

He seems delighted. "That's wonderful! Where? I'm in Palo Alto."

"Oakland. Well, technically our place is in Piedmont, if you know the area."

He gazes at Leo, clearly smitten. "Well, that's not so far, is it?"

I almost roll my eyes. I lie back down and close them, letting the sun warm every inch of me, and think about where I want to eat dinner, since Leo is clearly going to have plans.

"What are you doing tonight?" he asks, and I almost snort with satisfaction at having called it.

"Not much," Leo replies.

"There's a little gathering at my hotel this evening. I've been dreading it. It's going to be business contacts endlessly schmoozing. Why don't you two come and liven it up?"

I would rather die than sit through an entire evening of this. What Leo does, getting close to these men and ingratiating herself to them, is an art form I respect, but I'd kill them in their sleep. Every single one.

But then I reconsider. A hotel party full of rich people? I bet I can make something interesting happen there.

Leo glances at me, and I incline my chin in a miniature nod.

"Sure," she tells him. He looks like she's made his day. Aw. He's kind of nerdy for a billionaire.

I remember the last older man Leo hooked. He was an oil guy from Texas, and she walked away with enough to finance us for months. This Michael is a big fish. If she pulls this off, the sky is the limit.

I must admit, I'm impressed.

CHAPTER SIX

SUMMER

WEDNESDAY, JUNE 7

The hotel ladies' room is ultramodern, all white and stainless steel. Leo touches up her lipstick in the mirror while I adjust the neckline of my dress. There's a fine line between cleavage abundance and breast explosion, and I'm really toeing that line tonight.

She's wearing red, a pretty, silky dress with two layers—a skimpy slip under a chiffon exterior. The effect is bohemian but classy, a look that suits her so well, she should be allowed to trademark it. I'm in my usual black, a simple tank dress clinging to everything that needs clinging to. I call these my man-trapping dresses. I'm not as pretty as Leo tonight, but that's how it should be. It's unspoken code: We don't compete for the spotlight. This is her thing, so she should be the one to shine.

Leo fixes the outline of her red lips with a freshly manicured red pinkie nail and makes a kissing face at herself. She glances at me and laughs. "Really stuffing 'em in tonight, huh, girl?"

I grin at her in the mirror. "You brought me to a rich-guy party without my big purse. I need *somewhere* to stash my earnings."

She laughs. "You're off the clock. Try to have fun for a change. Maybe even get laid."

I wrinkle my nose at the thought of screwing one of these douchebags recreationally. "I'm good."

"You know what I'm going to say."

"Don't."

She throws her arms around me. "Say yes to life!"

"Stop!" I try to throw her off, but she's shockingly strong, with her wiry, former-track-star muscles.

I know she's going to do it before she opens her mouth, but I still cringe when she belts out that life is a highway and she wants to ride it. She releases me from the forced embrace and starts dancing on me, arms in the air, headbanging like the biggest nerd who ever nerded.

"Hold on, let me get my phone so I can record this for your Insta," I say, and then the door opens and a pair of young women walks in. Leo freezes mid-headbang, and the women look at her with matching skeptical, mocking expressions. They're in their early twenties and look very L.A., sculpted and smooth in their tight minidresses and five-inch heels.

"My friend is having a seizure," I inform them.

Leo laughs and smacks my arm. Her hair is a mess, but it looks better this way. She's like that—messy, but the mess is exactly right on her.

The women *click-clack* past us snootily. Leo loops her arm around my shoulders, and I wrap mine around her waist. "It's going to be a great night," she says. "I'm thinking this is a guy who's going to set me up with credit cards. And he's so high-profile, I'm positive there's tea to be spilled . . . and sold."

"They love confessing their sins to a pretty lady," I concur.

"Give them big eyes and naked tits and suddenly you hear every bad thing they've ever done."

"It's a universal truth." I fix a corner of my lipstick. "I've been thinking I've always wanted to get a guy to buy me a car. Something I could keep here in L.A. Something little and sporty."

"What name would you register it under?"

"I guess Summer Hendricks," I say, referring to my good fake ID. I'd gotten that license and social just last year. The last name is a fabrication; I don't have one of my own. I suppose, since my entire existence is not documented in any official way, that I don't technically have a first name either. "She doesn't have anything in her name except the Land Cruiser. I've been planning to sunset the Christina ID soon, ever since I got that speeding ticket."

"Well, let's go get you a car, then. And let's get me laid because it has been *weeks*."

"Gross."

"Grandma," she shoots back. We're slapping each other's arms as we exit the bathroom but pull ourselves together when we enter the dignified, upscale lobby. I've never been here before. It's a boutique hotel right on the beach, somewhere New York celebrities stay when they're in town and want to keep it low-key. It's forest themed, apparently, with hanging plants and a white marble floor that makes me feel like I'm in ancient Rome. We approach the front desk, behind which stands an attractive woman in a black suit. She sees us approaching and adopts a welcoming expression.

"You're here for the Forrester party?"

Smoothly, Leo says, "For Michael, yes."

"Right this way, please." She leads us toward wide-open glass doors beyond which is a stunning panorama of the dark Pacific Ocean. She chats in a friendly way, telling us about the beautiful weather we've been having as she takes us through a wide patio where people are lounging in comfortable-looking chairs and up a set of exterior steps to a second-floor outdoor space that's larger than the patio below it.

"Here you go," she says and fades into the background like she never existed. Leo and I take a moment to absorb the scene: fifty or sixty people mingling in small groups on couches, around cocktail tables, and by the railing that overlooks the ocean below. The Santa Monica Pier shines and sparkles so close, I imagine I can smell the concession stands. White flowers are everywhere— clustered on the tables, suspended from the railings, strung across the ceiling in twisted garlands. At the rear of the space, a string quartet plays soft, melodic jazz.

"Nice," Leo murmurs.

"The aesthetic is very upscale bridal," I reply, wondering what the intention is here as I scope out the room. Is he wooing new contacts, gathering together employees and investors, doing a social hour? I spot a bar under the overhanging trellis that covers the southern half of the patio and tell Leo, "Let's get a drink." As we take our time weaving through the crowd, I case it out, whispering my observations to Leo as we go.

"Old money," I tell her, nodding toward a middle-aged couple sitting on the edges of their seats like the chairs are dirty. "Connecticut or Boston. East Coast." As we pass a thirtysomething woman in animated conversation with a pair of stunning gay men, I tell Leo, "Industry people. She's an agent, they're, I don't know. Not production. Something on the talent end. Casting maybe. I think this party is kind of a meet and greet, a social thing. Not an only-business party. These people are all in different fields."

"What about them?" She points inconspicuously to a gathering of white men on a sectional couch arguing vehemently.

They're not particularly attractive, and they all have an unathletic pallor like they've never met the sun in person. "Tech," I tell Leo. "They're like your guy. Same industry, maybe they work for him. They could have some money, actually. Not billionaire money, but if they've got equity . . ." They'd be easy marks, too, a little naive and overly intellectual.

"Leo," a low voice says. We turn toward the sound. It's Michael, dressed in jeans and a faded black David Bowie T-shirt under a black blazer. His hair is a little messy, and when he kisses Leo on the cheek, I see that he's scruffy. She's beaming as he takes her by the shoulders and looks her over. "This is a very unfair dress." Turning to me, he says, "Summer. It's lovely to see you again."

"Thank you for having us. We were just about to grab ourselves a drink."

"Absolutely not." He waves a hand, and a server materializes out of thin air. "Please get the ladies whatever they like. And make sure neither of them even considers getting themselves a drink for the rest of the evening."

The server nods and turns to us. I say, "Red wine is fine. Thank you."

Leo says, "Sparkling water, please. With lime."

Michael gives her a little secret smile and tells the server, "Put her water in a martini glass." Leo laughs, and I lift my eyebrows. He knows Leo's trick, which is interesting; most men don't pick up on that.

Michael ushers us to a sofa near a heater, which he cranks up without being asked. He sits next to Leo and gives her his full attention. "So. You made it."

She rewards him with one of her thousand-watt smiles. "I'm glad I did."

I return to my analysis of the room, fighting a smirk. These two are going to be in his hotel room before this party wraps, guarantee it.

Our drinks arrive. I sip my wine while Michael and Leo have a low, private conversation about god knows what. Those tech guys could work. They're so caught up in their conversation, though, and I worry about coming on too strong if I interrupt them. As I'm considering and reconsidering, a pair of men in designer jeans with dates in tow approach us. "Michael," the one in front says, extending a hand.

Michael rises to clasp it. "Eric. Good to see you." To the other man, he offers his hand to shake. "Matt. How you doing?" He turns to their dates and says, "I'm Michael. It's so nice to meet you." I almost laugh. These are the girls from the bathroom. They give Leo and me dirty looks and introduce themselves as Amber and Kalani.

Just for fun, I say, "I think we've met. In the ladies' room. Leo was doing a karaoke number."

Michael laughs. "You were?"

She shows her dimples. "A little Rascal Flatts if you want to hear some later."

"I am a hundred percent in." He's completely charmed by her, and I get it. I'm charmed by her, too. I don't know how I lived without her. She's walking sunshine, a fire I can warm my hands in front of.

The women are not charmed. They're playing a game by a certain set of rules, and Leo and I play our own game by our own rules. In theirs, everyone is serious and careful with their image, and Leo's goofy flippancy is something they cannot tolerate.

Leo asks Michael, "Why did the old man fall in a well?"

He asks, "Why?"

"Because he couldn't see that well!" She makes finger guns at him, and he covers his face with his hands.

"Where did you learn such horrible dad jokes?" he groans.

Leo is smiling and Michael is gazing at her fondly, but something feels off, as though the moment is in vignette and the edges of the scene are darkening. I can almost feel reality tilt, just a little, the ground shifting under my feet. A note of dread creeps into my stomach, and I search for its source but can't . . . quite . . .

My mother used to say that people are like marbles in a jar, and the universe likes to shake it up. When you've been on the road long enough, you can feel when the jar is about to be shaken. It starts as a rumble, a ripple in the water you've been treading. Then the shake, and the person is gone.

Just like that.

Leo excuses herself to use the restroom, and Michael is immediately absorbed into the crowd. I'm left alone, eyes drifting back to the tech guys, with the distinct impression of being the fox in the henhouse. The men are still in the same place, on a sectional sofa debating something hotly. I consider my methods, land on one I've used before, and sidle toward them.

I smile warmly as I approach. "Excuse me, do you mind if I sit? I'm waiting for someone." I point to the unoccupied corner of the sectional.

Two of the men just stare up at me with vacant expressions—

it's the boobs—but one has the presence of mind to say, "Sure. Yes."

"Thanks so much." I sit gracefully, crossing my legs in just such a way that my skirt rides up. I swear I see them swallow. I sip my wine and, after a few minutes, make a show of checking my phone. I find an eggplant emoji from Leo, texted just a moment ago. That didn't take long.

A twinge of worry for her surprises me. I text her *Be safe.*

Always, she replies. I frown at the phone, not sure why her response unsettles me. Perhaps because it's so patently untrue. Leo is the most risk-taking person I've ever met.

Head in the game, I chastise myself. I'm proud of Leo, all grown up and handling her business like a boss, making it happen with her first billionaire.

I jiggle my foot, sipping my wine impatiently like I'm getting annoyed with waiting. I eavesdrop on the conversation between the tech guys but can't for the life of me make heads or tails of what they're talking about. It's like they're speaking half English, half something else.

I let my gaze land on the man nearest to me on the sectional. Because he's been looking at my legs off and on this whole time, we make eye contact. "Sorry," I say. I shake my head, laughing at myself. "Didn't mean to stare."

"It's fine," he replies, grinning delightedly. He's in his late thirties, maybe five years older than me, a moderately attractive man if you look past the horrible brown leather shoes and skinny arms.

"I promise I wasn't eavesdropping," I say.

"You'd be dead of boredom if you were." It's a charming little self-own.

"Why?" I ask.

"We're talking tech, as usual," he says, laughing at himself, another good sign.

I adopt a friendly, teasing expression. "Wow. You guys really know how to party."

"We're not exactly partiers," he confesses. "What about you?

Who are you waiting for? Your boyfriend?" He says the last word in a hopeful, guarded tone.

"Oh, no. Just a female friend."

He's clearly delighted. His two friends have continued the conversation without him, and he scoots a little closer to me. "So who are you here with?"

"Michael invited us."

That seems to delight him further. "Really? How do you know Michael?"

"Oh, do you know him, too?"

"We've been working together for years."

This is very, very promising. "Michael invited my friend as his date, and he invited me along for the ride. But you know what that means." I point to myself and say, "Third wheel."

He laughs. "That's terrible! And you don't know anyone else here?"

"Nope." I shrug. "It's okay. It happens."

He extends a hand to shake. "I'm Alan. Alan Fisher."

I accept the handshake in a demure, ladylike fashion that seems like it would appeal to a man who may be threatened by a woman with a strong grip. "I'm Summer."

He releases my hand and says, "So how does your friend know Michael?"

"I believe they met out in the city somewhere. And then we ran into him at the beach today, so here we are. And you? Do you live in L.A., or up in the Bay Area?"

"Oh, I'm mostly local, but I have a place in Palo Alto as well. The project I spearhead is based out of Southern California."

He has multiple residences. Excellent; I'm not wasting my time on someone middle-class. "And what project do you work on?"

He leans in, excited that I'm interested. "Are you familiar with wind and wave energy?"

"Like windmills? Wind farms, the kind you see outside of Palm Springs and off the freeway on the way up to the Bay?"

"Yes, kind of. But our technology is offshore, harnessing the wind off waves as well as the current beneath the surface."

"Wow." I don't know what else to say. "That sounds really . . . great for the environment. Clean energy."

"Yes! I suppose you don't follow Michael's work. This is his most exciting venture right now." I let him chatter on about clean energy technology, mansplaining the pros and cons of solar and plankton and whatever else. I finish my wine and sit there with the empty glass for a good half hour while he drones on about seaweed (I'm completely lost), until at last a waiter appears and says, "Miss? May I refresh your beverage?"

"Yes, thank you," I say, relieved.

Alan flushes. "I'm sorry. I should have done that."

"It's no problem." I'm smiling so much at this guy, my cheeks ache.

"Hey, listen." He clears his throat, and his cheeks turn red. "Would you like to get dinner? Maybe tomorrow?"

"I'd love to," I reply, like I thought he'd never ask. A plan takes form as I text him from my phone so we have each other's numbers. I don't have the attention span for these men that Leo does; I can give them a week max, and even then I nope out early half the time. But if I can get into his house, his wallet, his car, I can almost always find a way to make it profitable for myself without having to fake a relationship. Leo would say it's not faking it; she really enjoys her time with these men. She'd say their relationships are symbiotic.

He texts me back *Hello, it's Alan,* which is so incredibly unsexy, I can't help but hate Leo a little for landing an actually cute billionaire while I have to tolerate plankton analyses from *Alan.*

I decide to call it a night. I'm not going to clear the room of valuables—I don't shit where I eat—but, just to get even with the universe, on my way out, I find the young women who gave us dirty looks in the bathroom clinging to their much-older dates. While they're busy being sparkly and fabulous, I slip their wallets out of their purses and steal their credit cards.

CHAPTER SEVEN

LEO

WEDNESDAY, JUNE 7

I returned from the bathroom to find Michael surrounded by people who had swooped in like vultures, laughing and talking like each was trying to drown out the other, Michael expertly dividing his attention among them.

I hesitated at the outskirts of the crowd, uncertain. I didn't think it was appropriate to assert myself into the center of the group, and Summer had vanished. I did a quick visual survey of the party, which seemed to have doubled in size, and found her appraising a group of men, narrow-eyed. I couldn't help but smirk to myself. Off the clock, my ass. But that was Summer; you couldn't plunk her down into a rich-person party and expect her to sleep on the opportunity.

Michael's eyes landed on me and brightened. I gave him a little wave and made a gesture to indicate I could go hang out somewhere else. He shook his head and stood. "Excuse me, folks," he said, smoothly cutting through the crowd. He gripped my elbow and steered me away.

I protested, "I didn't mean to pull you away from—"

"No, for god's sake, please do. I'm dying out there. You were gone forever."

"I didn't want to interrupt," I mock-protested, giggling.

We were at the edge of the patio now, against the acrylic wall that allowed a view of the pier. The lights sparkled magically against the ocean below. "Don't be sorry." He leaned against the wall, his eyes never leaving mine. "I'm realizing I actually owe *you* an apology."

"You do?"

"I shouldn't have brought you here. I should have taken you out to dinner like a normal person. I think I was . . ." He looked down at his feet. He was wearing Converses.

"You were what?"

"Nervous, maybe?"

"About what?"

He rubbed the scruff along his chin. "I guess . . . I'm used to this." He waved his hand to indicate the party. "I'm used to a crowd of people, to beautiful women in groups who just want proximity to wealth. I think I felt safer bringing you here, but now I just want to escape." He smiled ruefully. "Sorry. That was maybe TMI."

I considered my response, feeling a pinch of sympathy. "I'm happy to come here. Or go to dinner. Whatever. I have a philosophy about these things."

"Tell me your philosophy." His eyes were so blue, burning into mine.

I felt a little hot in the face. "You're, like, really smart. You might think it's stupid."

"I won't." He looked hungry to hear it.

Encouraged, I said, "Well, it's four words."

"Don't date old men," he tried, counting the words on his fingers.

I laughed. "No."

"Break old men's hearts," he tried again.

"Shut up. God, you're not even old."

"Then what is it?"

"Say yes to life." I grimaced. "Is it stupid?"

"Explain it to me."

"I have this theory about doors," I began. "Are you sure you want to—"

"You're *killing* me."

"Fine. I believe that life is a hallway with a series of doors. Some are open, some are closed. You can bang on the closed doors all you want. You can kill yourself banging on them. But there are no knobs on this side of the doors. None at all."

His eyes were huge. His fingertips crept toward me, traced a line on the back of my hand. "Go on," he said, his voice low.

I felt vulnerable, naked, and the feeling sent a thrill through me.

"Some doors are open," I went on. "You're walking along and there's just an open door. That door takes you into a new hallway, with new doors that are both open and closed." I thought about my sister, dead back home in Fresno—her life a closed door. I had beaten my fists on that door a thousand times, flung myself against it, battered myself into a pulp against it. A closed door.

"Why do you look sad?" he asked, clearly in suspense.

I focused on him. "When life opens a door, I walk through it. I don't stay in one hallway, staring at the closed doors. I let the open doors take me away."

His hands were on my waist then, and he pulled me toward him and kissed me. His lips were gentle and firm, and all the different parts of me revved up and started whirring to life. I lifted my hands to his thick hair and tangled them in it, let one hand trail down to the back of his neck, feeling the warm, firm heat of his skin. His tongue was hot on mine, and my whole body sizzled with images of where else it could go.

I pulled back. "Michael," I whispered. "We should stop, right? Aren't these people your work friends?"

He groaned, a low, hungry sound. "Do you want to go to my room? It's fine if you don't."

I did want to. "But what about your party?"

"Fuck the party. Do you realize that every single person here wants something from me?"

I ran my fingertips along the scruff at his jawline, thinking about all the things I wanted from him. "What do they want?"

He looked bitter. "Money. Introductions to other people with money. Status. Power. That's what everyone wants."

I nodded, trying to imagine what that would be like.

"What do you want from me, Leo?" he asked, not in a challenging way, but as though he was curious. "Tell me what you want."

"I . . . I don't know." In this moment, my plans to steal credit cards and pictures off his phone felt distant. I was thinking about the open doors and all the closed ones, all the lost things and people, the memories that were starting to fade.

"Come on. Dream big. Are you hoping I'll marry you, buy you a mansion in the hills, give you a bunch of kids so you can file for divorce and get a truckload of child support?"

"Fuck no," I answered without hesitation. "That's my nightmare."

"Because you don't live in Oakland, do you?" I realized now I hadn't given him enough credit. He wasn't just smart; he was perceptive. "Tell me where you live," he demanded.

"Nowhere," I replied, gripping his collar and pulling myself closer to him.

"That's right. You're an adventurer." He said it as though I was confirming what he'd already guessed. "You and your friend travel. You don't stay anywhere long. All those open doors."

"All those open doors," I whispered.

"You don't want a damn thing." He tightened his grip on me.

He was right. At my core, I didn't want things. I wanted freedom. Everything I did was toward that end—buying Summer and myself the freedom to live.

"I want *you*," I said, and that was true.

He kissed me hard, with so much pent-up need, his lips careful like he was worried his need would be too much for me.

"Let's go to your room," I said, and he took me by the hand and led me into the darkness.

CHAPTER EIGHT

SUMMER

THURSDAY, JUNE 8

A seagull screeching nearby snaps me out of sleep. For a dreamy moment, the echoing cry sends me down a memory spiral. I'm in a tent. I'm a little girl. Outside, people are laughing. It smells like a campfire.

My eyes fly open.

No, that was then. This is now. I can see from the slices of window peeking around the edges of the curtains that it's morning.

There are no voices, no friendly campfire. I'm alone. Where's Leo?

I sit up, breathless, the empty space on the mattress humming with her absence.

It comes rushing back. She's spending the night with her billionaire. I'll hear from her at noon, and she'll return to me ravenous and bubbling over with excited sexcapade stories.

I breathe a sigh of relief. Everything's fine.

I let my eyes roam over the wall of cabinets I built. They're white and neat, efficient, each containing its small portion of my

possessions. When I think of people with whole apartments—
houses—mansions—the idea of all that baggage, the weight of it,
feels absurd. Hasn't anyone ever told them? The world has what
you need. You don't have to own things to use them.

Case in point: I have to pee. I'm parked outside a Starbucks, and
according to my phone, it's seven o'clock and they've been open
for an hour. See?

I use the restroom, grab breakfast, and head to a nearby Laun-
dromat, where I spend a few peaceful hours immersed in the
homey scents of detergent and dryer sheets. I finish a book I've
been reading, a mystery set in Japan, which I leave behind for
someone else to find and enjoy. I like doing that, leaving little trinkets around the world and imagining who might pick them up.

I'm sitting on the mattress in the back of my truck, folding clothes,
when I check my phone again. It's four thirty and I still haven't
heard from Leo.

I text her. *All good? When are you going to be done? I have a date with
this horrible guy named Alan tonight.* I wait a minute, but she doesn't
answer.

She's probably in the shower, or her phone died, or she turned
it off so she could have sex without me intruding. I'm being a
house cat.

My mom always said, "We're alley cats, babe!" when I'd get sad
about one of our friends leaving our traveling group. She'd say,
"Alley cats come and go. They live their lives. Don't be a house
cat."

As she was leaving me for the last time, off to join her new boyfriend and his stupid new religion, she told me, "If it's meant to
be, we'll run into each other again." I was almost an adult, and she
had done her job, right? Baby bird, spreading wings, whatever.
Heartsick, I shoved her off and ran away, into a world I knew
would swallow me whole.

I imagine her alive, now in her fifties, some other man teaching
her some New Age faith. I try not to picture the alternative, but

the images intrude anyway: Her dead, buried in some dark and unknown corner of the world. Or, worse, in some morgue's freezer, a Jane Doe tag on her toe, turning blue, waiting forever for someone to identify her.

She had a short-lived boyfriend when I was a teenager, during our residency at a campground near Big Sur. He had a sweet dog, a fluffy brown mutt. Once, for the dog's birthday, he put a hot dog in a bowl by his campsite's hearth. From then on, the dog checked that same spot every day, ten times a day, hoping for a hot dog. It never forgot.

"Come on, Leo," I mutter, eyes on my phone. It's four thirty-seven. I should have heard from her by now.

I can't wait. I'm going to check on her. I shove the last few T-shirts in a drawer and climb into the driver's seat. Maybe I'm just a house cat through and through.

The hotel is bustling, and I make my way through the shiny lobby with its backdrop view of the ocean through the wall of windows. I approach the concierge, a dark-haired man built like a greyhound in a skintight shirt. "I need to call up to one of your rooms," I tell him.

He raises his eyebrows and flicks his eyes down to my sweats and flip-flops, wordlessly reminding me that I am not dressed for this hotel. "Did you want me to place that call for you? I can't connect you directly."

"That's fine. I'm just here picking up a friend. It's Michael Forrester's room."

He *click-clacks* the keyboard. "Unfortunately, Mr. Forrester already checked out. Are you sure your friend isn't waiting for you in the lobby somewhere? There's also a patio that wraps around the side." He points out the windows.

I stare at him dumbly. That can't be right. "Checked out?"

"Yes, ma'am." He pinches his lips together primly.

I check my phone. No word from Leo. "Are you absolutely sure?"

"I am." He indicates the monitor of his computer.

"Can you call up there?"

He sighs almost imperceptibly. "All right." He picks up the receiver and dials something. It seems to be ringing and ringing. He says, "Nope. No one there," and sets the receiver down.

I try to quell the wave of anxiety rising up inside me, a visceral reaction to being disconnected. I reassure myself that this is probably just Leo fumbling logistics, forgetting her charger, or it's her and Michael going to get lunch and forgetting to call me. Except it's five o'clock, too late for lunch, and she's supposed to check in when she wakes up after spending the night with someone.

I tell the concierge, "I'm going to look around for her, okay?"

"Good luck," he croons with fake sympathy.

I want to flip him off. Instead, I hurry through the lobby to the ladies' room where Leo had done her impromptu Rascal Flatts karaoke session. I peek under the stall doors, but no one is in here.

Back out in the lobby, I search every corner, go out onto the patio, into the restaurant. No Leo. I ask the restaurant hostess if there's a reservation for Michael, or if Michael has been in today. She says no.

I hurry up the stairs to the second-floor patio where Michael's party took place last night. It's been transformed into a lounge area for hotel guests and is mostly empty. I check the bathroom. Nothing.

My heart is fully pounding now, about to thump right out of my chest. I trot back down the stairs to the concierge, who is now helping a rich, angry woman resolve a dispute with housekeeping. I wait, jittery and impatient, and when he's done, he turns to me with a pained smile. "Any luck?"

"No. Can you have someone go up and check the room in person? I need to know for sure she isn't in there."

"Ma'am—" He stops. "You know what? Fine." He gets a walkie-talkie and tells someone, "Can you please check Room 514? We need confirmation that the guests have checked out. Please knock before entering. Thank you." He sets the walkie-talkie down. "We'll have an answer shortly."

I call Leo on my cell while we wait. It goes straight to voice-mail.

I try to be logical. Let's say her phone died. What would she do if she didn't have a charger? Maybe she would email me from one of Michael's devices. I check my email. Nothing. Anyway, it doesn't track. Michael is a billionaire. Her iPhone takes a standard charger, the same kind everyone uses. There's no way in hell he couldn't just have someone bring her a new one.

Maybe she didn't notice her phone was dead until they'd already parted ways. In that case, she'd go where the truck had been parked yesterday, assuming it would still be there. I hadn't told her I planned to do laundry.

The concierge catches my attention. "Ma'am? They've confirmed the room is empty. Someone else should be checking into that suite shortly."

"Can I give you my number? In case she comes here looking for me?"

He takes a deep, long-suffering breath. "Of course."

I give him the number and show him a photo of her. "I'm going home in two hours," he tells me. "But I'll pass the info along to the next concierge on duty."

I almost run to my truck, get in, and gun it, searching for the spot we'd parked in last night. It's not far away, just a few blocks in a different direction. That particular space is occupied now, but I find another across the street. I grab a protein bar out of the food cabinet and settle in the driver's seat, eyes on the spot that now contains a white Prius. If she comes, I don't want to miss her.

The sun is lowering in the sky. I have to meet Alan at eight. *I should cancel,* I think, but then something hits me.

He might be able to tell me where Michael is, or at least Alan can call him on his cell and find out.

Excited, I climb into the back and start getting ready.

—

The Japanese restaurant is trendy and minimalist with just a small white sign outside reading "sushi" in lowercase, upside-down letters.

A host with immaculately applied eye makeup opens the heavy steel-and-glass door for me. "Good afternoon," they purr, their voice actor-smooth.

"Hello. I'm meeting—"

"Summer." Alan steps forward from a place he's been hovering near the host stand, eyes shining with happiness as if he'd thought I might stand him up. I can see from his face that my outfit is landing exactly how I'd intended. I went with an expensive romper in white and styled my long hair in curling-iron waves; I'm cosplaying a basic wealthy woman from Newport Beach. "You look incredible," he says, pulling me toward him and kissing my cheek.

I allow it, giving him an extra moment with me pressed up against his chest, before I step back. I've decided my persona with him will be demure and sweet, one of the nice, nonthreatening girls he probably thinks don't exist in bodies like mine.

"Thank you for the invitation. I'm so happy to see you again." The words make his cheeks pink up, a little win for me. I'm itching to ask about Leo and Michael but force myself to be patient.

He's a bit cuter than I remember, with a nice face and pretty brown eyes. When set against the restaurant full of L.A. people, all tanned and fit and glowing like they're in possession of some secret health serum, he looks very indoorsy. He's a few inches taller than me, maybe five ten, and is wearing dry-cleaned jeans with a striped button-down tucked into them. It's like his mom dressed him for a date in high school.

A hostess shows us to a table in the back. Alan asks me if I've eaten sushi before. I tell him yes, but he still explains how the menu works. I smile and nod, eyes on the prize.

Once we've gotten our drinks, Alan leans forward across the table and says, "So tell me about yourself."

I sip my drink. I hate white wine, but it seemed right for this persona. "First, can I ask you something? I know I'm being a worrywart, but I haven't heard from my friend today. I know she spent the night with Michael, but he checked out of the hotel this morning, and there's been no word from her."

He cocks his head. "Is it possible she's got something else going on? Do you hear from her every day?"

I nod. "We're roommates. She'd never let me worry like this, not after a date."

He pulls his phone out of his pocket. "Well, this is easily solved. I'll call Michael."

Relief cascades through my chest, and I put a hand on his arm. "Thank you."

He beams, the hero, and puts the phone to his ear. It goes straight to voicemail, which sends a frown flickering across his face, but then he says, "Oh, it's the eighth, right? She can't be with him. He's gone to the island. We have an event there this week-end."

"The island?" I echo, confused.

"Tenet Holdings, Michael's company, has a research facility dedicated to wind and wave energy. It's one of our most—" He clears his throat. "It's a flashy project. They needed someone with solid credentials to oversee it. That's me. It's housed on an island off the coast, near Catalina."

I process this, trying to understand. "So he's there for the week-end?"

He nods, sipping his drink. "We have an investors' weekend. We do them biannually. We invite current and potential inves-tors to view updates and, you know, show off the tech. They bring wives and girlfriends, and we make a party out of it." He grins.

"Could Leo have gone with Michael to the island?"

He lifts his shoulders. "I doubt it, but I can't be sure. He's never brought a date before, but I guess you never know."

"Could you email him and ask?"

He winces. "Sure, but he'll be offline till Monday. He has a pol-icy of separating himself from admin and focusing on higher-level cerebral work when he's on the island."

I take a long sip of my wine and try to organize the thoughts flying through my mind. Leo would want to see the island if she found out about it. She can be very convincing and completely single-minded once she's decided she wants something.

Leo's been bored with me. She's been itching to do something new.

Where worry had set up shop in my stomach, anger and resentment are starting to amalgamate. I can see it: Leo caught up in the moment, finagling an invitation to the island, not even considering how scared I'd be after she didn't call or text.

"Are you okay?" Alan asks.

I snap my eyes onto him. "Yes. Thank you. You're incredibly kind." I decide I'm going to get this guy to take me to the island as his date, and when I get there, I'm going to have it out with Leo. If she wants to leave me, she's welcome to go anytime. But to walk away without even a text? To leave me afraid that something horrible had happened to her after the years I've supported and looked after her? No. Absolutely not.

My brain snaps into calculations, and I appraise the man before me. He was boasting about his position with Tenet Holdings, which speaks to an ocean of underlying insecurity. He was no doubt a nerdy kid. Lots of teasing, lots of belittling, lots of alpha males making him feel small. As a grown man, he'll always feel like he has something to prove. My approach needs to be about making him feel big, strong, special, alpha.

I make my eyes big and wistful. "You're so lucky you get to work on an island. Is it beachy like Catalina?"

He nods, proud. "It's gorgeous. Beautiful sandy beaches, lots of hiking trails. I'm there about half the time, and you do start to get island fever."

"If it's a research facility, where do you stay?"

"Oh, there's a massive residential side to the island. It's like a resort."

I realize what I'm hearing: The upcoming weekend will be spent in a resortlike setting with who knows how many wealthy investors. I start picturing diamond earrings and money clips.

I smile sweetly. "I absolutely adore all things related to the beach. Nothing makes me happier than lying out in the sun and swimming all day. I have a serious bikini collection, it's ridiculous." I laugh at myself, covering my mouth, pretending I've said too much and am embarrassed. "Sorry. You don't want to hear about that." This is how I make him feel like a big man: I use myself as currency.

His eyes are stretched wide. "No, it's nice," he replies, so eager, it's funny. As Leo says, it's like shooting fish in a barrel.

I shift position to give him a clearer view of my cleavage. "So do you have a date lined up for this weekend? A wife or girlfriend? I'm not out to dinner with a married man, am I?"

"Not at all. I'm as single as they come. You know . . ." He hesitates. "Well, maybe not. Never mind."

I'm so close. I can feel it. "What is it?"

His cheeks turn pink again. "Sorry. That's—"

"You have to tell me now!" I grab the material of his striped shirtsleeve. He grins and shakes his head, and I cry out in protest. "Alan, you're mean! You have to tell me what you were going to say!" If I met myself right now, I would despise me.

His face is fully red, a deep blush. "I was just going to say, I am allowed to bring a plus-one to this weekend if I want to. But then I realized, this is our first date. I didn't mean to imply—"

"That's so sweet!" I actually croon the words. "You are so incredibly kind to think of me for that. But please don't worry. I totally understand, you don't feel ready to bring me there for a whole weekend, it's our first date, I get it—"

"No," he protests. "I was more thinking, I wasn't sure if you felt comfortable."

We stare at each other for a moment, and then we laugh at the same time. "This is funny," I say. "We're both worried the other person is offended or something."

He reaches for my chin, tilts my face toward him, and kisses me softly on the lips, which is where this was always headed. I allow him to linger on it, working hard not to pull away or make grossed-out facial expressions.

When he pulls back, I look him in the eyes for a moment, then avert my gaze down to my wine like I can't stand how attracted to him I am. "Well, now I'm shy. It's so hard meeting people in the city, and most of the men you meet are shallow and stupid. I just really like you."

"Don't be shy." His voice is gritty. He's gotten a taste and is picturing me naked. "It's crazy, I know, but you'd be welcome to come with me this weekend if you want to see the island. There are beautiful beaches, a spa, lots to do. I'll be busy working a lot of the time, and you'd have your own room, so I wouldn't be constantly bothering you. No worries if you don't want to, but I thought I'd offer, just in case—"

"Alan." I put my hand on top of his. "I would love to."

And that is how it's done.

CHAPTER NINE

LEO

WEDNESDAY, JUNE 7

The golden lamplight cast soft shadows over our bare skin, limbs intertwined in the tangled bedclothes. I was lying on my back, one hand stroking Michael's hair, and he was resting his head on my chest, tracing ticklish fingertips across my stomach. "Tell me again where you're from," he said after we'd been quiet for a blissful stretch of minutes.

"Fresno." The hotel room had so much open air, and my voice disappeared off into it. This was the penthouse, and it had vaulted ceilings and a skylight through which I could see the stars. It was wonderful, the opposite of claustrophobic. If I stayed the night, I'd sleep like a baby.

"And why did you leave?" His hand rested on my hip, fitting itself to the curve of my hip bone.

"It's a sad story," I warned him.

He propped himself up on an elbow so he could see my face. His hair was messy, a stray lock flopping down over one of his deep blue eyes. "I can handle sad."

He seemed like he could, so I told him the truth. "My sister died when I was sixteen." I didn't say her name. I never said it out loud.

He winced. "I'm sorry."

I nodded.

"So you left after high school? Too many bad memories?"

"Not quite." I hesitated, then went with the truth again. "Everything fell apart pretty quickly after she died. My parents. Everything. I left when I was seventeen. Never finished school."

He put a hand to my forehead and stroked the hair back from it. "That is a sad story."

"We were a normal family. House in the suburbs, I ran track. My mom stayed home. Lots of baking . . ." I trailed off, unable to say more. I'd reached my limit. The past was too close right now. I preferred to feel like I'd put a lot of miles between it and me, like I'd traveled so far from it that I couldn't even see it in the rearview mirror anymore.

When Amanda died, I'd realized that everything my parents had worked so hard for—stability, family—was bullshit. There was no safety in this world, no permanence. Family could be snatched from you overnight as easily as losing jewelry in a swimming pool.

When we got the news, I left my house at two o'clock in the morning, walking through the dark streets alone. I should have been terrified to leave the house, but no. It worked the opposite. I'd realized that nowhere was safe, and that my days on this earth were numbered whether I did everything right or wrong.

That year, my mom descended into an alcoholic stupor. My dad became a gaunt phantasm haunting the rooms of our dusty house. School was worse, filled with pitying looks and the ghost of Amanda's presence, agonizingly real everywhere I turned. And then there was my own face; my whole life, people would stop us at the mall, in restaurants, at Disneyland, always to tell us how pretty we were and how much alike we looked. But now Amanda was dead and neither of my parents could look at me without their eyes filling with tears. They were grieving her death, but they were also grieving the loss of who they thought I was. The Leo they knew wouldn't have done what I did, and every time I made eye contact with either of them, the weight of my guilt struck me over and over again until I was like a boxer knocked down one too many times, unable to lift myself even to my knees.

So I left. A few years later, I met Summer, and I had a sister again. And here we were, five years on the road together.

Michael was looking down at me with sympathetic eyes that were a deep shade of navy in the dim half-light. "You okay?"

I nodded. I wasn't going to cry. The past was a million miles behind me.

He leaned down to kiss me, and the soft hair on his chest tickled the smooth skin on mine. When he pulled back, he said, "Let me take you on a little adventure."

I grinned. "Now you're speaking my language. What kind?"

"Do you like boats?"

"I do like boats. Why do you ask?"

"Because I have one and I want to show it to you. We can take a nighttime ride."

I gasped, delighted. "Like a sailboat?"

He pressed his lips together for a moment. "If I tell you it's a yacht, will you hate me?"

"Only a little," I answered honestly.

"Fine, it's a fishing boat," he said with a laugh. "An *old* fishing boat."

I grabbed a pillow and hit him with it. "It's totally a yacht, you asshole."

An hour later, we were on the open ocean, the night wind blowing in our hair. It was not a yacht after all, but it definitely wasn't a fishing boat. It would only fit three people, and it was clearly built for speed. It was beautiful, pure white with sleek lines and a high-tech control panel Michael turned on with his thumbprint.

He piloted it with ease, steering through the waves with a concentration that gave me a glimpse into what his professional demeanor must be like. I sat beside him, watching the water soar beneath us. The moon hung directly ahead, hovering above the water like an alien starship. With the rush of the wind and the overwhelming feeling of weightlessness, I could almost believe we were leaving the earth, heaven bound.

Suddenly, I realized—he hadn't asked me to sign an NDA. That was unexpected. Men far below his level of wealth had had me sign them before even entering their hotel rooms. By no means was I going to encourage Michael to produce one; I could do way more without it. But it made me wonder if he wanted something deeper, something more akin to a relationship than I could provide.

"Where are we going?" I asked, not that I needed to be going anywhere in particular.

He glanced at me sideways, looking ten years younger than he had in the hotel. He was like me—he lived for these moments of spontaneous combustion.

"Is it okay if it's a surprise?" he asked.

"Why, are you taking me to Mexico? I don't have my passport."

"Nowhere out of the country, I promise." He wrapped an arm around me and pulled me closer. "You want to steer?"

He showed me how to turn, how to speed up and slow down. My face was stretched into a smile so wide, my cheeks hurt.

"You like it?" he asked, laughing at my delight.

"I love it!" I screamed, and then I shrieked a wordless cry of happiness into the moon-filled sky. It was gone as soon as I'd released it, snatched away by the wind.

We coasted the waves for an hour, the moon our bright-faced companion. "I've decided I need a boat," I told Michael, speaking loudly enough to be heard over the wind.

"Where would you keep it?"

"Not important."

He chuckled. "Veer right a bit."

"Where are we headed? Can't you give me a clue?"

"One moment . . ." And then, as though summoned, a low, ragged shape appeared at the horizon. "There," he said.

I glanced at him. "Is that . . . an island?"

He nodded. "It's mine."

"Your *island*?"

He cracked up at the shock in my voice. "It's for work. We have a research facility. But it's also for fun. I have a house here. It has a private beach. It seemed the perfect place to bring you in the spirit of adventure."

"An island," I echoed. "Are you kidding me?"

He pressed a kiss into the crease between my neck and my shoulder. "Leo," he murmured, giving me chills. I wanted him again.

"You drive," I told him, sliding away from the controls. As he took the wheel, I slithered onto his lap, straddling him. I kissed him deeply, electricity running through me. He groaned and flipped a few switches. The boat coasted to a stop and bobbed on the gentle waves. He took his hands off the wheel and gripped my hips, pulled me toward him. I gasped, clutched at his hair, and kissed him again. "I need you," I said into his mouth. That seemed to set him loose—he was pulling my dress up and sliding my underwear aside, unzipping his jeans, clumsy and desperate, and then he was inside me and I was moaning into his lips, the rocking of the boat sending shivers of pleasure through me. We were completely detached from the world, floating in a dark and empty space where nothing existed but the present moment. I felt myself falling harder and faster toward climax and thought, *How can I ever go back to my life before tonight, before knowing what it feels like to drive a fast boat into the open ocean?* And then his hands were on my ass and he was pulling me closer, and I was coming, and my name was on his salty lips, the wind whipping my hair into a tornado.

Afterward, we fell still, his arms wrapped around me. We held each other like that for a few long minutes, my heart beating against his, my face buried in his neck.

He cleared his throat. His voice was gruff in my ear. "Do you want to see the island?"

I pressed my hands to his cheeks and kissed his lips. "I do."

He stroked my tangled hair. "Is the island your next open door?"

"You know it is."

CHAPTER TEN

SUMMER

BIG SUR
FIFTEEN YEARS AGO

I woke to the smell of early-morning fog steaming off the red-woods and the ocean chill that always accompanied our trips to Big Sur. I lay in my sleeping bag, staring up at the nylon tent ceiling. Something was off, but I couldn't put my finger on it.

I was alone, but that was normal; my mom hadn't shared my tent all year, since her new boyfriend joined us. His name was Mage and he was older than her by a good ten years, a grizzled, skinny man with a gray-blond beard and khaki shorts that hung loose on his bony hips. She loved him, though, as much as she loved all of them, and he specialized in some sort of spiritual mind-body healing thing that made her hang on his every word.

I estimated the time to be six thirty, about an hour after day-break. I wondered again what was different, and then I realized—there was no campfire smell. Ever since Mage had joined us, he woke up at dawn and started the fire. He believed in precivilization sleep rhythms and slept from dusk until dawn with a wakeful period in the middle of the night, which was usually when he and my mom had loud sex that echoed embarrassingly around the campground. Their friends didn't care, of course. They thought it was "all good."

I sat up, pulled the hood of my sweatshirt over my head, and extracted myself from the sleeping bag and pile of blankets, my warm cocoon. I wanted coffee and apparently was going to have to start the fire myself.

I zipped open the tent door and shoved my feet into the wet flip-flops that waited for me outside. Grumpy and groggy, I closed the tent and straightened up, then jolted in surprise.

The night before, six tents had been clustered into our three campgrounds along with one large van—my mom's—and an old SUV owned by her friend Jim. Now, only my mom's van remained, all the tents packed up, no luggage or food left behind. My mom stood talking to Mage by the bumper of the van, and when she saw me, she held a hand up to him and headed toward me. He hoisted himself into the passenger's seat and closed the door.

I stepped carefully through the dirt and rocks, meeting her halfway. "What's going on? Are we moving to a different campground?" I noticed she was fully dressed in one of her long floral skirts and oversize cable-knit sweaters. How long had she been up? It took over an hour to break camp completely.

She put her hands on my shoulders and looked up into my eyes. I was two inches taller than her now. "I'm so proud of the woman you've become," she said.

I felt myself giving her a "what are you talking about" face and said, "I'm not a woman, I'm a teenager, weirdo."

"You're as old as I was when I struck out into the world." She was eternally trying to sound deep and poetic. I rolled my eyes.

"You ran away from home. It didn't make you a woman. Why are you being weird right now? Where are we going?"

She dropped her hands and clasped them in front of her. "Mage and I have a destination in mind, but where you go is up to you."

I frowned. "I'm sorry, what?"

"It's your time. Time to strike out. The world is yours." She beamed like she was giving me a birthday present.

I felt my jaw hanging open. "Is this a joke? Strike out where?"

"Every baby bird leaves the nest. Don't you feel that restlessness, that urge to explore? Can't you feel it in your bones?"

"All I feel right now is confused, and I also have to pee," I answered honestly.

She laughed. "You're going to be great. You have all your things." She gestured to my tent, and when I followed the motion, I saw that she'd set my suitcase, bags, and books beside it on the ground. "And here." From the pocket of her skirt she pulled out a wad of cash and pressed it into my hands. "A thousand dollars." She flushed. "I'm sorry, I know you're perfectly capable. But I'm a mother. I had to help you just a bit."

"But—" My hands wouldn't close over the money, and it started to flutter away. She grabbed it and returned it to me, and I forced myself to grip the bills into a messy double handful. I looked down at them, shock roaring in my ears. "What is happening?" I asked at last. "Are you abandoning me here? For real? You're leaving?"

"There is no abandonment. There are just two women making their way in the world."

"But how will I ever find you again?" I protested. "What if I need to get in touch with you?"

"The universe is like a jar of marbles—" she began, but I cut her off with an angry snarl.

"Do not give me that marbles bullshit. You're leaving? With *Mage*? You're choosing that dirty old man over your own *child*?"

"You're not my child anymore. You're all grown up now." Her eyes glistened with unshed tears.

I met them, red-hot anger roasting me from the inside. "I'm not a fucking baby bird. I'm a human teenager. What you're doing is wrong. You're a horrible mother. You've been a horrible mother from day one." Tears were streaming down my cheeks, and I wanted to throw the money at her, but I knew I'd need it because the reality of my situation was starting to sink in. "You don't want to set a time to meet? Once a year, we can meet here or something. Anywhere. Wherever you say, I'll meet you there." I had gone from rage to begging, sobbing, because she really was going to leave me in the woods by myself without even a car or a last name.

Gently, she pulled me into a hug. "If the universe shakes the jar and we end up side by side, I'll see you then." She pulled back, turned, and walked away. I watched, frozen in place, as she got in the van. The brake lights shone orange as the engine started, and tufts of dust plumed from the tires as she drove away, bumping over the dirt campground road. She turned a corner, and then she was gone, swallowed by the trees. The air was still except for a single blue jay, sitting on a pine branch above my tent, screeching merrily.

I felt exposed. The other campsites, though not close, rustled with life. Someone was starting a fire; the scent of smoke wafted through the cold morning air. Someone else was rinsing dishes in the spigot.

I turned and hurried to my tent, still clutching the money in both hands. I tumbled in, not bothering to remove my shoes, and zipped the nylon door shut. Frantically, fingers quivering, I counted the money, dividing it into piles by denomination. I counted the twenties, then the tens, the fives, the ones, and the process calmed me.

Nine hundred thirty-seven dollars. That was what she'd left me.

I sat on my pile of blankets and stared at the money. I was alone.

CHAPTER ELEVEN

SUMMER

LOS ANGELES
FRIDAY, JUNE 9

The yacht is full of assholes getting what I call "rich-people drunk." I sip my champagne and fake-laugh at the stories being told by Alan and the two couples surrounding him. My eyes keep drifting to the horizon, waiting to catch a glimpse of the island. The sky is a perfect baby blue, as empty as the space next to me where Leo should be.

These are old money people, the folks who write the checks, not like Michael and Alan, who are the self-made men who do the work. The two couples I'm smiling for right now are Steve and Julie and William and Caroline. Steve and William are interchangeable, in dark slacks, tailored shirts, and blazers that don't match, so it doesn't count as a suit. Steve is in his late forties, about ten years younger than William, who may as well be his future self. Looking at their wives' designer boat clothes, I thank the gods of theft that I was able to shop for this trip with the credit cards I picked up the other day.

Right now, William is telling a long, winding story about being hosted by a rich family in Brazil and how they were treated like celebrities by everyone they met, and Caroline is interjecting little comments like, "They had a beautiful banquet hall," and "They were just so *respectful*." Assuming Leo is on the island and getting a tan, inconsiderately enjoying herself while I'm panicking for days and nights alone in my truck, I'm going to first strangle her, then yell at her, and then we're going to steal the diamond rings off these bitches' fingers. Julie in particular has beautiful jewelry; she's younger than her husband and has been professionally sculpted like a work of fine art.

Goddammit, Leo.

I couldn't sleep last night for worry. I feel haggard, dragged out, exhausted, and starving but nauseous. The boat ride isn't helping, no matter how fancy this stupid yacht is.

"So, Summer, what do you do? How did you meet Alan?" William asks, turning the conversation on me so suddenly, I almost show annoyance. I rally, awarding him and his glaring wife a bright smile. "We met at a party, actually, in Santa Monica."

"Michael's quarterly get-together," Alan fills in, putting a possessive hand on my hip, clearly proud of the trophy he's collected.

"It was fun," I reply. To William, I say, "As for what I do, I work with social media influencers."

"How fascinating," Caroline murmurs bitchily, sipping her white wine.

To get revenge, I keep my eyes on William. "When I was in high school, I intended to go into nursing. Do you think I'd have been a good nurse?" I ask him, blinking my eyelashes prettily.

"Absolutely," he replies with lecherous enthusiasm, and I think Caroline might throw her glass at me. Julie seems to repress a smirk. Maybe she's a little bit cool.

"William, let's go talk to the McAllisters." Caroline pulls her husband away, and Alan turns to me with stars in his eyes.

"You're being very patient with all this," he says, wrapping his arms around me. "This isn't fun for you, is it?"

"It's fine. They're kinda boring, but I'm here with you." In my mind, I'm rolling my eyes so hard, they might get stuck this way.

He kisses me, and I go along with it, trying to stay in character but unable to stop mentally critiquing his form.

Over his shoulder, a dark form materializes at the horizon. I pull out of the kiss and point. "Is that it?"

Alan glances up. "Yep! We're almost there."

I walk to the railing and grip it tight. The waves slash foamy trails as the yacht glides steadily through them. It's easy to forget how fast we're going. This boat is so heavy, it cuts right through the water.

The island is larger than I expected, and soon I can see cliffs, rocky coves, and a small marina. None of the other guests seem the least bit surprised or impressed, but I'm sort of in awe. I've visited Catalina, but there are thousands of people on Catalina at any given time. Alan had said there would be "at least fifty guests" here this weekend, which had been comforting, but now I'm realizing how few fifty is on a whole-ass island.

Cliffs tower above us as we motor into the docks. I tip my head back and notice a structure at the very highest point. It's all sharp angles, redwood and glass, easily the size of a shopping mall. A long, narrow staircase zigzags up the cliff, disappearing into the rocks.

"Is that the house?" I ask Alan, pointing up at the structure.

"Yep! This is the south side of the island. The research facility is on the northernmost point. The east side has the best beaches. You can work on your tan." In the marina, a sleek speedboat is docked beside a chunkier, scientific-looking vessel.

Nearby, a group of people in pastels erupts into a chorus of laughter. They clink champagne flutes, which sounds like breaking glass. I wonder if we're going to lug all our bags up the stairs to the house. I can't imagine it. Rich people don't lug things. As I think this, I see a shape moving evenly down the side of the cliff. The shape resolves itself into that of a glass cube. It's an elevator whose shaft has been sliced out of the cliff wall.

Now I understand. The wood-planked dock continues over the pebbly beach, becoming a wide walkway. It branches left to meet the stairs and right to meet the elevator. Sure enough, the elevator comes to a stop and its doors open, letting out a handful of people in matching white shirts and black pants. They jog along the walkway toward the dock. This must be the service staff.

Alan reappears, having extricated himself from a conversation with a couple of Williams. "You ready? They'll take your bags up to your room."

"They'll know whose bag is whose?"

He smiles condescendingly. "They'll be hosting four dozen people this weekend. If they can't coordinate people with their luggage by now, they're in trouble."

I don't like it. But as I watch, the men and their wives start disembarking. Alan guides me with a hand at the small of my back, something I loathe, and I clutch my purse to my side.

"Mr. Fisher." A strikingly handsome man about my age greets Alan with a warmth that makes it clear they know each other well. "Welcome back." He has perfect white teeth and black hair gelled into an immaculate undercut.

"Thank you, Javier. This is Summer. She's my guest for the weekend. She's in the west wing with me."

"Welcome," Javier says to me. He extends a gentlemanly hand. Do I need assistance walking down the three steps to the dock? No, I don't, but I allow it. There's something subtly flirtatious about him, something that goes right over Alan's head.

"Thank you," I tell him. "It's beautiful here."

Javier grins at the horizon. "I have the best job on earth."

Alan nods. "You sure do." To me, he says, "The staff live half-time on the island, and the other half of the time, they get to do whatever they want. Full-time pay, half-time work."

Javier shrugs. "Like I said, best gig on earth."

I bet when they're on the island, they're on call twenty-four hours a day. So it's not actually that much extra time off, but whatever. Rich people like to congratulate themselves for keeping poor people alive.

Javier walks us to the elevator, chatting with Alan about the weather—should be clear and sunny, perfect for their unveiling of whatever technology all these investors are here to see—and about the guest list. Javier says, "This is the first group of people to arrive. The captain is returning to shore to collect the next one now. By evening, we should have about fifty guests in for the weekend."

"How many bedrooms does the house have?" I ask.

"Twenty-eight in the main house," Alan replies. "There's another set of living quarters for people working in the research facility, but that side of the island is segregated from the residential side for security reasons. Not to worry, you won't be getting the long, scientific tours."

We're waiting in line at the elevator now. It's much larger than I expected and fits fifteen people at a time, zooming them up the side of the cliff fast and smooth. My stomach turns over as I watch the glass cube shoot upward, reflecting the bright light off the ocean.

"Is that thing safe?" I ask Alan, breaking character.

"Oh, completely." He launches into a technical description of the shaft and the lift mechanism, and it takes everything in me to keep my eyes wide and interested.

When it's our turn, we're at the rear of the group getting on, which means there's no one between us and the glass doors. They swoosh shut behind us, and I turn to look out at the ocean. With a yank, my belly button is pulled out from behind me and we rocket skyward. It's like a roller coaster, the yacht and the dock falling away, the sky growing huge, a blue bubble in which we're floating.

And then it stops. We're easily a hundred feet up. The boats are small below us. Faintly, at the very horizon, I see a dark line that I think is the mainland. The sight gives me a little shiver of relief.

But wait. The doors are going to open out onto thin air. How are we—

The opposite wall slides open, leaving the glass doors closed. I spin, relieved, ready to claw my way out. People are moving slowly, and I almost shove them aside. With a grateful gasp of fresh air, I stumble onto an expansive lawn where a white flagstone walkway cuts a tidy path through the acres of grass to the mansion.

People are pausing at what looks like a checkpoint where two staff members are searching people with a metal detector wand like TSA does at the airport.

"What's happening?" I ask Alan.

"Oh, they have to confiscate all electronics," he explains.

"Like our phones?" My voice shoots up an octave in shock.

"Of course. The island houses proprietary technology. You've heard of corporate espionage?"

"But what if I need to make a call?" What if Leo calls me? I feel naked and vulnerable without a phone.

"Oh, don't worry! You'll have a phone in your room. It's just to prevent cameras, recording devices, stuff like that."

"What if I need to check my voicemail?" I ask. "What about texts?"

"There isn't service out here anyway. Check your phone, you'll see."

I look at it. He's right. No service. I want to slap him for not having mentioned this.

It's my turn now. A well-built blond man in the black-and-white uniform says, "Please hand us your purse." His female counterpart pats me down while he extracts my phone and zips it into a clear plastic baggie. "Write your name here," he instructs me, handing me a Sharpie. Everyone else has already done this. I see the bin at his feet with the pile of bagged iPhones in fancy cases.

I sigh heavily and write *Summer* on the bag. I don't like this. Not at all. For starters, if they're paranoid about thievery and searching us when we come and go, any plans I had to load myself up with diamonds and credit cards are out the window. I feel momentarily castrated, but then I think, perhaps there are ways to hide small items. I can't imagine they'll search every single inch of my suitcase, and it's not hard to fashion a hidden pocket in the lining. I've done that with many dresses I've worn to various events. Something to consider.

A group is taken to the mansion's east wing; a pair of older, important-looking couples are ferried off to the central wing, including William and Caroline. She shoots me a smug look, and we're taken to the west wing along with Steve and Julie. So far, I don't see Leo or Michael anywhere, but I keep my eyes peeled every step of the way. It takes a full five minutes to turn the corner to the east wing, which butts up against a forest. As we approach it, Alan tells me, "You see how the walkway splits in two?" He points toward the trees, where one leg of the flagstone walkway turns into a wooden footpath. "That's the way to the beach. The woods are on a hill, and they slope down to the ocean. The water's really nice. No waves; it's a protected cove. And there's a shark net, so you're safe."

Julie falls back to walk beside me. "Alan loves playing tour guide, especially when he has a captive audience." She's my height and slim, with full breasts that weren't cheap, brown hair threaded tastefully with highlights, and spray-tanned skin. She wears a diamond pendant that I estimate at three carats and a set of matching studs in her ears. My hands itch to slip them off her. *Not yet.*

"This place is massive," I say. "Bigger than I'd pictured."

She smiles. "I'm happy to show you around."

"Thanks."

"So you're dating Alan?"

"Yes, but it's new."

She looks me over. "God, you're gorgeous, though. How did Alan even have the nerve to talk to you? Usually he's so shy with women."

This might be a subtle way of figuring out if I'm here for Alan's money, which is a fair assumption. "I approached him, actually," I reply.

"Ha!" She shoots a knowing look at Alan's back. "Called it. He's such a chicken."

"We were at a party and everyone was very . . ." I shrug. "Kind of pretentious. Alan seemed nice. We got to talking. I find him refreshing. He's so sincere."

"That he is." She has a fond look on her face. "Steve has known Michael since MIT. They've worked on a ton of projects together, with Alan as well, of course."

I make a mental note: These are close friends of Alan. Don't do anything to make them suspicious. "So tell me about yourself. What do you do?"

Julie starts in about her former career in web design and how she quit to clear some space in her life to have a baby, but now she isn't sure she wants to be tied down by motherhood. I'm sure it's all very relatable for normal women who don't live in trucks. According to books, now that I'm in my thirties, I'm supposed to care about things like this.

The west wing has a humbler entrance than the main house, a small portal of geometric glass and wood through which you enter the foyer. Inside, it's clear an interior designer with an all-white fetish was given free rein and a blank check. The foyer leads into a large living room, which branches off to hallways in two directions. Steve and Julie head left, Julie waving at me as she goes. "See you at dinner!"

I follow Alan and Javier into the hallway, feeling unsettled and desperate to reunite with Leo. Alan takes my hand and gives me an excited smile.

"Here we go," Javier says, opening a tall wooden door. "Miss Summer, this is you. And Mr. Alan, you'll be right across the hall." He indicates a door twenty feet farther down. "Your room is keyed to this." He hands me a card, like in a hotel. To Alan, he says, "Your room has been keyed to your permanent card."

"Got it right here," Alan replies, patting his back pocket. He gives me a peck on the cheek. "Why don't you freshen up? I need to make some calls and check in. We should leave for dinner in an hour. Can you be ready by then?"

"Of course." I'm grateful he's not going to follow me into my room and demand sex. I don't yet know how I'm going to get out of that one.

I beep myself into my room, close the door behind me, and am engulfed by silence. It's more of a suite, with a sitting area off the bedroom outfitted with low, beige couches. The walls are stark white, and large picture windows look down onto the rolling, forested hills. Below them, I get a glimpse of the ocean.

I find my suitcase beside the bed, open it up, and discover that my clothes are a little rumpled and out of order. They searched my stuff. I'd expected as much, but I still feel violated by the intrusion.

I find the phone on the nightstand, examine the list of extensions, and press zero. A warm female voice answers, "Housekeeping, may I help you?"

"Yeah, I was wondering if I could call another guest from my room."

"Of course! You'll just dial the four-digit extension. Do you need me to look that up for you?"

"Yes, please. Her name is Leoneli Ramirez."

"One moment . . ." A pause. "Can you spell that?" I spell it and wait. "I'm so sorry, but I don't have anyone on the guest list by that name."

"Well, she's a guest of Michael's. She might be under his name."

"Oh," she replies, surprised.

"Can you put me through to his room?" I'm not expecting a yes, and I don't get one.

"I'm sorry, but no, we can't patch you through to Mr. Forrester directly. Would you like to leave him a message?"

"Sure, yes. Just tell him I'm trying to get in touch with Leo."

"Will do. I'll let him know he can reach you on your extension."

I put the phone down, eyes on the forest outside the window, feeling like I've taken a wrong turn and gotten myself very, very lost. My Land Cruiser, stashed on the third floor of LAX long-term parking, feels worlds away.

Leo, where are you?

CHAPTER TWELVE

LEO

WEDNESDAY, JUNE 7

The island rose up out of the dark, lullaby ocean, its cliffs like the hunched shoulders of celestial giants congregated in prayer, the ocean lapping their knees. The jagged landforms grew as we approached, silhouetted dark-on-dark against the blanket of stars that had been hidden behind light pollution in the city. My breath escaped in a quiet hiss of appreciation. It was so perfectly Californian, the shape of the land, all spiked outcroppings and staggering drops to the water below. It would be breathtaking by day. How incredibly strange that this land shouldn't be public.

"How can someone own an island?" I asked Michael in a hushed voice.

He was calm and serene, navigating parallel to the bluffs looming high above us. "What do you mean?"

"It's, like, a landform. It's its own tiny continent. It feels like something you shouldn't be able to *possess*."

He glanced at me, eyebrows raised. "Do you feel like that about owning land in general?"

I thought about it while we drifted past more cliffs, their ser-
rated architecture obscuring more and more stars. "I guess so. Like
if I own a house, do I also own all the land beneath it going down
to the earth's core?"

He didn't answer. He was focused on getting around a rocky
point where the water was choppier and sprayed a fine salty mist
up into our faces.

"I don't technically own it," he said once we were clear. "Tenet
Holdings does."

"But you own Tenet Holdings?"

"I'm the majority shareholder."

I had no idea what that meant, but it seemed boring.

A small marina came into view, all the slots empty. A cliff rose
high above, and at the very top of it, I glimpsed lights. A house? If
people were here, why weren't there any boats?

As we left the open ocean for the marina, the waves softened,
and the night was even quieter than it had been. I leaned forward
to peer up at the top of the cliff, but we were too close now and
the lights had disappeared behind the overhang. "Is that a building
up there?" I asked.

"That's the residence, yeah." He guided the boat into a slot and
killed the engine.

He hopped out of the boat onto the dock in a fluid, practiced
movement. He reached out a hand to help me, but I brushed it off.
"I'm a country girl," I reminded him, putting a hand on the boat
and jumping lightly onto the smooth wooden boards, shoes in
hand.

He gripped my shoulders and held me at arm's length, looking
me up and down. I must have been a disheveled mess, hair tangled
from wind and sex, dress rumpled, makeup worn off. On his face,
I thought I read fondness, and I smiled at him and tried to smooth
my hair.

"Is anyone in the house up there? I'm a disaster."

"You are perfect," he said. "And don't worry about your hair.
No one's here. Are you okay barefoot? I can have someone bring
down some sandals."

"I thought you just said no one's here," I protested.

"The house staff, I mean. And there's the research team at the facility on the other side of the island. You'll never see them."

I considered this, eyes flicking back up the cliff. "It's a huge house, isn't it?"

"It is. We have a lot of fundraisers and things like that. We have to be able to house large groups." He grinned, boyish, and pulled me by the hand. "Let me show you my elevator. I get excited about this."

I allowed myself to be led up a long wooden walkway that hovered above the sand to a glass elevator built into the side of the cliff. He pressed the button, the doors opened, and he ushered me inside. It was unlit, and I watched in quiet awe as the nighttime ocean, bright with moonlight, sparkled beneath us while we rocketed upward. I heard a gasp of excitement escape my lips. It was like flying. I pressed myself to the glass, arms extended on either side so I could imagine I was airborne.

We reached the top, and the back doors opened. I turned to Michael, who was watching me with a happy gleam in his blue eyes. "I like your elevator," I told him.

As the doors opened, he gripped my hand to guide me out, and we stood facing a ridiculous compound of a house across an expanse of lawn, with wings that stretched out in a U shape on either side. It was very modern with lots of glass and wood sliced into angular geometry.

"Well?" Michael asked.

I feigned a grimace. "It's not very big."

He chuckled. "You're teasing me."

"Do you feel comfortable here? Does it feel homey to you?"

"Oh, no. This house is for entertaining." He took my free hand and pulled me close to his side. "It has a great master bedroom, though. A really large bed."

I crooked an eyebrow, amused. "You probably get a lot of use out of it."

"Never." The corner of his mouth twitched, and I shook my head, not buying it in the least. I yawned, tired and unable to stifle it. He smiled down at me. "Let's get you into a hot bath. How does that sound?"

"It sounds amazing."

We were closer to the main entrance now, a two-story construction of glass and wood that belonged at the entryway of an art museum. One of the double front doors opened, and a model-handsome, muscular man a bit older than me in a white shirt and black slacks smiled at Michael, white teeth sparkling. "Welcome home, Mr. Forrester."

"Thanks, Javier." Michael nodded to me. "This is Leo. She'll need clothes and toiletries sent up to the master suite."

Javier turned his professionally whitened teeth on me. "That will be no problem. I can guess your dress size, but what is your shoe size?"

I blinked at him for a moment, a little creeped out. "Uh, a nine," I answered at last.

"Perfect."

Michael and I passed through the entrance into the foyer, which opened into a stadium-size great room with a massive stone fireplace and beams crisscrossing along the vaulted ceiling. I stood there for a moment, taking in the size of the place.

"What?" Michael asked as Javier hovered discreetly.

"I mean, you could only fit two apartment buildings inside this room. That's annoying."

He pulled me toward a hallway. To Javier, he called, "Have them bring us refreshments. Nothing with alcohol." To me, he said, "Any other food restrictions? Allergies?"

"I don't eat meat."

"Vegan," he called to Javier, and we were now in a hallway so wide you could drive a bus through it. He led me to a set of heavy double doors. Two small boxes were attached to the wall, one that looked like a sensor you'd beep with a card and a smaller flat black one that Michael pressed his thumb to. The doors swung inward, and we proceeded through them.

"What was that?" I asked, eyes on the large, antique paintings that lined the walls. They were all done in the same style, bright and colorful, a departure from the white-on-white of the rest of the house.

"Security. I often have a houseful of guests I don't know well. No one's allowed back here. It's my only way to feel some sense of privacy."

I walked beside him quietly, feeling like I'd wandered into some strange other universe and that, back in my home dimension, Leo was tucking in for the night with Summer in the back of the Land Cruiser.

This could be a cash cow, a voice whispers in the back of my head. This was his private space. No doubt there would be some hidden goodies in here that could be sold to the media or at least pawned for a good profit. That said, sometimes with these men, you could get more as gifts than by thievery if you played your cards right. I was starting to feel Michael might be that type of man, and my chest warmed at the possibilities, picturing Summer's pride and satisfaction.

We passed closed doors, a library, a conference room. At last, we entered a living room, large and airy, with a whole wall of windows. A comfortable-looking leather couch was set up across from the windows alongside two accompanying armchairs. An open door to the left led into an office. I got a glimpse of a desk and more uncovered windows.

"This way," he said, and my bare feet sank into a deep, soft area rug in a huge bedroom. The bed was gargantuan, clearly custom-made, low to the ground and soft-looking, with white bedding and a bamboo headboard that stretched up to the vaulted ceiling. "Stay there," he instructed, flicking off the lights.

With the room dark, I could see that the picture windows looked directly out onto the ocean far below. This side of the house must have been close to the edge of the cliff. Far away, the bright moon sent rippling reflections down onto corduroy waves hundreds of feet beneath us. "Just wanted you to see that no one can look in through these windows," he explained.

He turned the lights back on, sat on the edge of the bed, and kicked his shoes off. "The bathroom is through there if you'd like to get in the soaking tub. It's all yours."

"Are we going to hang out here tomorrow as well, you think?" I asked. "Or do you want to go back to L.A. in the morning?"

"I'd like you to stay for the day if you'd be willing. We can do some snorkeling, hang out on the beach." His blue eyes twinkled, and I could imagine the type of day he was actually hoping for.

"That sounds amazing. Let me just text my friend Summer so she doesn't worry." I dug through my purse, looking for my phone.

"That won't work. You won't have any service."

"What do you mean?"

"We don't support third-party cell reception here. We have so much proprietary tech, we prefer to use our own network."

I felt my eyebrows draw together. "But I have to tell Summer where I am. She'll be worried."

"Oh, don't worry, we'll make that available to you. You just have to be on our network."

"What does that mean?"

"We have house devices you're welcome to use. But for now, why don't you write down Summer's number and a message, and I'll have Javier pass it along so she doesn't have to wait. Good?"

I breathed a sigh of relief. "Good. Thank you."

He handed me a pad of paper and a pen, and I wrote down Summer's number and *Hey, it's Leo. I'm going to spend tomorrow with Michael. Phone doesn't have reception, so this is coming from his—*

I look up. "What's Javier's job title? Manservant? Butler? Dental hygienist?"

He looks up from a stack of papers, amusement playing at his lips. "House manager."

"Personal . . . shopper," I say, pretending to write it down.

. . . coming from his house manager, Javier. I'll check in with you tomorrow evening. Call or text this number if you need anything and they'll get the message to me.

I handed Michael the paper. He folded it in half without look-ing at it, which was sweet.

A musical chime sounded. He stood. "That'll be Javier. Why don't you get in the bath? When you're done, I'll have all kinds of treats set up for you."

I smiled angelically up at him. "You're nice. Maybe I'll let you impregnate me after all."

He cracked up, and I made my way into a massive bathroom entirely finished in white marble. As promised, there was a huge soaking tub with Jacuzzi jets and decorative glass jars filled with bath salts. I dismissed the implication that I was one in a long string of women to have enjoyed this bathtub. Who cared? It was my tub for now.

I started the water, laughed at my disheveled reflection, and did some nosing around in the cabinets while the bath filled up. No sign of a wife or girlfriend; there was one electric toothbrush, one fancy electric razor, one men's grooming kit, and a collection of men's moisturizer and hair care products.

I stripped, throwing my clothes into a careless heap, and sank into a lavender-scented bath that smelled and felt like paradise. I soaked until my whole body felt loose and warm, thinking about the movie *Pretty Woman,* where the main character takes a bath in the hotel bathroom. Michael did have some commonalities with the male lead in that movie. He was like a combo of that guy and Christian Grey, but more normal and without the weird issues. That I knew of.

"Michael?" I called. "Michael!"

A few moments passed, and then he poked his head around the doorframe. "You rang?" Music drifted in. He was playing some-thing I vaguely recognized. Radiohead?

"Are you trying to *Fifty Shades* me? Are you going to get me all happy and comfy and then introduce me to your sex dungeon?"

He put a hand to his forehead like I was exasperating. "I don't have a sex dungeon. Unless you want one. I can build you a dun-geon if you insist."

"And you should know something." I pointed a stern finger up at him, trying to look haughty, which is not easy when you're butt naked and your eye makeup is melting off your face. "I am not a virgin."

He chuckled. "Get your skinny ass out of there. I'm starving and there's tons of food."

"I've been with other men!" I yelled as he closed the door. I chuckled, satisfied. I liked him a lot. This could be the beginning of a beautiful symbiosis.

CHAPTER THIRTEEN

SUMMER

THE ISLAND
FRIDAY, JUNE 9

I put the finishing touches on my hair with the curling iron, picturing Leo's face when she sees me. Her expression will tell me a lot. She might look disappointed, or angry, or delighted . . .

It's pathetic how badly I'm hoping she'll look delighted.

A knock on the door echoes back through the suite, and I groan quietly and set the curling iron down on the marble countertop. A whole night with Alan. A whole weekend with him, for god's sake. *Leo, you owe me.*

I open the door and fake-smile warmly at Alan, whose eyes light up like it's Christmas morning. I'm in a figure-hugging black designer sheath that shows a rational amount of cleavage, not fully tits-out. "You look beautiful," he says, pulling me in for a kiss. I knew he would do this and didn't put on lipstick yet. I let the kiss go on for a minute, his hands running up and down my back, a daring little caress to my hip telling me he's hoping this will go further later tonight. At last, he pulls back. "I'm a lucky bastard," he says.

I beckon him into my room, leaving the door ajar so he doesn't get the wrong idea. "Give me a moment to put on my lipstick."

He checks his phone while I take a minute in front of the mirror. It's not password protected, which is weird. It's a strange-looking device, not one I remember him having. "They let you keep your phone?" I ask.

He lifts his chin self-importantly. "I have the highest security clearance. This is a specialized phone, encrypted, on the local network. Similar to a satellite phone but much more sophisticated." He pockets it and comes to stand behind me, hands on my hips as I paint gloss on top of the pink lip stain I just applied. "Normally, I stay in my suite of rooms at the research facility on the other side of the island. But I wanted to be close to you." He kisses my cheek from behind, and I feel his erection poking me in the butt.

I step aside and give him the dimpled, innocent smile he seems to like best. "Don't muss me. I worked hard on all this." I gesture to my dress and hair.

"I know, I know. Be a good boy."

I shiver with revulsion, take a black wrap off a hanger, shrug it over my shoulders, and grab my little black purse on our way out. A golf cart is waiting for us, and Alan says, "Hop in!" while getting into the driver's seat and starting it up. "I didn't want you to have to walk all the way to the main house in heels," he explains, which is sadly more thoughtful than most of the men I've actually dated. He cruises along the footpath, pausing when we approach Steve and Julie walking. "You guys want a ride?" he calls out.

"Hell yeah," Steve says, and they climb into the seats behind us. Julie is in a royal-blue cocktail dress and strappy heels, her neck and wrist adorned with strands of bright white diamonds that make my mouth water. "How are you, Summer?" she asks, settling in.

"Good!" I turn to smile at her. "You're looking beautiful tonight."

"So are you! Alan, your date is going to outshine all of us."

"Please," I reply. "This dress is nothing. Who are you wearing?" I'm proud I remembered to ask this. It's all about the little touches when you're playing a character. Julie starts in on this up-

and-coming designer she discovered on her last trip to Manhattan, and I'm saved from having to talk for the rest of the ride.

The main house is crowded, and the path to the grand entrance looks like the sidewalk outside an opera house, with sparkly, perfumed people chattering breezily. I force myself to keep my face neutral. If I were in this crowd under any other circumstances, my mind would be racing, thinking about opportunities for theft. Instead, I'm just a ball of anxiety, hoping to spot Leo.

Alan parks the golf cart in an empty space right off the footpath like he owns the place, and we get out and join the crowd.

"Who are all these people anyway?" I ask Alan as we climb the steps to the front entrance.

"A combination of investors we're trying very hard to impress and members of the scientific and tech communities," he replies in my ear.

"Well, tell me if you want me to be particularly nice to anyone," I say, the dutiful would-be girlfriend.

"Just be yourself," he answers, which is hilarious.

The great room has been divided into two main areas. By the fireplace, drinks are being served both by a bartender set up in the corner and by servers with trays of champagne. On the other side, ten large, round tables have been set up to create a dining area. The sun is setting outside the windows, and the ocean is glimmering orange and purple.

"Champagne?" Alan asks me.

"I'd prefer red wine if you don't mind," I reply, and he goes off to get us drinks at the bar. Relieved to be free of him for a moment, I search for Michael and Leo.

And then I see him. He's at the top of the front steps, chatting with a group of older men. Gone are the Radiohead T-shirt and jeans, replaced by a crisp suit with a soft-looking sweater in navy blue underneath. He still has his stubble, and his eyes glow bright blue.

Leo isn't beside him.

I step closer, scanning the people, my heart racing in anticipation, expecting to see that familiar face, the toss of dark brown hair, the wide smile that always seems ready to take off in flight.

But no. She's nowhere.

A blossom of panic blooms in my gut.

I feel for the first time that she's lost, scattered out in the too-wide world. It's a horrible, familiar feeling, and it terrifies me because I know from personal experience how possible it is to lose someone forever.

A hand on my arm makes me jump. Alan gazes at me, starry-eyed. "Didn't mean to startle you. Here's your wine." He hands me a large, delicate red wineglass and I dip my nose into it and inhale deeply, the scent reassuring. "You okay?" he asks.

"Of course! It's all just so beautiful."

"I know. It's a gorgeous place." The sun has almost set, and the ceiling fixtures brighten to compensate for the darkening sky.

Julie slides out of the crowd and clinks her glass against mine. "Having fun yet?"

"Oh yes, it's . . ."

"I'll leave you girls for a moment," Alan says, eyes on a pair of men talking to Michael. He hurries to join them and greets the men with enthusiasm, shoulder to shoulder with Michael.

"Investors?" I ask Julie.

"Who fucking knows." She crooks an eyebrow at me. "Now, how bored are you really?"

I force myself to stop looking for Leo and give Julie my attention. "On a scale of one to ten?"

She cackles and lifts her champagne. "Down the hatch, girl."

I sip my wine. "I never get drunk in a crowd," I tell her, which is both the truth and a piece of advice.

"Why not? Everyone's so obsessed with themselves, they're not paying attention to anyone else."

I say, "Exactly," which is a little inward joke. She's precisely right, which is why I limit myself to half a glass of wine, so I can take advantage of everyone's preoccupation and relieve them of some of their more valuable possessions. This crowd is ideal—the women are covered in diamonds, and the men's loose-fitting suits are such easy prey . . .

Julie says, "Come on, please talk to me. Otherwise I'm going to have to go hear about the stock market from some old guy who wants to *accidentally* feel me up. Or I can discuss laser face peels with some lady who thinks Pelotons are for the nouveaux riches."

I can't help but laugh. "Okay, okay. I'll save you. Talk away."

She follows my eyes, which are back to roving around the faces in the crowd. "Are you looking for someone?" she asks. "You seem distracted."

I decide to go with the truth. "I actually thought my friend would be here. Have you seen a young woman with dark brown hair in a long bob? Really pretty, very thin? She was with Michael the other day. I thought he'd bring her as his date for the weekend."

She shakes her head. "Michael never brings dates to an investors' weekend, and I've never seen him with anyone fitting that description. Did your friend say she was invited?"

"Not exactly . . ."

She waves her hand. "Many have tried to climb that mountain and failed. Trust me. So, let's talk. For real, what's your game plan? You want to get Alan to sponsor you for a while? You'll have to be super explicit with him about your expectations. He's kind of dense."

My eyebrows shoot up. "Excuse me?"

She puts a cool hand on my arm. "It's fine. No one's listening. They're talking about clean energy and the pressure of being the decision makers. 'It's lonely at the top,'" she drawls in an imitation of a masculine voice. "'Private jets aren't safe enough, but it's not right for someone in my position to fly commercial, can you imagine?'" She fakes an old-man belly laugh.

I reevaluate her from head to toe. She's probably thirty-seven, at least ten years younger than Steve, and has all the features I'd expect the wife of someone like Steve to have: skin smooth from facials, subtle surgical enhancements—beautiful breasts swelling above the neckline of her dress, lips a bit fuller than nature intended—but her eyes are twinkling mischievously, and it hits me that I'm looking at someone not unlike myself.

"What attracted you to Steve?" I ask. "How did you meet?"

"He was married to someone else at the time." She takes a delicate sip of her drink. "And now he's married to me."

I chuckle, eyes going back to Michael, who's now deep in conversation with two women who must work for him. One has a clipboard, and both have walkie-talkies clipped to the belts of their dark suits. Preparations are under way in the dining area, with black-and-white-outfitted people rushing back and forth.

"So?" She nudges me. "Alan doesn't have a current wife, so you're ahead of the game there. Although it's fun when you're the mistress. All that sneaking around gets them hot. They pay big money for that."

I return my eyes to her. "But what about now that *you're* the wife? Does *he* sneak around?"

She opens her mouth to answer, but the lights cut out completely. The crowd gasps and cries out into the darkness. My heart seizes, and my whole body tenses.

Then a light flickers on, up in the rafters above the dining area. A second one joins it, and then a third. They brighten just enough to reveal three figures clinging to the ceiling beams.

A series of gasps and whispers from the guests. I strain to understand what I'm seeing.

The lights brighten a bit more, and I see that the figures are women, dressed in sparkly black bikinis. What the hell?

They drop in unison, plummeting to the floor and stopping in midair. They're tethered to sashes, which are connected to the beams. I breathe out a sigh of relief. They're acrobats, the aerial ones who work with silks.

Music turns on, a song I almost recognize. It sounds a bit nineties, very low and bassy, some kind of trip-hop. I remember Michael's Radiohead T-shirt.

The women begin a routine that involves them spinning and

whirling, strong legs slicing the air. The audience claps and cheers as they perform in the semidarkness. Beside me, Julie sips her champagne, blasé like she's seen it all before.

With a deft, sneaky hand, I reach for Julie's wrist. I've been subconsciously tracking the clasp on her bracelet, which you squeeze and release, a very easy kind to undo one-handed. While all eyes are on the acrobats, Julie's filled with sardonic amusement, I carefully, without looking, hold the bracelet in place with two fingers and unclasp it with my thumb. The trick is to keep the bracelet from moving and alerting the wearer. You must suspend it in place until you remove it. I feel the catch loosen, and then I pull it off her wrist without any friction against her skin. It's a cool little weight in my palm.

I sip my wine and slip the bracelet into an invisible pocket I'd hand-sewn into the dress months ago; this is one of my favorite dresses for occasions like these. My heart is racing. There's no high on earth like this, not drugs, not sex. Nothing.

All right. I've had my fun. Now I need to focus.

"Excuse me one moment," I whisper to Julie, and I slip between people toward Michael. I feel fluid in the crowd, like water flowing around stones, and with stolen diamonds in my pocket, I might just be invincible. When I reach him, I put a hand on his forearm. "Michael?" I murmur, just audible over the music.

He looks down at me for a startled moment. Then he blinks away his surprise and gives me a warm smile. "Oh, hello!" He leans in and does a friendly air-cheek kiss. "You're Leo's friend Summer, right?"

"Yes. So good to see you again."

He looks puzzled. Up close, his blue eyes are beautiful, rimmed with long dark lashes. He says, "How did you—"

"I'm with Alan. We met at your party. He asked me to be his guest this weekend."

"Ah. Well, welcome. I hope you enjoy."

"I was thinking Leo would be here. Is she?"

Now he looks completely taken aback. "No. She didn't—Why would you think—"

"I haven't spoken to her since your party. I thought she might have come here with you."

His brow furrows. "No, I'm sorry." He clears his throat. "We went on a short ride on my boat, but we docked in Marina del Rey, and she said she was taking a cab home from there."

I'm stunned. "When did you drop her off? That same night?"

"The next morning, around nine o'clock. I had to get her back early because I needed to get over here by noon." He sees the concern on my face and says, "I'm sorry. I wish I could help."

She's been in L.A. this whole time?

One of the acrobats falls, spinning through the air. The crowd reverberates with gasps of horror, but it's a trick. She jolts to a stop at the bottom of her silk, mere feet above one of the round tables set with crystal and china. The audience breaks into applause.

One of the suited workers approaches Michael and whispers something into his ear. She rushes off, and he tells me, "It's my time to make a speech. Enjoy the show. I hope to see more of you this weekend." He turns to follow the woman back toward one of the hallways. I watch her fiddle with his lapel, putting a microphone on him. The acrobats are wrapping it up, doing their last tricks, and the music is dying down.

Michael hops nimbly onto the fireplace hearth, and a spotlight hits him, obviously tucked up in the ceiling somewhere. He looks like he's about to give a TED Talk.

"That was incredible, let's give them a round of applause," he cries. Everyone claps as the acrobats trot off into the darkness. The crowd falls silent, and Michael turns to us, hands clasped in front of him, shoulders square and relaxed. "Thank you so much for your presence here this weekend. We're standing at a juncture. Everyone in this room is a mover and shaker, disrupting the status quo and standing in the gap for a world on the brink."

Alan appears at my elbow and slips an arm around my waist. He shoots me a wink and returns his attention to Michael. We're a crowd of uplifted faces, drinking from the fountain of his words.

My mind drifts as Michael drones on about clean energy. Leo isn't here. She's been in L.A. this entire time I've been searching for her? Why didn't she call me?

It doesn't make sense. She ditched me? Just like that, after five years of being what I had considered sisters?

Maybe she didn't ditch me. Maybe she got lost, or maybe she got . . .

No. I'm not going to finish that sentence.

I turn, bumping into a gray-haired man who shoots me a sharp look, and slip through the crowd to the back, where Javier stands, hands in pockets, watching Michael's speech with no expression on his face. He's probably seen this a thousand times. I give him a little wave as I approach, and his eyes flick down my body as he greets me.

"May I help you?" He removes his hands from his pockets and clasps them in front of him.

"I hope so." I beckon him into the hallway so we won't be overheard. "I need to get back to L.A. Can someone take me in one of the boats?"

"I'm sorry, but no."

I'm not used to hearing no, not from men in service positions who have previously been staring at my breasts. I feel my eyebrows lift. "Excuse me?"

He stammers. "I–I mean, not no as in, no, but no as in, we don't have any boats to take you back in. It's a closed weekend. The yachts are chartered from Marina del Rey and have already returned."

I study his face for signs of deception. "When I arrived, there were two other boats docked at the marina. I assumed they belonged to the island."

He shakes his head. "They're docked on the mainland as well; they belong to the same company. As I said, it's a closed weekend."

A burst of applause from the great room almost makes me jump. "I don't understand," I reply. "You're telling me that if one of these investors came to you with the same request, you'd tell him, sorry, it's a closed weekend?"

He nods vigorously. "Yes, ma'am. We hold investors' weekends quarterly, and they're always closed. We're demo'ing proprietary technology. It's a high-security event. It's for everyone's safety, to protect investments. They're all aware."

I narrow my eyes and stare him down for five seconds. It's a trick I learned. Most people are uncomfortable with prolonged eye contact. He's no exception. He blinks in rapid succession, then begins explaining in a hurried string of words. "Of course, we maintain a relationship with a medevac in case of emergency. If we have a medical crisis, we have a doctor onsite, and we can have a helicopter or small plane here within the hour. All our guests over the age of fifty sign a waiver to—"

I hold a hand up. I've heard enough.

I'm tired of men. I wish they weren't simultaneously so easy and the most difficult, dangerous thing in the world. His brown eyes are wide with feigned innocence, but I can see lies scrawled across his tanned face.

"Thank you so much. I'm sorry for taking your time." I have to keep my voice low or I'll scream.

I back away from Javier, tucking myself into the nearest group of people who are listening to Michael's speech, mouths partway open like they've been hypnotized. I move to the back of the room and then the hallway that leads out into the next wing. Once the crowd is behind me, I find my shoulders relaxing, my steps widening. The *click-clack* of my heels on the bamboo floors comes faster, choppier.

I burst out into the night. The breeze tosses my hair around my face, and I kick my shoes off, dangling them in my hand, and jog across the lawn toward the glass elevator. Javier was lying, and I'm going to prove it before he has a chance to move the boats he swore aren't at the dock.

I press the elevator call button. The doors open, and I step in. The ocean is a vast black vista glinting in the light of a new moon. I press a hand to the glass, reassuring myself that it's real as the elevator descends smoothly, a rock falling from the sky. For one weightless moment, I let go of the glass, and I'm sure I'm dying, plummeting in a free fall—but then it slows, and the doors slide open, letting me out onto the wooden walkway.

Shoes in hand, I hurry along the path, boards creaking under my bare feet. It slopes down, makes a turn, and I jump down onto the sand, running toward the docks.

They're empty.

I stop, feet buried in cool, sucking sand. It's not quicksand, but only just.

There are no boats.

The docks rock slightly, or maybe it's an optical illusion as the waves foam around them. Not a single boat. Not one.

I find myself sinking to my knees, staring out to sea.

Above the ambient ocean noise, a faint whirring catches my attention. I search for the source and almost miss a small, airborne object as it sails smoothly past, about twenty feet above my head. It's gone so fast, I'm not sure I saw it at all.

A drone?

I guess they weren't kidding about this weekend being high-security.

The waves are gentle, ebbing and flowing, licking at the sand, unconcerned. I'm reminded of all the things my mom said about the universe. What if she was right about everything? That stupid jar full of marbles. If you wait for the universe to give it another shake and land you next to someone you love, you'll be waiting for an eternity.

I guess all I can do is get through the weekend, go back to L.A., and try to find Leo. Is this going to be my mother all over again? Mauricio searching through Jane Does, showing me photos of dead women?

If I never find her, I'll have to assume . . .

What? That she left me? Or that she hitched a ride with a strange man and he decided to take her path in a new, darker direction?

There has to be something I can do. Leo has family in Fresno, a Social Security number, a last name. If I report her missing, the cops will be able to find her in their computers. I can't just sit here. I have to do *something*.

CHAPTER FOURTEEN

LEO

THURSDAY, JUNE 8

We tumbled into the house from the beach, sandy and suntanned and exhilarated. It had been an incredible day—we had woken up late, and, after a long brunch, had taken the Jet Skis out and explored the coves. A blissful hour was spent driving Michael's speedboat all around the coastline, past the research facility, which loomed like a nuclear power plant on the opposite side of the island. It was creepy out there, acres of windmills rising out of the water, their roots deep in the waves below.

Afterward, we snorkeled in pristine coves populated by colorful fish, watching sea lions sunbathe on a huge rock off the coast, where the horizon was the entire Pacific, stretching out to the vast expanses between California and Japan.

When we returned to the house, Javier was waiting in the front hall as though he'd had a psychic vision we would be arriving momentarily. Ever pleasant, he said, "Mr. Forrester, may I bring you some beverages once you've gotten cleaned up?"

Michael said, "Sure, and get dinner set up."

"Yes, it's all handled."

To Javier, I said, "Can I just check on something? Did someone text my friend Summer?"

He nodded, almost a bow. "It's been taken care of."

"Did she reply?"

"She did, this morning at ten o'clock. She said, 'Sounds good.'"

Relief. I'd been worrying about this all day in the back of my mind, thinking Summer may not have read the text from an unknown number. I followed Michael to his rooms, almost skipping with happiness.

"You hungry?" he asked, looping an arm around me.

"Starved."

"Good. I have something special planned for dinner."

"Really?"

"Yep." He winked at me, a little secretive.

Outside the picture windows in his suite, the sun was setting, turning the ocean orange and purple. I stood there to witness it, thinking big thoughts about existence and impermanence, thoughts tainted by memories of my sister and all the distance between now and then. He came up behind me, and I said, "I don't know how you ever go back to the mainland. I could stay here forever."

He rested his cheek on my head. "This is where I go to be free. To be myself."

I dressed for dinner in a black dress and heels retrieved from the rack of clothes Javier had brought in for me. The dress fit perfectly, just a simple, stretchy sheath that somehow still managed to look expensive. The heels were high enough to give me the long-legged look I leaned on heavily when buttering up men. I emerged from the bathroom, made-up and ready to go, and found Michael on the couch, typing fast into a laptop. He glanced up, did a double take, and snapped the laptop shut.

"Let's stay here," he said, eyes intense in the low lamplight.

I laughed. "You're going to have to feed me first."

He sighed, looking at my legs again. "Fine." He was in another pair of jeans and a black T-shirt, and he grabbed a blazer off the couch. Slipping it on, he said, "It would be a shame to waste the surprise, anyway."

"Surprise?"

"I may have gone overboard." He made a chivalrous, after-you gesture, and I headed for the door of his suite.

"What did you do?" I was dying of curiosity. I loved surprises. And this gave me hope; gifts were good.

"You'll see," he replied, a mysterious smile pulling at the corners of his mouth.

We walked the mile of hallways to the great room, my heels loud on the bamboo flooring. I tried guess after guess. "You brought in a buffalo and we're going spear hunting," and "We're going to be skydiving off your private rocket ship."

When we arrived at last, I gasped. A fire was crackling in the massive fireplace, a cozy table for two set up in front of it. The walls were lit in pinks and purples by hidden spotlights. From the ceiling dangled long, silky sashes, an unusual touch.

"Please, sit," Michael said, gesturing to the table.

The chair was soft and comfortable, big enough for me to sink into, and the fire turned Michael's skin into warm honey. "This is heavenly," I told him, hiding my disappointment and hoping for more tangible gifts after dinner.

Three staff members appeared out of the darkness. One wheeled a cart full of silver-covered plates and two positioned themselves on either side of the fireplace with hands crossed in front of themselves, as though their entire job was to stand there and be available in case we needed anything.

The woman wheeling the cart was a brunette in her thirties with a pretty, patient face. She said, "Good evening, Mr. Forrester."

"Yes, thank you."

She poured water like a fine-dining server, one hand behind her back. "I can offer you mocktails if you like, sir."

He must have told them I didn't drink. I realized now that he hadn't had a drop of alcohol since we'd been together. "Go ahead and have a real drink if you want," I told him. "It won't bother me."

He shook his head. "I'm fine." To the woman, he said, "Sparkling water with lime for me, and whatever she'd like."

"That's perfect for me as well," I told her.

The appetizers were fancy, finger-size bites of pastry that looked French. As I tried not to devour them ravenously, the lights dimmed. A quartet of musicians had appeared out of nowhere, tucked into a corner of the room. They lifted their instruments and began to play an interesting, haunting melody. I laughed in disbelief. "Do you have musicians onsite, or did you bring them in? Either way, that's the most extra thing I've ever seen."

He grinned at me. "I flew them in."

"For tonight?"

"I'm trying to impress a much-younger woman."

I started to make a joke, but then movement drew my attention upward. At the top of the sashes, bodies were unfurling. They had been up there this whole time, stationed at the ceiling, and now the pink and purple lights began to flash and flicker, a light show in time to the music. The bodies unfolded and whirled; they were acrobats, three of them, the central woman a platinum blonde with long, muscular legs.

"I was wrong," I murmured. "*This* is the most extra thing I've ever seen."

He chuckled. "Do you like?"

"It's incredible. And truly a first." The brunette had returned with her cart and was sliding plates onto the table. She named the dishes as she set them down, but I didn't hear her words.

Michael was watching me. "Do you wish you could do what the acrobats are doing?"

I laughed. "You already know me."

"I think so." His eyes were doing the thing again, where their concentration on me was so hot, it burned. I couldn't look away. Suddenly, I wanted his hands on me and wished we were in his room and not surrounded by all these servants and musicians and acrobats. I felt their eyes on me and wondered if I was imagining it. After all, I was sure Michael had done this sort of thing before. He could do it every weekend for all I knew.

Michael took my hand and grazed his lips across the inside of my wrist, up my forearm to my elbow. My breath caught in my throat, and the tingle of his lips on my skin went all the way to my core. "Let's go to your room," I said. "We'll come back in a minute."

"It's far away," he replied, and then he slipped out of his chair onto his knees. He turned my chair so I was facing him and kissed my knee. I was confused, full of music and pink light, the firelight flickering in time with the purple strobes, the ceiling stretching up into darkness.

"Michael, what—"

He pulled my legs apart and kissed the inside of my thigh. I gasped, eyes flying up to the acrobats, to the staff members standing in the shadows, hands clasped in front of them. "Michael—" I tried to protest, squirming back in my chair. He pulled me forward, his head under my skirt, and when I felt his mouth on my panties, I gasped again. I opened my mouth to protest, but it was too late, my body throbbing as he pushed my underwear aside and ran his tongue along the sensitive skin. I felt the presence of the staff, of the woman with her cart standing just out of sight, waiting for her cue—the musicians, who played on like nothing was happening—the acrobats. My eyes went up to them, their bodies twisting and hurtling through the air. Pleasure racked my nerves, but then the blonde's eyes met mine, just for a moment as she spun through a series of somersaults, and I tried to pull Michael away by the hair. He drew back a few inches and frowned up at me. "What's wrong?"

"These people are watching us," I whispered.

"They don't care," he murmured, almost laughing. "We could do anything. Trust me." Again, I thought about NDAs. All these workers must have signed them. Why hadn't I?

His lips were back on me, his head under my dress, and I heard myself moan, the rhythm of his mouth hypnotizing me, dizzying me. It all felt unreal, the strobe and the firelight and the acrobats a movie playing on a 360-degree screen.

It was too late; I was too far gone now, too deep in a mental cave I'd wandered into without realizing it. Michael was unzipping his jeans, pulling me into his lap, and we were joined on the floor, his hands gripping me, his mouth on my neck, everything a dark swirl of colors and music luring me deeper and deeper underground.

"Don't worry," he murmured, and my body was obeying him, on a journey without me.

CHAPTER FIFTEEN

SUMMER

SATURDAY, JUNE 10

The sky goes from black to gray outside the picture window beside my bed. Lying on my side, I watch the dawn as it lightens the tops of the trees, delicately caressing them and the foggy surface of the ocean far below.

I get up, pushing the down comforter off me. I've been awake for hours. I may as well make coffee. There's a coffeemaker on the bureau by the window, and I fix a strong pot. It's dead quiet, and the rug under my feet is deep, soft, and fluffy, a pristine white to match the walls and duvet cover.

While the coffee brews, I study a map of the island that was clearly left out for guests. The island is shaped like an imperfect cookie with some bites taken around the edges and a point poking out near the top. Down at the very southern end, a long rectangle is titled *Residence*. Beyond this is an outbuilding marked *Spa/Gym,* another marked *Facilities,* and a swimming pool and hot tub. A dotted-line path runs from the exit of the west wing, making its

winding way down to a cove marked *Private Guest Beach*. I trace
my finger along its route, making a note of its course.

Most of the island seems to be uninhabited. A road travels
around the island's left perimeter from the residence in the south
to the point up north where another building is labeled *Research
Facility*. The right, or eastern, side of the island doesn't have any
roads or paths marked, and the light topographical markings tell
me it's mountainous. There's a bold dotted line cutting horizon-
tally across the island, separating the top third containing the research facility from the rest, and I imagine that's some kind of
security fence or wall.

I drink coffee as I dress in a bathing suit and sweats, planning on
heading down to the beach and away from all these people; I always feel clearest by the water. I miss my Land Cruiser and the
cozy warmth of Leo, passed out beside me, always still sleeping
when I wake up. I haven't truly slept since she left three nights
ago.

What will it be like if I can't find her?

I won't let her fade off into the ether without a fight. I'll call the
police and report her missing, though I doubt it will do much
good. I've been down that road before.

My eyes drift to the phone in my room. I'm sure calls are monitored, since they're so worried about confidentiality. Would it
matter if I called the police from it? They would know I had . . .
Do I care?

I think I do, but I can't put my finger on why.

A knock sounds on the door, breaking into my thoughts. "One
sec," I call. I cap the mascara bottle and hurry through the suite to
the door, checking the time on my way: seven fifty-five.

Alan is standing on the threshold, dressed for business in a navy
suit and tie. "Hey, pretty lady. I missed you last night." He steps
forward, forcing me back into my room, and kisses my throat,
tongue grazing my collarbone. "Feeling better?"

"I am, thank you. So sorry I pooped out early." I'd come
straight back here from the docks, claiming a migraine.

"We'll catch up tonight." His face is dark with lust. "I have to give tours today or I'd stay here and never leave." His hands drift up to my breasts, and he squeezes them, which almost makes me laugh. Is he honking them? Why do men do this? Is it some sort of latent breastfeeding thing? Why don't women do it, then? Women are breastfed. He looks up from my boobs and sighs. "Later," he says.

"Sounds good," I murmur in response, vowing to find a way out of whatever horrible naked boob-honking ritual he has planned for me. My hand lingers on his belt, then lowers to his pocket, where a distinct hard edge locates his phone for me.

As he returns to nuzzling my neck, I slip fingertips into his pocket and rearrange his hair with my other hand. As I slide his phone out, I brush my body against his crotch and straighten his tie. It all but melts him. He shivers and grips my ass.

"I'm so glad you're here," he says.

"Me, too." Poor guy.

"Hook up with Julie today. She said she'd take you to the spa. Go ahead and get pampered. Enjoy yourself."

The way he says it grosses me out. "That sounds like a plan. What time do you think you'll be done?"

His mouth twists wryly. "It's an all-day thing. Taking groups through the research facility, showing them our new solutions. Lunch, then investors-only cocktail hour. We'll all come back together for dinner again, though, at eight."

I'm relieved to be free of him all day. "Plenty of time for me to get pampered."

He kisses me again, long and wet, and then retreats out into the hallway. The door clicks behind him.

I run to the bathroom to brush my teeth and wash his spit off my neck, and then I examine the phone. It's similar to an Android, as he'd said, but thicker and heavier. I press a button on the side and get a home screen. When I touch the screen, a simple black background and a series of apps are revealed. I don't recognize any of them, but one has an icon of a telephone receiver. I touch the phone app and pull up the call log.

Paranoid, I lock the door, then sit in the bathtub with the

shower curtain pulled shut. After a few seconds of hemming and hawing about how to get the number to the police station, I call the hotel, whose number I'd committed to memory, and ask them if they can find me the number to the Santa Monica Police Department. The guy clearly thinks it's weird, but he searches for the number and gives it to me. I type it in and let it ring, chewing anxiously on a thumbnail.

"SMPD, can I help you?" a woman says curtly.

Keeping my voice down, I say, "Yes, I . . . I wonder what I should do about . . ." I'm stammering. I take a centering breath. "My roommate went on a date with a guy Wednesday night, and she hasn't come home. He says he dropped her off in Marina del Rey on Thursday morning, but she hasn't called or texted, and her phone is off, which is really unlike her. I want to file a missing persons report."

"One moment please."

I listen to hold music until someone else picks up the line. "Santa Monica PD, Officer Baldwin speaking," says a male voice.

I repeat what I'd told the woman, and he asks a few clarifying questions. "When did you last see or hear from her?"

"Wednesday night. We were both at a party at a hotel in Santa Monica. She had a date with a man staying there. He says they took his boat on a ride the next morning, and then he dropped her off in Marina del Rey, where she thought she got a cab back to Santa Monica."

"Do you know the man's name?"

"Yes, it's Michael Forrester. I had been thinking she was still with him on Thursday, so I didn't realize anything was wrong until he told me he'd dropped her off in the marina. Her phone is off. She's not answering." I stop. I'm beginning to repeat myself. Nerves are audible in my stretched-thin voice.

There's a pause.

"Did you say Michael *Forrester*?" His tone is dubious. "The tech guy? The billionaire?"

"You know who he is?" This could lend credibility to my story.

"Ma'am, is this a joke?"

I frown. "No."

"All right. Well, your next step would be to come in and file a missing persons report."

"Can I do it over the phone? I'm out of town right now—"

He sighs like he's praying for patience. "You need to come in and file a report."

"But I'm not there," I argue. "Please. It's really important."

"If you're not in town, how do you know she isn't with a different friend? Are you not even at the house you claim she hasn't returned to? How can you know she isn't home and has her phone off?"

"Because we—" I don't know how to answer this. *Because our house is a truck* doesn't seem like it will get me very far. "I would know," I tell him.

There's a long pause. "What's her name?"

Gratitude rushes through me. "Leoneli Ramirez."

The sound of clicking. "Middle name?"

"I don't know."

"Parents' names?"

"I'm not sure. She had a sister Amanda, but she passed away ten years ago."

More typing. "Oh. One moment . . . She . . ." His voice trails off. I wait. "Huh. I'm familiar with this case. A famous cold case. We studied it in the academy."

My skin prickles. "Cold case?" Why would the police study a car accident—had it been a hit-and-run? A drunk driver? I've never asked Leo for details about her sister's death. It seemed too painful to dig into, and she'd never offered more information.

The officer says, "Oh, yeah. I remember this. Amanda Ramirez. It was a big story out of Fresno."

I'm afraid to say something that will reveal how little I know about this, so I just make a sad noise and murmur, "Yeah, it's been really hard for Leo."

"Well, of course. It always hurts the family the most." He's softened now. "Look. I'll take down her information. When will you be back in L.A.?"

"Monday. And—"

The phone goes dead. It's a black brick in my hand. No apps, nothing. It's been powered off.

"Shit," I whisper, sure this means Alan has noticed it missing and remotely deactivated it.

I need to get rid of it.

I scramble out of the tub and shove my feet into my running shoes. Phone stuffed into my bikini top, I leave my room at a fast walk, breaking into a jog once I'm outside on the path. I wince and hold my boobs, wishing I had on a sports bra. My heart is pounding, and I keep looking over my shoulder, imagining Alan or Javier chasing after me.

The path takes a turn and winds along the clifftops overlooking the ocean, where the sky has lightened to a pearly gray. I slow to a walk, approach the edge of the cliff, and hurl the phone out into space. It bounces off the rocks into the churning waves below.

I stand there, chest heaving, and realize my hands are shaking. I shouldn't have stolen Alan's phone. I could have just called from the landline. Why would anyone here object to me reporting Leo missing?

As soon as I ask myself the question, I have the answer: in case Michael was lying. I don't trust anyone except Leo, least of all men like Forrester.

The cop's words about Amanda being a cold case come back to me. Even if the car accident had been a hit-and-run, I can't see why they'd study it at the police academy. The implication is obvious: Leo lied to me. Her sister may not have died in a car accident. She was likely murdered.

Why hadn't Leo ever told me the truth? I thought we told each other everything. She's my one person, the only one I can rely on to be honest and . . .

I try to push the thought out of my head. I'm sure she has her reasons for keeping this private.

My previous plan to wait out the weekend seems weak now that I have confirmation that the cops will be as useless as I'd imagined. There has to be a way to get back to L.A. Just because Javier can't think of a way to get me back doesn't mean it doesn't exist.

He'd mentioned a doctor, a medevac. I wonder if I could fake an illness to get myself helicoptered back to the mainland. I consider this, thinking through different injuries and sicknesses.

I decide it depends what kind of medical equipment they have here on the island. If they have imaging capabilities, I'm going to have a harder time faking something. Besides, how the hell am I going to casually ask Javier or some other staff member what kind of medical equipment this doctor has?

It comes to me in a rush. *Julie.* She's been here before. She might know.

I turn and hurry back along the path. I jog up the few stairs and into the building, let myself into my room, and head straight for the phone. I press zero and it rings twice.

"Housekeeping," a female voice answers.

"Can you connect me to Julie's room?" I hope they know Julie by first name because I've forgotten her last.

"Certainly. One moment." Hold music, soft and soothing. I tap my feet. The young woman comes back. "Ms. Julie is at the gym and then going down to the beach, ma'am."

"Which beach?"

"There's a path that leads from the exit door closest to your room, down to a set of stairs that will take you to it. Would you like one of us to come escort you?"

"No, thanks. I'll find it."

"There's a guest map on your nightstand if you prefer to make your own way."

After hanging up, I sit on the edge of the bed, anxiety knotting in my stomach. I wonder if Alan will be able to see his phone's location with an exactness that would show him what I'd done or if his call log is monitored remotely. I suppose I'll find out.

CHAPTER SIXTEEN

SUMMER

MONTEREY
FIFTEEN YEARS AGO

I fidgeted in the hard plastic chair, heart thudding dully in my chest, already regretting coming here. Across the desk, a detective stared at me, his face a mask of annoyance. "When you file a missing persons report, you need to tell us where they're missing *from,*" he said like I was an idiot. "You're telling me your mother has been nomadic for twenty years. How can she be missing if she has no home?" He made air quotes with his fingers when he said the word *nomadic.* He was a white man in his fifties with a grizzled, salt-and-pepper military haircut and skin leathered from the sun. I guessed him to be a backpacker or other serious outdoorsman. It made sense; a lot of people around here were hiking and water sports enthusiasts.

I wrapped my arms around myself and glanced back behind me, where the lobby and its exits lay. I could leave anytime. I returned my attention to the detective and summoned a calm, reasoned persona. "We moved from place to place, but we always stayed in Big

Sur a few times a year. That's where we were camping when she left."

"So she left you at the campground. She went off with her boyfriend."

I nodded.

"And you're how old?"

I hesitated, sure the answer wouldn't go over well but determined to tell the truth. There had to be a way out of this trap my mom had set for me. I had to find a way to be a legitimate person, to get a job, a house, a driver's license. "I'm not sure. She doesn't believe in birthdays or 'counting time.'" It was my turn to do air quotes. "She believes that humans existed for thousands of years without clocks, and we should return to that 'simplicity of being.'"

His eyebrows were going to hit his hairline. "So you have no idea how old you are?"

"I think I'm seventeen." I sat up straighter, folding my hands on my lap. I'd chosen my outfit carefully: jeans and a black sweater, something the teenagers he knew probably wore, something that made me look competent. I was playing a part like I always did with strangers, my mom's instructions ingrained into my every mannerism.

He cracked his gnarled knuckles. "Here's the truth. Tracking your mom down is going to be rough. Putting an APB on a plain white van throughout California is . . . really not viable."

I nodded. I hadn't been expecting them to track her down that way.

He continued. "And she's not really missing. She hasn't been kidnapped; there's no crime to investigate. She ran away, essentially. She abandoned you. This is more a case for social services."

Alarm rippled through me. I knew about social services. They were the ones people called if they felt your parents weren't doing a good enough job with you. They took kids and put them into orphanages. My mom was always coaching me, reminding me that above all else, I did not want to get caught by social services.

But she was a liar, wasn't she? A liar and a woman who abandoned her daughter. How much worse could this get?

It turned out it could get a whole lot worse.

Hours later, I was in front of a pair of social workers, women in their thirties or forties taking notes in black-covered folios. I had been moved into an interview room, one of three in a hallway that branched off the rear of the police station's central lobby. I had been told I wasn't a prisoner, but the door was closed, there were no windows, and it was starting to feel like I had blundered into a blind alley.

"What's your mother's last name?" asked the younger of the two women who faced me across the table.

"I don't know."

"Please think carefully. You may have seen her driver's license, maybe heard her mention it to someone."

I shook my head. I was exhausted; I'd been here for hours. No one had fed me, and I felt shaky to my core. Everything I had been able to carry with me from Big Sur was hidden in the woods outside the city, and I was starting to feel a pull toward it, anxious about having left it there, worried about thieves. The one photo album I owned was in my backpack, but everything else I had was there: the tent my mom bought me for my birthday last year (Was she planning this even then?); the small collection of trinkets I'd picked up during our travels; the many little irreplaceable things that still tied me to my mom.

"You don't know?" she clarified, exchanging a glance with the woman beside her, who had a pinched face and graying brown hair in a bun.

"She wouldn't tell me. That was her before life, and it's something she wanted to leave behind."

The women had a nonverbal conversation with their eyes, and then the older one said, "We'll find you a place to stay, but it won't be fast and it won't be easy. At your age, it's likely you'll be placed in a group home until you turn eighteen."

Panic rose like high tide, and I pictured the ocean, the waves roaring into tide pools, submerging them completely. I'd always wondered how the crabs didn't get washed away.

Maybe they did.

"What's a group home?" I heard myself ask in a shaky, uncertain voice that didn't sound like my own.

"It's where a number of young people live together under one roof. There's always an adult there as well," the younger woman explained, clearly assuming the presence of a strange adult would somehow make me feel better. I knew firsthand that adults were more dangerous than kids could ever be.

I took a deep breath. "What about the fact that I don't have an identity? A last name? How am I going to fix that?"

Again, they exchanged a glance. The older woman said, "This is highly unusual. It's possible we won't be able to prove you were born in the United States. If that's true, we could be looking at deportation, but without a country of origin . . . I've honestly never seen a case like this. Of course, it will have to go to court. You'll be assigned an attorney, an advocate."

"Deportation?" I echoed, disbelief coloring my voice. "Where would they even send me?"

"That's what we'll have to work with the court to decide. It hopefully won't come to that."

Now I saw what would happen. I'd have to go through the legal system. Judges, lawyers, courtrooms. Homes that functioned like prisons, like this room did.

I should never have come here. My mother was right. So it would be like this then, me spending my entire life combing through all the lessons she'd taught me, searching for the grains of truth, sifting out the lies.

My heart was a galloping horse, anxiety its black-clad rider. The social workers weren't looking at me; they had their heads together, murmuring. I'd hoped these people could help me get what I'd never had: an identity, stability, the building blocks of a life. But now I realized that my mother had determined my fate for me. She'd written a check I'd spend my whole life cashing, because I would never come to a place like this again looking for answers.

I forced my mind to steady itself. I had a solution. Unlike my mom, I always had a plan A, plan B, plan C, and plan D.

"Excuse me?" I ventured, keeping my voice subdued and meek. "I need to use the restroom. I think it's out in the hallway, right?"

The younger woman looked annoyed. "I'll take you."

"I can walk myself," I protested.

"Sorry, but we can't let you go alone." So I was a prisoner after all.

The bathroom was across the lobby, through a corridor I'd noticed when I'd cased out the station. I'd sat in the waiting area for half an hour, examining every corner, drawing a mental floor plan just in case I needed a quick escape. I'd learned this the previous year from one of my mom's friends, a woman named April with platinum blond hair and pierced eyebrows. "I don't go in if I can't get out." She had been leaning up against the sticky wall in an underground nightclub in Sacramento where we were picking up a brick of weed April planned on selling.

I let the social worker lead me away from the interview room toward the front counter, which split the room in two. Behind the counter were desks manned by cops, the area protected by a bulletproof glass partition. On this side, a straggly line of civilians wound across the open floor space and a few bored-looking people waited in the plastic chairs by the wall. Ahead lay the hallway with the restrooms and, beyond them, the back door to the parking lot.

As my jailer turned left to bypass the line, I reached inside my pocket and pulled out a plastic Easter egg. I palmed it, waited for the right moment, then tossed it with a flick of my wrist. It flew low, hit the counter, and the air exploded with the sharp *pop-pop-pop* of snappers. I'd fit ten of them in the egg; it sounded like fireworks, like miniature gunshots, like an explosion.

The room flew into chaos. People screamed, scattered. Cops bellowed; the woman I followed fell to her knees, covering her head.

I pulled a new egg from my left pocket and threw it in the other direction, initiating a second spray of cracks and pops and screams. I joined the panicked civilians, crouched over and running for an exit. I passed the social worker, who now sheltered under a chair, and was almost bowled over by two cops who ran from behind the counter, guns drawn. Through the hallway I ran, past the restrooms, through a swinging glass door, and out into the cool ocean air in the parking lot.

Freedom.

I trotted to the street, turned right, and walked south as fast as I could. I needed to get to the woods where I'd hidden my things, and then I . . .

And then what?

I guessed this was my life beginning. If I was going to live like my mother, I'd need a car, but before that, I'd need a license. I'd read in books about people getting fake IDs that were good enough to fool the police. If I wanted to stay free, I'd have to do it the wrong way like I'd been taught. It was the only way I knew how to live without dying small deaths daily, a wild bird fettered in a small and lonely cage.

CHAPTER SEVENTEEN

SUMMER

THE ISLAND
SATURDAY, JUNE 10

I carry a towel down a half-mile hiking trail to the beach. The air is warm and clear, the sky a bright, uninterrupted blue. It reminds me of La Jolla or Malibu, somewhere the paths are immaculately tended, and I feel suddenly angry at the beauty and how few people have access to it. In Southern California, it's a glaring, insulting truth—all the best places are reserved for the rich. All the clean, healthy ocean air—that's for them. The poor live inland, in the smog and sweltering heat where the air reeks of asphalt and exhaust and, when you go far enough east, cow shit. It makes me proud not to belong to any of it, to be outside the classist world of housing. I go where I want. If I want to spend my time on the cliffs of Malibu, that's where I go, rich or not.

My mom wasn't interested in class or poverty. She just cared about her lifestyle, the romance of being "a true bohemian." It was an easy thing to fall in love with after what I gathered was a pretty boring upbringing in the Midwest, a big two-story house, and a potentially paid-for college education she threw out the window to follow a "spiritual leader" to California when she was a teenager.

The trail lets out onto a small beach, and the blue sky opens up to meet the vast blue Pacific. This beach is tucked inside a cove, as the map had indicated, with a little dock that stretches into the tranquil water.

I find Julie reclining artistically on a large white towel in a black bikini, looking every inch the exercised, massaged, spray-tanned rich lady. She crows delightedly when she sees me. "Summer! Join me!"

"I heard you might be down here." I make my way across the warm sand. It's soft and clings to my toes; this island has slightly darker sand than Southern California, a little more like dirt, and I decide I don't like it.

She props herself up on her elbows. "I'm a whore for the beach. This is all I do when I'm here. Gym, beach, spa, repeat."

I spot four Jet Skis bobbing in the water, tied to the dock. "They just leave the Jet Skis out like that?" I ask. "What happens during high tide?"

"I think they bring them in every night."

I look dubiously up the path, sliding out of my cover-up. "That's a lot of work. How many people are on staff here?"

"Oh god, tons." Her eyes land on my bikini. "Jesus, girl. Keep that dress on when the husbands are around."

I laugh. "You have plenty of assets of your own."

"Yeah, but God gave you those for free." She starts rummaging in her purse.

I stretch out in the sun, considering how to lead the conversation to the island's resident doctor. I don't want her remembering that I'd asked. It has to come up naturally.

"What happened to you last night?" she asks, extracting a joint from her bag and lighting it.

"I had a migraine," I reply, echoing my lie to Alan. It occurs to me that this is a great segue. "I could have really used some Excedrin or something, but I didn't have any, so I just went to bed and toughed it out."

"You should have asked me. I have painkillers."

I clear my throat. "Alan told me there's also a doctor here in case I need anything."

She hits the joint deeply, and I'm not quite sure she heard me. The familiar smell of weed wafts over me. It always reminds me of my childhood, of campfires surrounded by my mom's endless chain of friends and their bongs, their acoustic guitars, their tangled, ratty hair.

"Want some?" She passes it to me.

"Sure." I take a hit, don't inhale, and pass it back. One of my life skills is pretending to smoke and drink things. The tiny waves lap peacefully and we lay there for a while, sun bronzing our skin, as she finishes the joint. After a bit, she pulls a thermos out of her bag and takes a swig from it.

"I'm so incredibly bored," she murmurs. She hands me the thermos. I take it and sniff.

"Vodka cranberry?" I guess.

"Cosmos."

I laugh. "It's not even eleven."

She rolls onto her side and rests her head on her hand. Her eyes are shadowy through the dark lenses. "Self-care is over. I choose chaos."

I take a sip. "Jesus Christ, that's sweet." I hand it back to her. "It's like drinking straight grenadine."

"I know. No lunch for me today." She sits up. "I'm so fucking *bored*. Let's get on the Jet Skis."

"Um . . ." She's left sober way behind in the rearview mirror. "Maybe in a little while, okay?"

She's already halfway down the beach. "Chaos!" she cries back to me.

I sigh.

But I know what I have to do. I have to buddy up with her, get on the stupid Jet Ski, and get her talking. The drunker she gets, the less she'll remember about our conversation.

———

The water whizzes beneath us, the vain sky gazing at its own sapphire reflection. I'm clinging to Julie's life-vested waist, hoping the added padding on both of us doesn't make it so I can't hold on to her properly and go spinning off the Jet Ski into the endlessly deep water.

"See over there?" she calls, oblivious to my terror. She points to the curve of the cliffs and forest, which have come into view now that we're out of the protected cove. "That's the uninhabited part of the island. Michael keeps more than half of the land undisturbed as a nature preserve. It's mostly on the east side, but it snakes around here as well."

"Cool." I feel nauseous.

I can feel her laughing through her vest. "Are you okay back there?"

"Doing great." Picturing that joint she smoked and that thermos of cosmos, wondering if I'm living the last minutes of my life.

She says, "Good!" and then guns it, revving the engine and driving twice as fast. I let out a shriek and she laughs. "Chaos!" she cries.

I yell, "Can we drive slower and still have chaos?"

"Fuck no!" She goes even faster. We're skipping above the water now, and I hear all kinds of alarm bells ringing.

"Seriously, slow down. I don't think we're supposed to take this thing out into the open ocean!" I yell above the wind blasting our faces.

"We're still in a cove!" She yells the words over her shoulder. "The little cove we started in is tucked into a larger one! We just have to stay away from the point."

"We're too far out. I don't like it!" I shout back.

"You want to turn back?" Something in her voice sounds teasing, threatening, and I hesitate.

"I mean, yeah."

"You got it!" She revs up the engine and then does a hard U-turn, which makes the Jet Ski tip onto its side. I scream, terrified, and she hollers in glee.

The Jet Ski falls back onto its belly, and I think we may survive after all, but the force sends us the other way, tipping right. She steers left to correct, but it has the opposite effect. My scream is cut off by the hard yank of gravity, ripping me off the Jet Ski and sending me flying. I'm airborne for two heart-stopping seconds before I hit the water, go under, and then bob to the surface, buoyed by my life jacket.

I'm disoriented, salt water stinging my eyes as I bob uselessly on the waves. I wipe my hair out of my face and look around. "Julie?"

The Jet Ski is on its side, floating on the water twenty feet from me. We're far from shore, in deep, dark water.

"Julie!" I scream. A small wave splashes my face, choking my cry off.

"Yo!" The cry comes from behind me.

I spin, searching. She's doing a strong crawl toward the stalled-out Jet Ski, a grin stretched across her wet face. "Chaos, bitches!"

I swim toward her. "I'm going to kill you," I tell her through chattering teeth. She pushes the watercraft upright—damn, she's strong. She pulls herself on, straddles it, and holds out a hand to help me. I ignore her hand and climb onto the slippery beast, and then I shove her back and sit in front of her. "I'm driving. You're fucking crazy. Aren't you supposed to be, like, a respectable member of society or something?" I imitate what I'd seen her do, starting the engine. It's easy to operate, much simpler than driving a motorcycle, which I've done a bunch of times.

I turn the handles, and we start back toward the dock at a reasonable pace. After a few minutes, she says, "It doesn't matter what I do. I'm invisible."

That piques my interest. "What do you mean?"

"I'm over thirty. I don't have kids. As long as I behave myself at cocktail parties, I'm as free as a woman can be. I can go wild inside my little cage."

It doesn't sound like she feels free. It sounds like she has depression or something. "Do you have friends and family of your own, apart from Steve?" I ask.

"Meh, kind of. My parents are back in Connecticut. Nothing

feels real. You know? I grew up in a normal suburb. Everything was simple. I mean, we had money, but it wasn't like this. This kind of life is . . . it's lonely sometimes."

I consider that as I drive. Now that I'm at the wheel, I can appreciate the warmth of the sun drying the cold water on my skin and the beauty of the trees creeping down the virgin coastline. I'd always suspected that very rich people led lonely lives. I've read books about people at different levels of wealth and have observed them in countless parties and clubs, and I always wonder how much all those possessions must weigh. It must take a toll, owning so much, being responsible for lugging it all through the world.

I say, "You could get a divorce, go live your life the way you want to."

"Right." She laughs. Her arms tighten on my waist, and we ride quietly for a bit. We're getting closer to the dock now, and I'm not totally sure how to stop.

Her hands stray to my upper thighs. Surprised, I look down at her French-tipped acrylics, digging gently into the tanned flesh. She leans forward and rubs her hands down my legs toward my knees, then back up again, resting them on my hips. Into my ear, she murmurs, "I like you."

I'm taken aback. I blink at the blue water, thoughts whirling through my head: *This would be a much more appealing situation than Alan. I wish I had come to the island with her.* Then: *Wait. She's married. This is a bad situation.* Then: *But she probably does stuff like this all the time without telling her husband.* And finally: *This can only be good for me. The more options I have, the better.*

I turn slightly, letting up on the acceleration, and look back at her. She brushes a little kiss onto my cheek. "Do you like me?" she asks, her breath warm on my ear.

I shiver. I kind of do, actually. I consider my words carefully. "You've had some booze, and you're high. So I'm pleading the Fifth."

She laughs again. Her hands return to my waist, snaking up under the life vest and tickling my bare ribs. The Jet Ski rocks beneath me, and the friction of the seat beneath my bathing suit combined with her hand on my leg makes me shiver.

We're almost at the docks. "How do I stop this thing?" I ask.

"Just lay off the accelerator. It'll cruise to a stop. And then pull this one back." She reaches past me, which crushes her against my back, and shows me. I follow her instructions, slowing down and coasting into the dock. She lets out a triumphant whoop when I get us into our original slot. "Nice! You're good at this. See? It's not so scary when you're in the driver's seat." She hops up onto the dock. I follow suit, my legs a little shaky.

"God, you scared the shit out of me," I say, and then we're both laughing. Back on the sand, we fall onto our towels, dripping, and lay there in the sun for a few minutes. I shrug out of my life vest—hers is already strewn on the sand beside her—and say, "Give me that thermos. I need a drink."

She passes it over, eyes closed, soaking up the sun. "I'm glad you came. I think you're a kindred spirit."

I rest my head in my hand. "What do you mean?"

"You don't fool me," she replies. Despite her claims of sobriety, her eyes are red, her smile too broad.

"How so?"

"You're no sweet little angel who's just *so* happy to meet a *nice* guy who happens to be fucking loaded."

"What am I, then?"

"You're like me. It's a relief when there's another one of us on these things. We can have fun. We don't have to hang out with the old money women. All they talk about is fundraisers; they're so above it all."

"That does seem boring," I agree.

"So tell me about your friend, the one who's seeing Michael," she says in a warm, gossipy tone. "What's she like?"

I search for a way to adequately describe Leo. "She's very free. She's just . . . completely herself."

She looks annoyed. "Is she pretty?"

"Beautiful." It stings. I miss Leo so much it hurts.

"Are you, you know . . . together? Do you mess around?" She says it with a wink, in a cheesy way that makes me cringe.

"Not at all. She's like a sister."

She seems to mull that over for a minute. "Who's the older sister? The alpha?"

I chuckle. "That would be me."

"Let me guess, you're always taking care of her, getting her out of scrapes. That's why you don't know where she is right now. You're the steady one, she's the flaky one. Blah, blah, blah."

I roll onto my side to face her. "How did you know?"

"It's always like that. There's always one friend who cares more, who tries harder. That's why female friendships are doomed. Eventually she'll get tired of you mothering her and you'll get sick of cleaning up after her. The other option is being too much alike and competing for everything until you hate each other." She reaches a manicured finger to play with the string on my bikini top. "Do you want to go back to my room? I have a massive spa tub."

I laugh, but what she said about Leo and me makes my stomach hurt. "You're drunk."

"Not really."

Frustrated, I decide to come out with it and risk being obvious. "Hey, where can I find the island doctor? In case my migraine comes back? Is there an office or something?"

"Yeah, it's somewhere in the research facility. There's a whole medical clinic in there. X-rays, drugs, anything the old guys could possibly need. Can't have them dying on the island. Imagine the lawsuits." She groans. Her words are slurry and thick. "I'm so fucking *bored,*" she murmurs as though to herself.

That's bad news. If there's a lot of medical equipment here, it might be hard to come up with something that would make them helicopter me back to the mainland. I consider appendicitis, but surely that will be impossible to fake. I wonder if I could actually injure myself, intentionally break an arm or something, but that seems drastic.

Besides, Leo might not even be truly lost. Julie's words come back to me, about the possibility of Leo getting sick of being smothered by me. I wonder if Leo is truly sick of my looking out for her, if she's just taking her opportunity to find her own way in the world. Could she have done that—gotten back from her date with Michael and opted to do something else without me? I remember her friend in Italy and what she said about going to see her.

But, no, that's ridiculous. All her belongings are in my truck. She would have had to come back for her stuff at least. Right?

Leo might be bored, and she might want to go to Europe and live a more exciting life, but I can't picture a reality that includes her abandoning all her possessions and not even saying goodbye to me. That is, unless I don't know Leo as well as I think I do.

I stand, gathering my towel. Julie doesn't stir as I shove my feet into my flip-flops and hurry across the sand. I think I'm going to cry, and I'll be damned if that's going to happen in public.

I shut the door to my room and slide down to the cool bamboo floor. I need to cry, but the sadness is stuck inside my chest, unable to well up into sobs. Instead, it swells to occupy every inch of my torso, taking up all the room I need to breathe.

I'm trying to reconstruct the chain of events. I picture Leo and Michael, laughing on their way to his boat, zooming around, and then him dropping her off at the marina. From there, she'd have been exhilarated, winded, and she'd have called me to come pick her up.

Maybe she realized she'd forgotten her phone in the hotel room, or on the boat. Maybe she thought she'd walk to Santa Monica; it's only a few miles north.

But, no. She'd have been in her party dress and heels. It doesn't add up. Why hadn't Michael ordered her a taxi or had one of his cronies give her a lift? Nothing makes sense.

Again, a whisper of intuition reminds me that I don't trust

men I don't know for a reason. Michael saying he'd dropped Leo off at the Marina del Rey harbor didn't make it true. I remember being told that Michael never brings dates to these weekends. Maybe he doesn't want anyone to know he brought a girl here. Maybe . . .

I cock my head, mind racing.

Michael's not alone on this island. He can hide things from his invited guests, but the staff . . . They see everything, don't they?

I wipe my eyes, but they're dry. I push myself up and dig in my suitcase, hunting. I need to see Leo's face. I need to feel like she's real, to remember how wrong Julie is. I end up unpacking everything onto the bed, and at the bottom, with the two used paperbacks I'd packed, I find the mini photo album I take with me everywhere.

I sit on the edge of the bed and crack it open. The first page contains a Polaroid of Leo and me, arms slung around each other's shoulders on one of the piers in San Francisco. The bay is glittering behind us. My hair is shorter, skin paler. Leo looks so different—her hair is in tangled dreadlocks, and her eyes are red and hazy. She is skeletal, so thin she looks ill, but her face is bright with humor. This is the first photo we ever took together.

Never letting my eyes leave Leo's, I reach for the phone and press zero. The female housekeeping voice answers, and I ask if she can bring me something to eat for lunch.

"I'm actually already on my way," she says. "You caught me just as I was heading to you."

"Great, see you in a few." I set the phone down and flip to the next page. It's me in the driver's seat of my truck, wearing a bikini top and cutoffs, showing off my tan. It's summertime, and redwoods can be glimpsed out the window behind me. We'd been on a trip through Sequoia. I touch the picture, wishing I could go back.

I know the next page will be the worst, but I force myself to turn to it. Yep. There's Leo, in a sundress, hair in a pixie cut— she'd lopped off the dreads because she had lice and I was not about to have lice in my truck; besides, she has naturally straight hair and has no good reason to wear it in locks. In the photo, she's standing in front of a shop window in Santa Barbara, and she's giving the camera her signature let's-get-into-trouble smile.

Fuck what Julie said. Our friendship is not doomed. Leo and I were meant to be sisters. We were given to each other, a consolation prize for everything we'd lost.

I set the album on the bed, open to the photo of Leo, and flick my eyes to it as I repack my suitcase, neater this time than last. Everything in its place, I feel a little more in control.

A light knock sounds at my door, and I shake myself, putting on my game face. I set the photo album in a visible spot on the bed, open to the photo of Leo smiling. At the door, I'm greeted by a fair, washed-out woman I recognize from my first night here. "Ashley?" I try, hoping I have it right.

She's clearly surprised. "Yes, and thank you for remembering. That's very kind of you." She pushes a cart into the room and lifts a tray from it onto the foot of the bed. "We have house-made hummus served with a dish of kalamata olives, sliced Persian cucumbers, goat cheese feta, and gluten-free wafer crackers."

"Thanks." I dig a couple of dollars out of my wallet and offer them to her. I toss my wallet on the bed beside the photo album, drawing her eyes unconsciously to it.

She locks onto Leo's face and her eyes go wide, shoulders stiffening.

"Ashley?" I ask, still holding the bills out.

She looks up at me, and her eyes are full of questions. Her mouth hangs ajar as though she'd started to say something and stopped herself mid-word.

"That's my friend Leo," I say, scrutinizing her face. "Do you know her?"

"I'm sorry, no. Thank you. I hope you enjoy your . . ." She glances at the hummus tray as though she's already forgotten what it contains.

"Wait a second." I touch her arm. "It really seems like you've met her."

"No, of course not." She's lying. It's so false, anyone could hear it a mile away.

But the implication is astounding. She recognizes Leo. And she's afraid to admit it.

There's only one conclusion I can draw. Leo was here.

CHAPTER EIGHTEEN

LEO

FRIDAY, JUNE 9

I lay curled on my side in the soft, king-size bed, Michael asleep beside me, one of his arms thrown over his head. With my back to him, I was watching dawn creep over the ocean far below. The view was spectacular up here, the entire Pacific glistening wide like it had been poured out just for us.

I'd seen sunrises like this before, always from a clifftop perch on the PCH, snuggled up on the tailgate of the Land Cruiser, a cup of something steaming hot in hand. Those were amazing moments, much more special than this. Maybe it was better because we'd had to steal those sunrise moments; we weren't handed them by mansions with calculated floor plans.

It had been only two days, but I missed Summer. I missed the Land Cruiser. I missed the feeling that we could get up and be on the road to anywhere. *I feel itchy,* I'd tell her, and she'd say, *You want trees, ocean, or desert?* It was ironic that after losing my sister and making a run for it toward an untethered, bohemian life, I ended up with a new sister. I wanted to tell Summer about Michael and see her reactions as I described each part: The boat, the island—she'd die when she heard about the island. I wondered what she'd say about last night's public dinner-sex. Probably one concise word: *Ew*.

Thinking about it, my stomach soured. It felt dark and twisted, what we'd done with all those people watching. I'd had sex in public places before—parking lots, a bathroom at a party, a hot tub, but never with any actual people around to witness. Last night was different. Had I liked it? It had been unnerving, so each push and pull had felt stronger, and Michael was so calm and commanding, the whole thing like an out-of-body experience.

Michael stirred behind me, and his hand rested on my hip. "How long have you been awake?" he murmured, voice gruff with sleep in a way that made me feel melty.

"Just a few minutes. I've been watching the sunrise," I replied softly.

I felt him prop himself up on an elbow so he could see over my shoulder. "It's going to be a beautiful day."

"Mm."

"You okay?" He kissed my bare shoulder. His face was scratchy.

I hesitated and then told the truth. "I feel weird about last night."

"What about it? You didn't have fun?"

I rolled onto my back so I could face him. He looked peaceful, dark hair messy, face shadowy with beard regrowth. "The dinner was magical," I clarified. "You totally spoiled me. But . . . the sex part."

"Oh." He sounded surprised.

"I just . . . I can't believe I did that. With all those people watching."

He waved a hand. "As long as I sign their paychecks, we could walk around naked with bells on for all they care."

And just like that, I felt my nagging doubts fade away. I reached up to run a hand through his hair. He snuggled closer and leaned down to kiss my cheek, my neck, my forehead. His stubble was ticklish, and I felt myself squeak out a giggle, which made him chuckle. He settled back onto his pillow, and I cuddled up to him, enjoying the soft dusting of chest hair.

"I have to do some work today," he said, words rumbling in my ear. "I'm hosting an investors' weekend. They're arriving this evening. I have to spend some time at the research facility with the scientists getting everything set up."

I nodded, contemplating the setup. "Do the scientists work here full-time?"

"Yes. You'll never see them, though. The island is divided in half, and they don't come to the residential side. I'll just be a few hours. Half a day at most. You can hang out at the beach, get a tan. No one here will make you wear a bathing suit."

I considered my words carefully, balancing my need to strike it big with the gnawing in my gut.

"Michael, I . . ." I cleared my throat and forced a smile into my voice. "I love it here, it's beautiful, but to be honest, I should be heading home soon."

He kissed my shoulder, his hair tickling my skin. "No problem. I'll get you back as soon as I can."

We spent the next hour in bed and then showered and dressed. I selected a black bikini, shorts, and a T-shirt from the clothes Javier had provided. Everything was designer and fit impeccably. It made me wonder how many women Michael had brought here, what with the seemingly endless supply of clothes in what had to be an array of sizes. It didn't matter. I was always one in a long line of young women who temporarily occupied these men's time. It was fine with me, and it was fine with them. This was the ritual: a swept-away weekend followed by rewards. I needed to keep my focus on the rewards.

With Michael busy, I decided to spend some time on the beach, hiding from the servants who had seen my shame last night. On my way out, in the foyer, I ran into Javier, who was rushing inside with a set of keys in hand. He smiled professionally, but his eyes twinkled at me in a way I hated. "Do you need any help finding the beach?" he asked.

I wanted to sink into the ground beneath me and die. Grudgingly, face hot, I nodded.

He turned to point out the front door, to the right. "You'll follow this path. Past the swimming pool, there's a trail straight down. Would you like me to walk you over?"

"No." I slipped past him and out the door before he could say another word.

It felt great to be outside. The sun was warm, and the ocean's cool, salty breeze intermingled with deciduous trees and a faint whiff of pine. It was so much like the forest-ocean smells in Northern California, I felt suddenly and intensely homesick. Summer and I both went through that: missing Southern California when we were up north and missing Northern California when we were down south.

I followed the clean, white walkway all the way around the house—god, this place was huge, more like a college campus—and found the pool, which looked like it belonged on a magazine cover.

To the left of the gym, I saw what looked like a wooden footpath headed down into the trees. I hurried toward it, and yes, it did disappear into the forest, turning into a staircase. I followed it, sandaled footsteps slapping hollow drumbeats on the planks.

The path opened onto the beach, and I sighed with relief. It was completely secluded, a private cove with a little dock on the left. The water was calm here, just right for paddle boarding or rowing around in a kayak. The sand was soft, a dark beige, and I kicked my shoes off and found a good spot. I laid out my towel, shrugged out of my shorts and shirt, and sprawled out to enjoy the morning sun. For a few blissful minutes, I lay there, enjoying the sounds of wind and birds and the soft lapping of tiny waves.

I didn't remember a time I'd felt more alone, at least not since joining Summer. She'd caught me at a low point, when I was couch surfing and had no idea how to do life. I knew I couldn't stay in one place and work a regular job, but I wasn't cut out for panhandling and drug dealing like the people I was hanging out with. But then I'd met Summer, like an answer to a prayer, and we'd worked together to figure out what I could do. I wasn't great at pickpocketing; Summer made it an art form, but I was clumsy with my fingers. I wasn't a natural con artist like she was, but I was good with men, especially older men. What would become of me in ten years, when I was no longer the much-younger object of desire?

I shrugged off the worry. I'd figure it out. Summer would help me. We'd rebrand somehow. In the meantime, I was living in the now, and—

"Excuse me?" A timid voice cut into my thoughts, and I bolted up to a sitting position. A young woman with a colorful towel in hand was standing above me. She said, "I noticed you were using one of your bathroom towels, and I thought you might enjoy a beach towel. It's larger and will keep more sand off of you." She handed it down to me.

I accepted it. "Thanks," I said, not in my most friendly voice.

"Can I get you anything to drink while you sunbathe? Maybe some ice water?"

"I'm good."

A fearful expression crossed her face at my tone. To her, I was one of the bitchy rich ladies Michael had brought here before me.

I tried to make nice. "I'm just going to lie out and relax. I'm totally fine."

She pointed to the footpath. "I'll be right there if you need anything. My name is Ashley."

I followed her gesture. "You're going to just stand there?"

She nodded. "I'm here to get you anything you'd like."

"You really don't have to do that," I protested.

She backed away. "Please let me know if you change your mind."

I watched her retreat, frustration mounting into anger. I didn't need to be babysat, and I didn't know why rich people were so fragile they needed someone at hand to fetch them things every moment of the day.

I lay down and tried to ignore her, but her presence was like a weight behind me. I sat up again and looked over my shoulder. Sure enough, there she was, tucked into the trees at the base of the footpath, hands clasped in front of her.

"For god's sake," I muttered. She was going to stand there the entire time I was here.

I sat up and threw on my clothes. I grabbed the towels, crossed the beach, huffing through the dunes, and handed her the beach towel. "Here. I'm going on a walk." I brushed my sandy feet off with the bath towel.

"Would you like a bottle of water for your—"

"I'm good," I snapped, shoving my feet into my sandals.

"I can take that bath towel as well if you—"

"Why are you doing this?" I asked, unable to contain the frustration. "You don't need to hover like this."

Her face went beet red. "I do, though."

"You don't!"

"I'm just doing my job. I'm here to . . ." She glanced up and around, maybe looking for help. "It's good to have someone else around," she finished.

"I told you, please leave me alone. How much more blunt do I have to be?" Last night was roaring around in my head; she'd been there. I remembered her, standing by the fireplace, hands clasped, eyes focused on the ground.

Unable to face her another moment, I threw down the bath towel and stomped up the path. She was following me, I was sure of it. I glanced back. Sure enough, she was hurrying to keep up. I walked faster, heart speeding up, quads burning. I wanted to laugh and scream at the same time.

I'd been wild too long. I was not going to be followed, monitored. That was not how I lived.

Suddenly, I grinned, the adrenaline from anger rushing a wave of mischief through me. Now she'd given me a challenge.

I broke into a run, which was not easy on the steep incline, got out of her field of vision, and then hopped the railing in one swift movement, landing on the soft forest floor. Pine needles poking through my sandals and my heart full of adventure, I sprinted into the woods.

Country Girl on the Run at Billionaire Island was the title of the movie I was currently starring in, I thought giddily. Young inge-nue meets wealthy older man only to find herself . . .

Never mind. That felt more like a horror movie.

I slowed to a fast walk, figuring I'd given her the slip, and grinned to myself, panting. I was walking with the downhill slope to my right, the mansion somewhere above me to my left. Occa-sionally, the trees broke, and I caught a glimpse of ocean between them, a sparkling, bright blue expanse. I loved the woods, always had, despite everything that had happened. None of that was the trees' fault. An image flickered unbidden: a withered corpse in a yellow dress.

And then it hit me like a baseball bat to the gut: a visceral, Technicolor image of Amanda, almost skeletonized, found in the woods by Shaver Lake. I'd seen the crime scene photos. They were burned into my brain.

I tripped and fell, landed on my palms, and stayed there in the dirt, trying to breathe, trying not to vomit. I spat a mouthful of saliva onto the ground and squeezed my eyes shut.

She'd been wearing a yellow dress, one I hadn't seen before. They'd made my parents look at her corpse, made my father say the words: This dead girl was his daughter. They'd asked me if I recognized her dress; they'd shown me close-ups. I'd screamed, thrown up, run from the house, and walked for hours.

The cops had no idea who might have done it. Maybe a vagrant, they said, but some things didn't add up. For one, she was wearing a lipstick shade that didn't match anything in our house. She never wore red lipstick; she couldn't keep it from smearing. I'd been the one to notice this, and they'd tried to reassure me. "See? It's good that you looked at these. You're helping." I wasn't helping. I was lying to them. I knew a lot of things, but none of them made it past my lips until it was much too late.

I bared my teeth against these memories and sat back on my heels. I inhaled deeply, counted to seven, then exhaled slowly. This was what I'd been taught to do in moments like these. It was like that with PTSD; it came on suddenly and swallowed you whole.

They never figured out if she'd been raped. Her body had been too decomposed by the time they found her.

Strangled.

Stabbed.

My wonderful sister, ballerina and birthday cake baker, the one who had taught me everything from riding a bike to putting on mascara—wiped from the earth, just like that. An asteroid may as well have crashed down from the heavens and destroyed everything in my life.

The deep breathing was working. The image of Amanda rotting in a yellow dress was fading. I pushed myself to my feet, knees shaking. This was the worst attack I'd had in years. Then again, it was my first time alone in the woods without Summer to guide and distract me.

I wandered downhill, hoping for a clearer view of the ocean and a break from the trees. I passed a rocky outcropping and then a steep, small cliff. I saw a clearing ahead and headed eagerly for it, thinking I'd found my unobstructed view at last. Instead, I stepped onto a beaten path that bordered a tall fence.

It was easily ten feet high and topped with a slanted row of barbed wire. This was familiar to me; ranchers used this type of fencing to protect their property lines. I could look left and right along the path and see the fence fade into the distance.

I noticed that signs were posted on the fence every thirty feet or so. I approached the nearest one. It was black and white, with a red image of a lightning bolt. CAUTION, DO NOT TOUCH, ELECTRIC FENCE.

I lifted my eyebrows. Jeez. I knew he had specialized technology on the research side of the island, but an electric fence? These were murder on wildlife, and this was an island, after all. How big of a problem was security?

I wandered along beside the fence for a while, wondering if it was possible to walk all the way around the island or if I'd get cut off at some point. How big was the island, anyway? A mile across? Two? It felt so huge and empty.

A faint sound drifted on the wind. Singing? Or maybe a coyote?

I stopped, listening, wondering if there were coyotes on the island. It seemed unlikely, but what did I know?

The sound rose again, louder. It was a person, someone calling out, a summons.

Ahead of me, a figure appeared. Black pants, white shirt. A man. My steps slowed. As he approached, I recognized Javier.

I turned, wanting to go in the other direction, but two people were advancing, walking fast. One was Ashley from the beach, another an older woman I recognized from the house.

Javier called, "Leo! Hang on!" It was his voice I'd heard above the wind. He closed the last few feet and said, "You can't be down here. It's very dangerous. The fence carries a strong electrical charge."

"I figured that out all on my own," I retorted. "How did you know I was here?"

He pointed up at the tops of the fence posts. "Security cameras. This is the border between the research facility and the residential side of the island."

I followed his gesture, but I didn't see any cameras.

He beckoned me. "Come on back to the house. At two o'clock, we're going to get lunch set up for you on the patio. Do you like sashimi?"

What would Summer do? Would she manipulate, trick, or assert dominance? She was so wise about dealing with people, and she was such a quick thinker, but she always said, "Sometimes you have to trust your gut."

I squared my shoulders and took a step toward Javier. "Take me to Michael. Wherever he is, I want to see him now."

He lifted his eyebrows. "Mr. Forrester is in the lab, but I can reach out to him."

My voice was low and measured. "Yes, you can. Let's go. Now." I pushed past him and headed back the way I'd come, leaving him and the wide-eyed women to either follow or not.

CHAPTER NINETEEN

SUMMER

SATURDAY, JUNE 10

Another black dress, another crowd sparkling with diamonds, another set of entertainers—tonight, it's a quartet playing classical Spanish guitar by the fireplace, and the great room is lit in shades of gold. I float in on Alan's arm, having endured another session of kissing and pawing in my room before applying my lipstick. He shines with pride like he's caught a massive fish, presenting me to different men, introducing them as "Jeff, a leader in hydro energy" and "Dr. Johnson, prizewinning physicist" and "Mark Lindberg, venture capitalist." The accompanying women always get "and his wife, Lucy," or "and his guest, Fabiana." I meet three women who are afforded the same "Dr. Maxine Kepner, CEO" type of introduction. Otherwise, like me, the women seem mostly decorative.

Through it all, I'm barely able to focus. I can't stop thinking about Leo. She was here. Michael lied.

I've been obsessing about this for hours, and I can think of two reasons she might still be here and Michael might be lying about it.

Reason one—He's never brought a date to this type of event.

He doesn't want to introduce flighty Leo to all these investors and have them think he's serious about her, which they would, given that he's never introduced anyone before. Leo could be happily sipping cocktails on a balcony somewhere, waiting for the party to be over, no idea I'm here at all.

Reason two—Something more sinister is happening. He could be keeping her here against her will, or . . . I don't know. Reason two doesn't compute. Men as rich as Michael don't have to coerce or force women to do anything. For the right price, there's always someone willing to oblige any fantasy. Reason one would explain so much more.

I consider my search options. As far as I can tell, the residential side of the island has three buildings: the huge main house where I am now, the spa/gym outbuilding, and a small maintenance building set behind the spa. If I had to guess, Leo would be sequestered here in the main wing somewhere, maybe in Michael's private rooms.

Steve and Julie appear beside us, and Alan and Steve greet each other with doglike excitement, immediately descending into chatter about today's tour of the facility and a shining moment during the demo. Julie arches an eyebrow. "Well, we've lost them." She sips her white wine delicately. She's back to being the Julie I first met on the yacht, collected and organized, hair perfectly coiffed, an ice-blue, one-shoulder cocktail dress fitted to her curves like it was custom-made, which it probably was.

If Leo were here, she'd crack a joke to ease my tension. "What did the salt say to the meat? You've been as*salt*ed. Get it?" My stomach pinches with sudden loneliness. The space beside me where she's supposed to be is so empty, it's like I have a black hole on a leash.

Julie makes eye contact with a woman in her fifties and smiles brightly. "Alison! I didn't realize you'd be here!" She gives me a polite, "Excuse me, please," with a secret squeeze of my wrist, and joins a group of gray-haired men and their Botoxed wives.

She's wild. I like that. And there's something unapologetic

about her. I suspect if she found out the truth about my lifestyle, she'd be okay with it.

Two other men have joined Alan and Steve, and they're hooting it up, so I take the opportunity to slip between partygoers, searching for Javier, resisting the temptation to slip things out of people's pockets as I go. I see Michael at the dead center of the group, surrounded by people, all competing for his attention. He looks calm and upbeat, dividing his attention evenly among them.

I find Javier in conversation with a pair of older women, and I wait for him to be done before I slide smoothly into step beside him. "Hello, Javier? I'm Summer, I'm staying in the west wing."

He gives me his attention, and I'm glad I wore the dress I did. Tonight, I didn't pull any punches with the cleavage. I remembered Javier's eyes straying to my chest yesterday, and I plan to leverage that to my advantage.

"Of course. How can I help you?" he asks. He's very handsome and well built, the white uniform shirt straining against his muscular arms. I bet he cleans up with these middle-aged women.

"I wanted to ask you about something. May I have a moment?" I gesture that we should step aside into the hallway, and he nods courteously and follows me. Out of earshot, I adjust my body language, smiling at him as though we're close friends. "I wanted to ask you a favor," I explain.

He lets his eyes flicker up and down my body. "How can I help?" His pose is professional, but there's something in his voice—he's hoping I'm looking for help in certain bedroom ways.

"Ashley, she works on your housekeeping staff, right?"

He nods, a frown flickering across his brow. "Is something wrong?"

"Not at all. I wanted to know how I could reach her if I ever need to. She's really great. Very polite, not overbearing." I know this about rich people: They have favorite servants.

It seems to make sense to him. "Ah. Well, we are all available to you anytime you need anything. If you like Ashley, I'll ask her to answer your calls whenever you need something."

"Thank you," I say. "I should just call the main line if I need her?"

"Absolutely. And I'd be glad to find her now, ma'am, if you like."

"No, I'm good, but can you please not call me ma'am? It makes me feel old." It's a flirtatious thing to say, and I hope he takes the bait.

He grins. "How can that be possible? You're younger than me." Jackpot.

I let my gaze drift down his arm as though I'm admiring his bicep. "I was at the beach today. Where were you? I thought I'd run into you."

"I was working." He crosses his arms to show off his pecs.

"Yes, but why weren't you working anywhere *I* was?" I pretend to pout. "Don't you know how boring it is here with all these people?"

The reminder of the other partygoers does exactly what I want it to. He glances nervously at the doorway, realizing he's been gone too long, worried someone will see him flirting with me. In that one instant while his attention is diverted, I slip the key card off its little elastic holder on his belt and palm it behind my back.

CHAPTER TWENTY

SUMMER

SATURDAY, JUNE 10

The corridors are empty as I hurry barefoot through them, shoes in hand. I'm going to search every single inch of this stupid mansion until I am sure Leo isn't here. After all this, if I find her sipping daiquiris in some hidden hot tub, I may actually murder her.

Out of breath, I arrive at the far end of the west wing, where the exterior door leads out to the pool. I glance around, searching for surveillance cameras. I don't see any.

The first door belongs to Alan's suite. I quickly confirm it's empty, let myself out, and beep into the room across the hall. It proves to be a storage closet full of sheets, cleaning supplies, and toiletries. Next is my room, which I ignore, and then, around a corner, another set of doors leads into a suite I'm pretty sure is Julie and Steve's. I pause in the bathroom by a huge setup of makeup and lotion, imagining how long Julie must take to get ready. The rooms are all decorated in the same minimalist, white-and-wood theme, all of them with the same bed frames and windows looking out into the darkness.

I beep into another set of suites and check every inch, tempted to steal designer purses and expensive watches. Hand hovering over a jewelry box, I consider my options, think about my plans for Ashley, and decide the diamond bracelet I stole off Julie's wrist will suffice.

I work my way through the rest of the west wing, through a kitchen and a laundry room with four industrial washers and dryers, and then I'm in the hallway that connects to the central wing of the structure that houses the great room. There are two stories here, and I decide to start with the second floor, since the party is happening on the ground level. I find a high-ceilinged library, a computer room that looks like an Apple store, a number of guest rooms, and utilitarian spaces that are clearly for staff use: a commercial kitchen, a second identical laundry room, a few storage closets filled with linens, cleaning supplies, and household goods. I find a lounge room with a pool and poker tables and a movie theater that seats twenty. This house is absurd, and I'm getting frustrated. I was hoping Michael's private quarters would be up here, but I still haven't discovered where the boss sleeps.

I stand in a suite that smells like a woman's expensive perfume and look out the window at the darkness. The central wing has a view out onto the ocean, and I imagine what it looks like during the day, an endless blue carpet, sparkling in the sun. Now, it's dark-on-dark, its presence only hinted at by the faint reflection of the moon glimmering gray on its surface.

I've been counting the bedrooms. So far I've found twenty-eight. The bottom floor of this wing may have some other bedrooms, but judging from the layout, I believe it's mostly dedicated to common spaces: the stadium-size great room, the kitchen, the indoor-outdoor covered patio in between. The only wing left to explore is the east wing. Could that be Michael's private area? I'd thought it must be for servants, but maybe they're not housed in the main house at all. At the far end of the second floor, I find a set of stairs and take them down slowly, bare feet soundless on the cool bamboo steps.

They let out into a hallway. To my left is the central wing's first floor, and the smell of food drifts faintly my way. To the right, the hallway dead-ends at a tall wooden door with a keypad.

I stand frozen, listening, waiting, searching the white walls for security cameras, but it's still and quiet with no cameras in sight.

I clutch my shoes tighter and pad barefoot toward the door. I lift the key card to the pad and notice something: This is different from the others in the house. It has a second, smaller pad beside it. I've seen these before; it's a thumbprint scanner. I assume it allows Michael to enter without a key card.

I lift Javier's card and swipe it across the red light, holding my breath. There's a now-familiar beep and a click—the door unlocking.

I turn the handle and push it open. In front of me is another hallway.

I step through and pull the door shut behind me. It clicks softly. My heart is pounding, each beat shivering up my diaphragm. I swallow it down, pulling my face into stillness.

The hall stretches before me, longer than I'd expected, decorated with large paintings unlike anything elsewhere in the house. They're colorful, perhaps all by the same artist. The first is a large portrait of a young blonde in a fancy dress. The style is old-fashioned, the kind of setup you see in museums: girl seated in a decorative chair, hands folded in her lap, hair arranged just so over one bare shoulder. She's sitting beside a table laden with a bowl of fruit and an open leather-bound book, the whole painting in rich shades of blues and reds. At first glance, I think it's an antique, but there's something about it that makes me think this is actually modern, just done in an older style. Her dress, for one, looks like a prom dress you might buy at a department store, and her long hair is layered, worn loose.

As I pass, the blonde's eyes seem to follow me, and then I'm confronted with the brown-eyed stare of another young woman, painted in a black dress and seated on a grassy stretch of lawn. My arms prickle with goosebumps, and I walk faster, past a seascape and a nude portrait of another girl who watches my passage. I come to the first door branching off the hall, beep it unlocked, and peek in. It's a conference room, with a large central table surrounded by cushy executive chairs.

I pass more paintings and open another door. This is a library, smaller than the first I'd found and sort of British-looking, with squashy leather armchairs and books to the ceiling with ladders to reach them. It looks out of place in this stark, minimalist house. The door across the hall is beside a portrait of a young girl with wide brown eyes sitting on a bench with her dress arranged out around her. This door leads to a kitchen, a bit homier than the restaurant-grade kitchen I'd found in the west wing. The kitchen has a patio through a set of French doors with an outdoor dining set.

I catch my own reflection in the French doors and freeze, heart pounding, sure I've been caught. But then my wide, scared eyes snap me into reality, and I rush to move on with my search.

The next door takes me to a bathroom, and then a smaller laundry room with just two washers and dryers, and now the hall dead-ends at a tall, locked door. I beep it open and hold my breath.

I'm standing in a living area, with a couch and armchair, a television, and a set of glass doors that let out onto a patio. It smells faintly of men's cologne.

This must be Michael's inner sanctum.

A short burst of laughter escapes me. I did it. I'm in. This is it; she's in here or she's not, and if she's not . . .

I hasten to the two doors on the far side of the room, acutely aware of every passing second. One leads to an empty study and I sigh, frustrated. The other leads to a bedroom with a large, low bed and a minimalist dresser. I look under the bed and in the attached bathroom that's not much larger than the one in my own suite. His set of rooms is humbler than I'd have expected. This is all consistent with the impression I'd gotten of him that first day, that he's kind of an unpretentious person underneath the billionaire boss-man exterior. This isn't any fancier than you'd see in most upper-middle-class homes. It's as if the rest of the house is built for his guests, to impress and seduce investors and sell his own success. I can picture him tucked away back here, working on his computer, reading his books, watching TV like a normal person.

Most important, Leo isn't here. I've now searched every inch of the house.

Discouraged, I check the walk-in closet. It contains a row of jeans, a row of blazers, an endless line of band T-shirts, and some sweaters. A couple of suits are stationed to one side, which I'm sure Michael avoids unless he has to. I back out of the closet and am halfway to the bedroom door when a beep and a click echo off the high ceilings. A door opens and closes, and Michael's voice murmurs in the living room, his baritone unmistakable.

My heart stops.

Oh, shit. Shit shit shit.

I back up fast, searching for somewhere to hide. The bed is low to the ground; I might not fit. The only options are the closet or the bathroom. *Closet,* my brain recommends. *In case he needs to go to the bathroom.* I'm already tiptoeing in and closing myself into darkness.

I press my ear to the door and strain to hear. He's talking, then pausing, then talking again. Maybe he's on the phone.

I can think of a few reasons he'd need to open the closet: He spilled something on himself and needs to change; he keeps something in here like a briefcase that he might need; someone saw me break in and he's here to do a search.

I retreat to the back corner and squeeze in behind the clothes. I hold still, barely breathing, clutching my shoes to my chest. Through the wall, I hear the faint murmur of his low voice.

It's not a short conversation; it goes on and on. I fidget, nerves rattling. *Get off the phone and back to your guests,* I pray, but then there's a new, terrible sound. Other male voices join him, louder, and an animated conversation starts up.

Oh god. He has friends. They must be out in his living room having a drink or something.

I lean my head against the wall and push the filmy garment at the end of the row of hangers away from me. As I do, I catch a whiff of perfume or deodorant off it, something feminine.

I run my hands down the garment. It's a dress, silky soft, an unusual thing for a single man to have, and from the feel of it, it's smaller than anything that would fit Michael. I press it to my face and inhale again. There's something familiar about this scent. I realize it smells like the kind of deodorant I use—it smells like me. I test it, sniffing my armpit and then the dress. Not just me. It smells like *Leo*.

The men break out into laughs. I crush the fabric in my fist.

Fuck it.

I leave my little hiding spot behind the clothes, tiptoe to the front of the closet, and feel around for a light switch. I find and poke at it, and the overhead light flicks on. My dark-adjusted eyes are shocked by the brightness, and I hold my breath, waiting to see if I've triggered any alarm. The voices drone on, taking turns interrupting one another.

I return to the back of the closet and pull the dress away from the suits it hangs behind. It's red chiffon, two layers, one transparent and one opaque.

This is the dress Leo wore on Wednesday night in Santa Monica. I see her in my mind's eye singing Rascal Flatts in the ladies' room.

Something bulky is hanging beside it, strung onto a hanger. I pull it forward.

It's Leo's purse, a small, black designer bag a prior benefactor had gifted her.

My hands are shaking. I open the clutch and feel around inside. I find a slim wallet, a lipstick, powder. Her phone.

I fumble with the phone, getting it out so fast I almost drop it. It's at 4 percent, and a picture of Malibu stares brightly out at me. Her wallpaper.

No service.

My heart sinks with disappointment. But of course, I was warned there was no service on the island. I try swiping left and dialing 911, pressing it to my ear so the sound doesn't give me away in here, but it times out, unable to place the call.

I pull out her wallet. Leo smiles back at me from her California driver's license. She's reduced to stats: five foot seven, a hundred and fifteen pounds, hair brown, eyes brown, no corrective lenses. The address is old, borrowed from a friend she used to stay with in Berkeley.

My breath catches in my throat, and for a second I think I might cry.

Leo was definitely here. My instincts proved themselves right again; Michael is a liar. She was here and she took her clothes off, and she . . . what? She didn't have a change of clothes. I guess the servants must have some clothes of their own they could have lent her, but why? And where can she be? Hiding out on the grounds somewhere, wearing something of Ashley's?

My stomach feels like it's eating itself, and I know there's a terrible possibility I'm not facing. Something could have happened to Leo, something horrible, something I can't let myself picture. All the dead women shown to me by Mauricio flash through my mind, the pale faces, the blue lips.

The voices drop in volume, and I realize the light is still on in here. I flip it off and return to my hiding place, clutching Leo's wallet to my chest, breathing in shallow gasps.

I could burst out of here and demand to know where she is, trusting that the men Michael is talking to won't let anything happen to me. They'll be shocked. They'll help me call the police.

Right. I'm so sure.

I clearly do not understand the playing field, and until I do, I need to be careful. Leo may not be in this house, but she never left this island.

What am I going to do, call the police and demand they raid Michael Forrester's private island searching for my homeless friend?

I stand there in the dark for a long time, chest aching, tears bottled up behind my face, the whole-body terror at a level I haven't felt since my mom left me.

The last time I saw Leo was Wednesday. It's now Saturday. I'm trapped here until tomorrow night. While I'm here, I can search for her. I can tear apart the island. And when I get back to L.A., I can talk to the police in person. Maybe the FBI will help. Maybe I can contact the media.

What will I tell them? What do I think happened to her?

I know from experience what my conversations with them will be like, but I have to try. I can't leave a single stone unturned.

I transfer Leo's wallet and phone into my purse. At least I'll have some evidence, something to show.

I realize the voices have stopped. I strain my ears. How long have they been quiet?

Did they leave?

I wait.

After what seems like hours but is probably only ten minutes, I creep out from my hiding place and press my ear to the door.

Nothing.

I slowly turn the handle, crack the closet door, and listen.

Silence.

I push the door open. The bedroom is empty, the bathroom door ajar like I'd left it. The suite's living area is vacant, the air smelling vaguely of cologne.

I pad through it, shoes in hand, a spike of fear in my gut. I need to get back to the party. I need to get away from here.

For the first time in years, since my mom left me and I was faced with a wide-open and hostile, impossible world, I feel completely unequipped to deal with what's been placed in front of me.

CHAPTER TWENTY-ONE

LEO

FRIDAY, JUNE 9

I was pacing around Michael's suite when the door opened and Michael walked in. He looked ready for a fight, face in that defensive expression men get when they know they're in hot water.

"Leo—" he began.

I held a hand up to stop him. "I need you to talk to your staff."

"What happened?" He stepped toward me. "Javier said he found you in a state by the electric fence. Do you know how dangerous that is?"

"Your staff is following me everywhere I go. It's creepy and I don't like it. And it's hurtful, honestly. What do you think I'm going to do alone at the beach? Swim to the other side of the island and break into your lab and, like, steal trade secrets? This is ridiculous. What am I, just some whore you brought with you, and you can't leave me alone with all your fancy shit?" I was angrier than seemed reasonable, and maybe it was because being treated like a shoplifter reminded me of why I'd come here in the first place. He wasn't completely wrong, and that hurt. It hurt a lot.

We stared at each other across the stretch of empty space, my chest heaving. At last, he nodded. "I'm sorry. I didn't think. They have their instructions, they know what they're supposed to do when I have a guest here, but I didn't tell them to change the protocol for you, and I should have. You're not just some guest."

I narrowed my eyes at him, but I felt myself softening. "I don't want to have to interact with these people today," I admitted. "I'm embarrassed about last night. I feel like they're all . . . watching me." There it was, the truth behind my anger. I was ashamed of our public sex, hurt he'd talked me into it, mad at myself for going along with something that made me uncomfortable.

He stepped toward me. "I want to show you something. Something I've never shown anybody before. Not even my staff. No one. And we'll have privacy. Okay?"

He was so handsome and genuine, his dark blue eyes melting me. "What is it?"

He took my hand, and I allowed it. "Leo, I love that you're so . . ." He seemed to search for the right word. "So free-range," he said at last, a smirk playing at the corners of his mouth. "I've never met anyone who could keep up with me. You don't know how special that is to me. I don't play games. I don't have the time or energy for it. If I didn't like you, I could drop you off in L.A. and never see you again. I have no motivation to be dishonest with you."

I had to agree with that.

"Let me show you this one thing. And then I'll take you back to L.A., and our next date can just be the two of us. How does that sound?"

My anger deflated like a popped balloon. "That sounds great. I should get back to Summer anyway."

He kissed my cheek. "That works perfect, then. I'll show you this, and then we'll hop on the boat. Would you like to stay in my hotel suite in Santa Monica for a few days, through the weekend? I can meet you back there after, and maybe you can accompany me to Switzerland? I have a working trip coming up next week."

Switzerland. A whole new world unfurled in front of me, full of globe-trotting and fancy hotels. I soared inside, picturing Europe. I'd always dreamed of backpacking from country to country. But where did Summer fit into this fantasy? I felt a pang of guilt.

"That sounds really nice," I replied truthfully.

"Come on." He took my hand and led me out of the suite. We walked down the long corridor, and he gestured to the paintings on both walls. "Did you notice these on your way in?"

"Of course. They're beautiful."

"I'm glad you like them."

"The portraits are kind of haunting. They all seem like they have this sort of . . . darkness behind the bright colors. Who are the subjects?"

"No one in particular. I collect this artist's work." He ran his finger along the edge of one as we passed by it.

He took me out of the house, no servants anywhere to be seen, and down the front steps. It was midafternoon and the sun burned bright in the sky. He said, "We'll be walking for about a mile. Will you be all right in your shoes?"

I was still wearing the sandals I'd put on for the beach. "I'm a country girl. I can go all day."

He seemed to like that. We were quiet as we walked away from the mansion, down a narrow dirt path into the woods. I hadn't noticed it from the house, but Michael traveled it like he'd done so a thousand times. It took us to a different fence, older and without the electricity warnings. He unlocked a gate, and the path led us into the forest, between shady banks of trees, at last breaking out onto a cliffside where it wound around the side of a rock wall with a steep drop to the ocean below. He paused at an overhang and pointed down at the water. "I've gone cliff diving here," he said above the rush of wind. "The water is very deep and calm."

I stood beside him and looked down. The blue sky was an endless dome above us, the water reflecting its color all the way to the horizon. We were on the south side of the island, and there was no land before us, nothing for countless thousands of miles.

"Did you know the water isn't really that color?" I asked him.

"It's reflecting the sky. If there were no sky to reflect, it'd be dark green and black."

"I know." It reminded me that he was a brilliant scientist, someone who knew all kinds of things I didn't. I felt embarrassed at having offered him this piece of trivia.

He rested a hand on the small of my back and looked deep into my eyes. "Would you jump with me?"

"Right now?" I asked, surprised.

"No. I mean, another time. Later. Would you?"

"Sure." I'd gone cliff diving lots of times.

He kissed the top of my head. "You're one of a kind." He took my hand and led me farther down the path, which took us back into the woods and became rougher, more of a cow trail. Predictions flew through my mind as I tried to figure out what he might want to show me.

He led and I followed, between trees and through thickets of bushes, until a structure appeared in front of us. It was a tiny, stone mountain cabin, and it looked much older than the house. He turned to me. "This is it."

I was skeptical. "Is it a sex dungeon? Are you finally getting ready to *Fifty Shades* me?"

He laughed. "I told you, no one else has ever been in here." He took a set of keys out of his pocket and unlocked the door. He swung it open and said, "This is my secret place."

I stepped inside, hesitant, and then I smiled, a huge whoosh of relief escaping me.

It was a single room with a wood-burning stove and one solitary window. Rolls of canvas leaned in a corner, and an easel was set opposite the small window. A large shelving unit contained paints and painting supplies, and a rusty-looking sink was splattered with color. Canvases were stacked up against the opposite wall, and I glimpsed the colorful style that matched the paintings decorating the walls of his suite.

"You're a painter," I said, turning in a circle. "You're the artist who did all the paintings in your suite. Why would you keep that a secret?"

He shrugged, hands stuffed deep in his pockets. "I need one thing that's just for me."

"You're very talented." I looked at the canvas at the front of the stack, a landscape done in a stylized fashion that made the palm trees look a little threatening. "It seems unfair. You're good at so many things."

He closed the distance between us. "Now you know everything about me. Everything. You're the only one."

It seemed a little melodramatic, but I supposed artists were always overly precious about their work. I wrapped my arms around him. "Well, I won't tell anyone that you're a really gifted painter. I can see how embarrassing that would be for you."

"It's lonely at the top," he replied, making fun of himself.

"Now I hate you." I pulled back and looked up at him. "So did you want to head over to the docks so we can get going back?"

He frowned, eyes traveling over my face. "That's it? You don't want to tell me any of your secrets?"

"Oh," I replied, surprised. "I don't have any. I'm an open book. You can ask me anything."

He was disappointed. Something in this interaction hadn't gone as he'd hoped. "Anything? I can ask you anything?"

His sharpened tone set me on edge. "Yes, sure. Why, what's wrong?"

His hands slid down to my upper arms. "It's time to tell me."

"Tell you what?"

I hadn't seen his face make this expression before. It was cold, and his hands tightened on my arms. "Stop playing dumb."

Red alert, screamed my entire body. I tried to squirm out of his grip but couldn't. "What are you talking about?"

"Stop playing games with me."

"What games? Michael, you're scaring me."

He stared at me for a few endless seconds, eyes dark in the dim light. "No one can hear you. No one knows you're in here. It's just you and me. No more games. *How did you find me?*"

Find him? He was a famous billionaire; he himself had tweeted about going to that hotel in Downtown L.A., and besides, *he* had liked *my* Instagram post. I couldn't step backward any farther. My shoulder blades ground into the wall. "Michael, I don't know what you're talking about."

He leaned down like he was going to kiss me, but then he wrapped his hands around my throat.

It was in slow motion. It couldn't be happening. It had to be a sex thing, a fake-out thing, anything but what it was. I froze while his hands tightened, my brain like a snow globe, swimming with questions.

And then it came into focus. His hands were tight. I could barely breathe. He was watching me like a scientist. I was under his microscope. I grabbed for the hands, clawed at them. "Michael, you're hurting me," I wheezed, but I was almost out of air.

"Tell me," he commanded, voice soft, a growl or a purr. "What did I miss?" He loosened his grip enough so I could reply.

"Let me go." It came out as a plea. I kicked, tried to knee him, but his hands only tightened. His body pressed against me like this was a sexual act. My knees wouldn't lift; he was using his size, pinning me to the wall. His breath came faster, hot on my cheek. This was happening. My life was a road, winding and chaotic, and this was its dead end.

No, my brain screamed against the tsunami of fear. My lungs burned. His hands were a vise. My neck ached, throbbed, circulation cutting off. I felt my head go dizzy.

I slumped, limp, letting myself go deadweight as though I'd gone unconscious. He reacted as I'd hoped, shifting his position to lower me to the ground. I didn't know what he planned to do to me once I was down there, and I didn't plan to find out. The moment his grip slackened, I wrenched sideways, thrashing my elbows and knees at him, becoming a spiky ball of limbs and joints. He compensated immediately, an angry grunt escaping him, but I was already sideways on the ground, scrambling away on my hands and knees. I knew he'd throw his weight on me, try to trap me on my stomach, so I threw my head back. It cracked his face hard— I felt the impact from the back of my skull to my sinuses. He cried out, and I launched myself forward, up, from knees to sprinting like the starting line of a race.

He was immediately behind me, tearing my hair out as he came close to getting me back in his grip. My throat burned, a jagged heat, as I scrambled for the door handle. It jiggled and I faltered, fumbled, yanked it open, and then I was on the path and nothing was in my way. The air was fresh, the ground was level, and I was a teenager again, running track with all my heart. After Amanda had died, I'd become feverish about the running, carving circles around the track day and night like I could take off and fly if I only tried hard enough, ran fast enough.

My leg muscles were electric, infused with the power of years of running away. I ran for my life, away from that cabin, back the way we'd come. I needed to think, though. Speed wasn't the only thing that mattered. I was running back to danger; this path would take me to the house. And then what?

After half a breathless mile, I risked a glance behind me. I was barefoot; I'd lost my sandals in the struggle and hadn't even noticed. My gait slowed, uncertainty heavy on my shoulders.

Should I turn into the woods and head for the house? Try to get the servants to help me?

They worked for Michael. They'd been following me for him, controlling me, tracking me. No way would they help me.

It came crashing down on me, the position I was in. I was stranded. Enemies surrounded me. There was no way out. I was running straight into danger.

From behind came a rustling—someone with shoes on, running on the path, shoving tree branches aside in haste.

I sprinted off at top speed, rounded a corner, and came to the ocean overlook where Michael had said he liked to go cliff diving. Immediately, it came to me, my best option. *No,* my brain argued. *You don't know if it's safe.*

Nothing is safe, I wanted to scream. *Look at me! Look at Amanda! Safety is a* joke.

Besides, I'd rather die here than endure whatever Michael had in store for me.

Breath coming in desperate shudders, I loped to the edge of the cliff, checked to make sure I hadn't left footprints—all clear, the ground was too hard—and surveyed the water below. It was calm and dark, a rocky cove right next to what looked like a protected beach butting up to a shady forest.

I took a few steps back, got a running start, and leaped off the cliff.

CHAPTER TWENTY-TWO

SUMMER

SATURDAY, JUNE 10

Heels strapped onto my feet, Leo's wallet and phone tucked into my purse, I pause in the hallway outside the great room and pull out my lipstick and compact with shaking hands. I fix my hair, which is a little tousled, and apply a new coat of dark pink to my lips. I look put-together, but my expression is off.

I take a deep breath and maintain eye contact with myself. I give one cheek a slap. I blink a bunch of times, hard and fast. Then I fake a silent laugh.

That's better.

I square my shoulders and make my way into the great room. People are standing in their little cliques, talking in voices that have grown louder since I left, their faces flushed with alcohol. The dinner tables have been cleared, and they're back to cocktails.

A hand grabs my arm, making me jump. It's Julie. "Where have you been?" she asks. She's with Steve, who's deep in conversation with a gray-haired man.

"Oh, I actually wasn't feeling that great," I reply. "I hid in the bathroom for a while. Another migraine." I wince and point to my head, unable to come up with a fresh excuse on the fly right now.

Her smoky eyes go wide in sympathy. "Another one? I'm so sorry! Did you get some meds? Remember"—she lowers her voice—"I have the good shit."

"I may need to try and get in touch with that doctor; only certain medications work for me." I move to slip away, but she slides her hand down my arm, a subtle gesture that doesn't look like anything from the outside but that touches every nerve on the inside of my arm.

She murmurs so no one can hear, "I'm dying of boredom and I think I'm going to scream."

"Try giving everyone secret nicknames. It helps."

She furrows her brow. "What do you mean?"

I nod toward the older man nearby. "He's kind of tall and regal, all white-haired and stern, right?"

She nods.

"I've been calling him the Ghost of Christmas Past."

She cracks up. "Oh my god."

"It's fun. Anyway, I'm going to find Alan."

She purses her lips. "Gonna have to put out tonight, eh? He's not going to buy the migraine excuse two nights in a row."

I shoot her a look, surprised at how perceptive she is. It makes her laugh again. "Get him drunk and give him a hand job," she murmurs. "It'll be the best night of his life."

I wrinkle my nose at her. "Ew."

"Better than the alternative."

I consider that, feeling queasy. She taps a finger to the inside of my elbow, gives me a seductive look, and releases me. I step into the flow of people and move through them, flashing back to all the times Leo and I have slid through crowds, grazing on valuables along the way. I think about her wide, frequent grin, her finger guns, the way she wakes from sleep so suddenly, about her dead sister and her fearless sprinting into the wide unknown.

I've arrived at one of the large picture windows. It's cooler here in front of the glass. Outside, it's so dark, I can see my own reflection better than I can see the woods or ocean. I look lost and alone.

"Summer, hello," a warm voice croons at my shoulder. I see his reflection before I turn to face him.

Michael.

My heart pounds. I blink twice and get my game face on. "Hello," I reply.

He leans his shoulder on the windowpane and sips his drink. "You look a little bored," he says, eyes crinkling.

"Not at all."

He gestures with his glass to the gathering. "It's okay. I'm bored, and this is my event." I examine the brightness in his blue eyes, the way his body is turned toward me, a casual stance. Is he hitting on me? That can't be right. I check his drink. Sparkling water, and he appears to be cold sober.

I decide to go with imitation. When in doubt, mirroring someone's mannerisms is the surest way to put them at ease. I relax my stance and return his playful smile. "I suppose it's a bit boring if you aren't familiar with the industry."

He wiggles his eyebrows. "And even if you are."

It's a joke. I laugh. "I'm trying to be a good sport. I actually didn't realize I would be here all weekend. I thought it was just an overnight."

"Oh, I'm sorry," he replies, courteous. "Do you have all the supplies you need? Clothes, toiletries?"

"I do, thank you." I'd wondered if he'd help me get back to L.A. I apply a bit more pressure. "I asked Javier if there were any boats back to the mainland, and he said it's not an option to leave before Sunday."

"Sadly, that's true. We charter them from L.A."

I make sure my eyes are bright as I tease him. "Wow, I thought you were the boss. Are you not in charge of the boats?"

He laughs, throwing his head back. "I wish! If it were up to me, I'd have the island all to myself. But the shareholders, you know."

He leans in just a bit. "Leo told me a little about you. I think it's fascinating, that you travel around without a home base. She said it's what you've been doing your whole life. What's that like?"

I blink in surprise, thrown off my rhythm. I'm shocked that Leo told him this. I run back through our conversation the night of Michael's party, and I specifically remember agreeing we were influencer matchmakers, an identity that had passed muster on numerous occasions.

A few seconds have passed, but he hasn't prompted me. Rather, he seems patient as he waits for my answer. At last, I say, "To be honest, I don't talk about it a lot."

"I'm so sorry. I didn't mean to pry." It's a lie. He's enjoying this.

I'm collected now. "It's no problem. Yes, we move around a lot. I guess you could call us digital nomads. Our work allows us to be remote, so we take advantage of that."

"Mm." He nods, sips his drink, and smiles at me with his eyes. "That sounds wonderful. I think many of us would aspire to that lifestyle."

"Well, I would encourage anyone to give it a try."

I imagine all the things that could have happened to Leo. Sex gone wrong, she ended up dead, he buried her in the woods. She drowned while Jet Skiing, and he got rid of her body quietly so no blame could be cast on him.

I gaze up at Michael, at his clear, deep blue eyes. He's incredibly handsome when you really look at him. Those eyes—you could get lost in them.

"Please let me know if you need anything," he says. He winks at me and pushes off the window, nonchalant as he grabs Javier and leans down to give him some instructions.

Javier hurries off to obey, messing with the lights by the fireplace. He dims the overheads, which must be the signal that dinner is over because people start to disperse, heading for the exits and their rooms. I observe all this in isolated, stop-motion moments. I'm thinking about something, watching the servants trickle in from the hallways to clear cocktail tables and help guests with their coats.

Michael doesn't do anything alone. Everything he does, his servants help him with. I bet he thinks they're infallibly loyal, but I wonder if they could be persuaded to follow a different light. After all, everything in this billionaire world is for sale . . . for the right price.

CHAPTER TWENTY-THREE

LEO

FRESNO
TEN YEARS AGO

The landline was ringing when I walked in the door from track practice. I threw down my gym bag and ran to the kitchen, catching it on the fourth ring. "Hello?"

"Dude, where have you been? I've been calling your cell since three."

I scowled at the wall clock. "I've been at practice, my phone is off because they make you turn it off in school, and what is your problem?"

Amanda laughed. "You're such a brat. Are you on the kitchen portable?"

"Yeah." I wedged it between shoulder and ear and opened the fridge. "Oh, hell yes, Mom made brownies." I grabbed the Tupperware and a gallon of milk and closed the fridge with my butt.

"Don't eat all of them," she cried.

"Aren't you going to be here soon?" We always went out to dinner as a family on Fridays at seven. It was our one restaurant meal

a week, a tradition. Amanda drove in from college every Friday
and spent the weekends at home, doing laundry and studying.

"So here's the thing." A note of hesitancy crept into her voice.

"What?" My mouth was full; I'd crammed in an entire brownie.
I grabbed a glass from the cabinet and poured milk, then slurped a
gulp, dripping some onto my uniform T-shirt.

"Are you being disgusting?" I could hear her scowling prissily.

"Maybe," I replied. Chocolate gluing my mouth shut, it came
out as "Muh-buh."

"*Anyway.* So I met some new friends, and we're going clubbing
in the city tonight."

I froze, eyes wide, milk tracing a thin rivulet down my chin to
my neck. I swallowed, wiped my face, and said, "I'm sorry. I think
I'm losing my hearing. It sounded like you just said you're going
clubbing in the city. With other humans."

"Shut up. I have friends."

I was baffled. She was an introvert; she hated crowds. "What
will you even wear?"

"I stole your black dress last weekend," she mumbled, fast and
guiltily.

I gasped. "The one I wore to Homecoming?"

"Yes! You aren't using it."

"But—" I halted, considering. "This means your little club
thing was premeditated. You *knew* you were going to do this."

She dropped her voice. "I met a guy. I wasn't sure it would be
anything, but I stole your dress in case he asked me out. I don't
have date clothes."

I snorted through a fresh mouthful of brownie. "Ain't that the
truth."

"Bitch." She laughed in spite of herself. "I mean, it's fair,
though. Imagine me on a first date in my favorite sweats."

I giggled, which made me choke, and then we were both laughing. When we calmed down, I said, "So you're going on a group
date kind of thing?"

"Yeah! He has some friends in from out of town and they want
to go to a fancy club."

"At least you know how to dance," I point out.

"I doubt we'll be doing ballet," she replied dryly.

"True. So what's your cover story?"

"I told Mom I was spending the night at Maddy's parents' house in Sacramento and would be home tomorrow in time for brunch. She's going to make migas."

"Yes," I hissed. Even with two brownies in me, I was still starving. Since I started running track in eighth grade, I could never get enough food. "Don't be late. Mom won't let me eat breakfast if she's making brunch. Ten o'clock latest."

"Fine."

"You slut." I sighed wistfully. "I'm so proud. And jealous. In a couple of years, I'll be ho-ing it up in San Francisco and *you'll* be covering for *me*."

"I'm not going to *ho it up*." I could hear the blush through the phone.

"You gotta lose your V card sometime," I teased. "You can't take it with you to college graduation."

"I've been in college for like six months. I think it's socially acceptable that I haven't had sex yet."

"No it's not. God, you nerd!" I was just messing around and she knew it. She laughed and told me she'd see me in the morning, and I called her a prude, and she asked how she was supposed to be a prude if I'd just called her a ho, and then I hung up on her.

That was it—the last time I'd hear her voice. I'd hear it over and over in my dreams, but I'd never hear it again upon this living earth.

CHAPTER TWENTY-FOUR

SUMMER

SATURDAY, JUNE 10

The crowd is dispersing when Alan materializes at my elbow. I force a pleasant expression onto my face. "How's business?"

His eyebrows draw together, and he doesn't meet my eyes. "It's just another dinner."

It's a grumpy, rude answer, and I look him over, suddenly terrified he knows I stole his phone. "You okay?" I don't have to fake my anxiety.

"I'm fine." He won't meet my eyes.

We make our way down the steps and along the walkway. A few other couples are nearby, chatting drunkenly as they head to the west wing. He speeds up, a hand moving to grip my elbow, surprising me with the possessive gesture. I try to keep up, which isn't easy in my heels, planning what I'll say when he confronts me. I could always go with the truth and tell him I'm worried about Leo, but then what do I do about Michael?

He leads me up the steps into the west wing, then to my bedroom door. He steps aside, obviously waiting for me to open it.

I'm not sure I want him in my room, not that it's much safer here in the hallway.

"Alan . . ." I begin.

He looks sharply at me, key card in hand. "What's the matter?"

"You seem off," I reply honestly. "Is something bothering you?"

He turns on me slowly, pivoting to fully face me. He steps forward, and I take an automatic step back, bumping into the wall. He says, "I saw you talking to Michael."

I feel a series of expressions fly across my face. Relief, for one. This is not what I was expecting. Finally, I say, "Yes. For a minute."

He beeps my door open with his key card and indicates that I should step inside. His card opens my door? That doesn't feel safe.

He gestures, frustrated. "You coming?"

I don't go into private rooms with angry men. "I'd feel better if we talked out here."

"I don't need my business discussed in public."

"Alan, what's wrong? You're clearly upset."

"I saw you talking to Michael."

"You mentioned that." My heart is jackhammering in my chest.

"Here's what I want to know." He looks around, making sure we're alone. "What do you girls see in him? Why is it always him?" He presses into me, chest to chest, an effort to dominate or intimidate. I hold my ground despite a full-body urge to run.

"Alan, calm down," I say, trying to control my voice. "Take some deep breaths. We can talk through this."

"Why are you acting like I'm going to hurt you?" he asks.

My mouth is dry. "Are you not?"

A half laugh explodes out of him. "Jesus. Who do you think I am? I have a right to be upset when you flirt with my boss."

I protest, "I wasn't flirting. He approached me. I was just being polite."

"You looked cozy enough." His tone is petulant, wounded.

I fold my arms across my chest and square my shoulders, a defensive posture, I know, but it makes me feel more in control. "I'm not interested in Michael."

He shoves his hands in his pockets. "You're not?"

"Not at all. If that's what you're worried about, you can stop." The door to my room stands ajar. I shoot a longing glance at it, wishing I could go in there and close it, lock it.

He puts his hands on my waist. I hate them there, but I let them stay. "Women always like him better. He has more money, he's taller, he's better-looking." He sounds fourteen.

I know what I have to do. I'm about to lose him, and I can't afford to blow this up right now. I steel myself, wind my arms around his neck, and pull him toward me for a kiss.

A low groan snakes out of his throat, and then he's kissing my neck, pulling me backward into my room. His suit jacket falls to the floor and I cringe. Julie's words come back to me—*just give him a hand job*. Disgusting, but maybe she's right.

In his pocket, something buzzes. He has a new phone?

He groans, "No, oh my god, not now," and digs it out of his pocket. It looks just like the one I threw into the ocean. He answers the call, clearing his throat. "This is Alan."

A pause.

"Now? Come *on*," he whines, that petulant note back in his voice.

Another pause.

He grabs his suit jacket off the ground. "On my way." He hangs up and tosses me a regretful smile as he pulls the jacket on. "Duty calls."

I can't believe my luck. "What's going on?" I try not to sound too happy.

We're interrupted by a strange whirring outside the window, a mechanical thrumming sound. I look out just in time to see a flash of movement. He says, "The wife of a big-ticket investor thought it was a good idea to bring her lapdog along with her on the weekend and it got lost. We've been searching for it since yesterday."

"But what was that outside the window?"

"Drones." He straightens his tie and smooths his shirt. "I wrote their program. One of them is malfunctioning, and I have to fix it." He crosses the room and kisses me, lingering on it. "Sorry we got interrupted," he murmurs, a hand reaching to cup my breast. "We'll pick up where we left off tomorrow, okay?"

I smile angelically, internally shuddering with revulsion. "Good luck."

He hurries out, and I return my attention to the window. Outside, the same muted whirring tells me the drone is still somewhere close by. I'm reminded of the drone I saw last night when I was at the dock searching for boats. I'd thought they were part of the security system.

I grab my room card and let myself out into the hallway. Barefoot, I walk through the exterior door and stand on the porch, studying the dark sky and trees.

A drone whizzes overhead, closely followed by another. They're like hexagonal helicopters, probably two feet in diameter. They head for the forest and disappear above the trees.

South, above the main residence, another drone heads in the opposite direction. I barely make out its dim gray form before it vanishes behind the house. In the distance, a faint buzzing tells me more are hovering on the other side of the compound.

This is a lot of effort for a dog. Alan is the head of whatever scientific project is happening here. Would he really get pulled into the search for a lapdog? Seems more like something Javier and the servants would be dealing with, but I suppose if he built the drones, it kind of makes sense.

I stand there awhile, listening for drones, occasionally detecting them at the periphery of my hearing. This island is doing something to me, messing with my instincts. Usually, I feel confident in my ability to read people and situations. Here . . . I don't know.

Leo's dress, hanging in Michael's closet. Javier, eyes sharp and sparkling.

Ashley, pale and timid. Afraid? If so, of what? Of things she's seen?

I return to my room and call housekeeping.

When she finally knocks, I'm pacing around, impatient. I pull the door open and am again struck by her frailty, the fairness of her skin, the way her hair lies flat to her skull, coiled into a low bun.

"Thanks for coming," I say.

"Of course. What can I do for you?"

"Come in." I hold the door open wider.

She fidgets. "I'm really not supposed to—"

"Come in," I repeat, and she obeys, which is what I'd expected. Her face has gone dead white, lips parted, eyes stretched wide.

I direct her to the love seat and sit beside her, considering my tactics. I've met a lot of women like Ashley. When someone rages at her, she'll turn inward. I'd be willing to bet she isn't this thin naturally; she probably struggles with anxiety, gets stomachaches, can't eat. There's an abusive caregiver in her past resulting in issues with confrontation and authority . . . a direct approach will yield results but create fear.

She's looking at me with big, nervous eyes, waiting for me to talk. I run my hands through my hair and lean back, an arm across the back of the love seat, taking ownership of the space.

"What's your job here?" I ask.

"Laundry and guest services." She sits up straight, then straighter as though she's hoping I'll see what a good girl she is and be nice to her.

"You remember when you were in here earlier? You saw a photograph of my friend Leo. You recognized her."

She flushes pink. "Oh, no. Not at all. I'm so sorry, I wasn't try-ing to—"

"Quiet." I think I've landed on how I'll handle this. I stand. "Stay there," I tell her. I squat by my suitcase and hunt around until I find and pull Julie's diamond bracelet out. It's cool and slinky. I show it to her on my palm as I return to my seat. "Pretty, right?"

She glances at it. "Yes, it is, but—"

"It's not mine." I sit beside her. "I found it on the beach. I think

Julie dropped it. I meant to return it tonight but forgot." I pause for dramatic effect. "Or maybe I found it on you. Maybe you stole it."

All the blood seems to leave her body. "I would never steal from a guest."

I settle closer to her this time so our legs are almost touching. "You grew up poor. Am I right? You're from a big family, and you were forgotten. Overlooked. Maybe you were the babysitter for your younger siblings."

After a long moment of staring at me with huge, scared eyes, she says, "How did you know all that?"

I let my eyes trace the diamonds' bright facets. "I'm good at that. People. Reading them, that is. Not relating to them. Anyway." I turn my eyes on her. "You know I'm here with Alan. I'd hate to have to tell Alan that I found this bracelet on you and recognized it as Julie's. I'm sure you need this job. Maybe you send money back home to your family?"

She nods mutely.

I set the bracelet on the cushion beside me. "I'm willing to negotiate an alternative. I would love for us to come to an agreement that makes everybody happy."

Tears are glimmering in her washed-out blue eyes. "What sort of agreement?"

"You remember the photograph of my friend Leo."

She doesn't answer.

"I know you recognized her. I need you to tell me how. When did you see her?"

She looks down at her hands. "I'm just here to do the laundry," she says in a small, squeaky voice. A tear drips off her nose into her lap.

I need to apply pressure. "Hey. I'm losing my patience. Tell me how you recognized my friend or I'm calling Alan right the hell now."

She cries harder, bringing her hands to her face.

I get up and pick up the phone receiver. "This is your last chance. Do you really want to fuck with me?"

She lifts her face to look at me in horror. "Please. I can't. Please."

"Why can't you?" I ask, one finger grazing the buttons.

"You don't understand. I can't." I realize she's actually trembling. This reaction seems over-the-top for someone who's just afraid of losing her job. There's more to it than that.

"Explain why you can't," I command, returning to her. This time, I squat in front of her so I'm level with her knees. I put my hand on one.

She shakes her head, still sobbing.

"*Explain,*" I repeat. "Right now. Or I call."

She has to breathe deeply a few times to get the words to whisper out. "He'll get so mad."

I consider this. "Who is 'he'? Michael?"

She nods, crying quieter now.

Interesting.

"Look at me." I tap her knees. She obeys. "We can help each other out. There's a way for us to both walk away from this, getting what we want."

"How?" she asks.

"Tell me everything you know about Leo. I'll keep it a secret, never letting anyone know you told me, and I'll return this bracelet to Julie myself. Like this never happened."

She doesn't say anything.

"Wouldn't that be nice?" I prompt. Nothing. I apply pressure once more. "I'm only here for the weekend. I don't give a single shit about these people, Michael, your job, none of it. I just want to find my friend."

She wipes tears from her eyes and nods, a microscopic gesture that sends triumph roaring through me.

I get up from my squat and sit beside her. "Good. Now tell me how you recognized that photo of Leo. She was here, wasn't she? She was here with Michael on Wednesday night. They came in on his little boat."

Her eyes search my face, intense and hungry. "If you already know that, then—"

"What I want to know is what happened while she was here."

She winces, looks at the door.

"The sooner you tell me, the sooner you get back to work and the smaller the chance that anyone will know you were ever here."

She huffs out a frustrated breath, wipes her face, and turns to look me full on. "Fine. Okay. She came on Wednesday with Mr. Forrester, like you said."

"They were having fun, right? Being a happy couple."

"They got in very late. I didn't see them arrive."

"Fair enough. When did you first see her?"

"The next morning. Thursday. She and Mr. Forrester were . . . enjoying their time. We made them brunch, and they went to explore the island. I believe snorkeling and boating. I was working."

"Good. Go on."

"After their day, they came back and had dinner." She breaks eye contact for a moment, then returns her eyes back to me.

"What was that? Something's weird about the dinner. Tell me."

She looks down at her hands in her lap. "I really can't say."

My temper flares, and I bite back curses. "Please," I say through gritted teeth.

"They were doing things at dinner," she bursts out.

I'm confused. I watch her, analyzing her expressions, and then I realize. "They were getting sexual at dinner."

"Yes." She's clearly relieved I guessed it.

"There's no time to be a prude, Ashley. What happened?"

"Well, he kind of . . . They . . ." She blows out a breath, then says in a rush, "They had sex at the dinner table. With everyone watching."

I raise my eyebrows. That's not like Leo. She doesn't mind going skinny-dipping, but she's not into public sex.

I decide to move on. "Fine. Okay, then what?"

"They went to his room. The next morning, Friday, he had to work at the research facility for a few hours. I was asked to accompany her and make sure she had everything she needed. She wanted to go to the beach."

"Which beach?"

"The same one you visited with Mrs. Lodstrom."

"Who?"

"Julie." Her eyes dart to the bracelet.

"Fine. Then what?"

"She became . . . irritated with me for following her. She clearly wanted her privacy, but I'd been specifically instructed to stay with her, so it was a very awkward situation. She became angry."

I'm nodding. This all tracks. "Then what?"

"She said she was going back up to the house. I followed her. That made her even more angry. She started running, and then she left the path and went into the woods."

My eyebrows shoot up. "She went into the *woods*? Why?"

"It seemed like she was trying to lose me. She went sprinting off the path out of nowhere. She was fast, too. Very fast. There was no way I could keep up."

I let out a dry laugh. It's totally something Leo would do. I can picture it so clearly. "And then what?"

"I never saw her again."

I wait a beat, then repeat it. "You never saw her at all after that?"

She shakes her head, and something in the gesture makes me wonder what she's thinking. "I called Javier and told him what had happened. That part of the island is undeveloped. It's all wilderness, and it's very easy to get turned around. He said he would organize a few staff members to look for her. Some of our staff have backpacking experience and serve as rangers in case we have any situations like this come up. Mr. Forrester likes to explore the wilderness quite often." She opens and closes her mouth a few times. "And that's it. She's been gone ever since."

I remember the pairs of drones, Alan's phone ringing, the urgency in the whole thing. I'd thought it was weird that they were doing all this for a dog.

Last night—down at the docks. I'd chalked the drones up to security, to the same billionaire paranoia that made Michael send all the boats back to L.A.

Now I understand. They're not looking for a dog. They're looking for Leo. She's out there somewhere, lost.

She could be alive.

CHAPTER TWENTY-FIVE

LEO

FRESNO
TEN YEARS AGO

I sat at the table, watching the migas get cold as my mom and dad argued bitterly. Above us, the wall clock read ten thirty.

"Let's just eat," my dad protested. "If she's going to be late, she's going to miss brunch. It's not a big deal, hon, she's a college student, she probably just overslept."

"We don't start eating until everyone's here," my mom insisted, her trademark stubbornness sending a twitch down my dad's neck.

I looked gloomily at the spread: the tortillas in their cloth bed, the bowl of homemade guacamole and the other of salsa, the beans, the rice, the platter of sliced melon because my mom believed no meal was complete without fresh fruit.

"She's probably just running late," I said. "Like Dad said, she's in college, not middle school. Can I please eat?"

"Rita, come on," my dad said. "Let the kid eat."

"Fine." My mom threw her napkin on her plate, stood, and marched off to their bedroom. I watched, eyes wide, worried this was a trick. When my mom said the word *fine,* it was usually the end of the world.

"Eat," my dad told me and almost knocked his chair over hurrying after my mom. Through the wall, I heard their angry voices resume their fight, more heated now that they thought I was out of earshot. I shrugged and filled my plate. *Look who's a ho after all,* I thought, itchy with anticipation to hear about Amanda's sordid night out, gleeful to be the good child for once.

The police and my parents faced me in the living room. It was dark now, day having passed into night, and the food I'd eaten hours ago had turned sour in my stomach. I sat miserably on the ottoman, my mom's hand rubbing my back.

"Can you tell me again what your sister told you?" the officer, a red-haired woman just a few years older than Amanda, asked me.

"She said she was spending the night at her friend Maddy's parents' house in Sacramento," I answered, feeling uncertain. I wasn't sure if I should keep up Amanda's story or not. She'd been MIA all day, which was extremely weird, but I was bound by sister code. I would die before I'd snitch. If our parents found out she'd lied and spent the night partying, she'd be grounded for the rest of her life. And yes, she was in college, but our parents were paying for it, which meant they felt they had control over everything she did.

"Do you know Maddy's last name?" the officer asked.

I shook my head. "They're in class together. That's all I know."

"So not roommates."

"No. She shares a room in the dorms with a girl named Teresa."

"We spoke with Teresa already," my mom told the cop. Her voice trembled with worry, and guilt ripped a new path through me when I looked at my dad. He was pale, a wreck, and Amanda had only been missing for a handful of hours.

"You mentioned that," the officer said kindly. My mom had repeated the same facts over and over again, clearly unaware she was doing so. To me, she said, "And you mentioned Amanda was wearing a black dress she'd borrowed from you."

"She wanted to look cute," I said defensively, because it was absurd that Amanda would wear this to a friend's family home, but I was determined that they have an accurate description of her. No one caught the inconsistency, and I was asked to provide a photo of the dress from when I'd worn it to Homecoming, which I pulled off the mantel and extracted from its frame with shaking fingers.

"We have enough to go on for now," the woman said, holding the photograph by a corner. "We'll be in touch, and please call this number when she turns up." *When*—that word was comforting. My sister was eighteen. She had probably just . . . gone away for the weekend, gotten caught up in the fun she was having. Right?

Wrong. I knew it and my parents knew it. Wrong, wrong, wrong.

CHAPTER TWENTY-SIX

SUMMER

SUNDAY, JUNE 11

I chug the last of the coffee, shove my feet into sneakers, and pull on my sweatshirt. I'm in workout clothes, which is as much cover as I can give myself if I get spotted. "Out for a late-night jog" is weak, but it's all I've got to explain being in the woods at two in the morning. I twist my mane of hair into a bun and fasten it with an elastic and a few bobby pins.

I study the map of the island one last time, fold it up, and tuck it into the pocket of my leggings. The island is jaggedly divided into two sections, one labeled *Residential* and the other *Research Facility*. I have to imagine there's some kind of barrier between the two, a fence or something. The beach is on the residential side, obviously, and the path leading from the west wing to the beach loosely parallels the dividing line between the halves of the island. If Leo went off the path where Ashley says she did, she'd have run into the barrier if there is one. I have a hard time imagining how she could have gotten lost under those conditions, but perhaps there isn't a physical barrier. Maybe the division between the island's halves is informal.

Out in the hallway, Ashley is nowhere to be seen, but I imagine I can feel her nervous presence. She'd skittered out of my room like a terrified mouse as soon as I released her. She better not get confessional and tell someone I'd cornered her. With someone like that, the chances are seventy-thirty of them keeping a guilty secret.

I don't know that I care. If Michael lost Leo somewhere on the island, and he's not sure if he's going to be able to find her or if she's going to die of exposure out in the wilderness, that explains why he's pretending she was never here. It makes him an asshole of the highest order, but it surprises me not at all. He can be that way, but no way in hell am I going to sit back and trust a bunch of drones to find her. I know her better than anyone else. I can at least try to retrace her steps and maybe even figure out where she went.

I glance out the window. The moon is bright, almost full, but it's nowhere near bright enough for it to be safe to venture into the woods. I could get lost, too, or end up walking right off one of this island's cliffs.

I can't leave Leo out there. If they're looking for her, so will I.

I hurry down the porch steps. A tired songbird lets out a muted chirp as I brush against a shrub it must be roosting in. I follow the path downhill toward the beach, its trajectory unfamiliar in the silver moonlight. I'd made Ashley tell me exactly where Leo had turned off, and I watch for it as I walk through the woods. In the shadows where the moon can't peek through, the dark is black, a color you don't get in any city, a complete absence of light. I stop once, holding my breath, a low sound buzzing overhead. The sound resolves into the faint whisper of wings. Bats? That's fine with me. Humans are the only animals I'm afraid of.

I walk slowly, searching for the turnoff Ashley had described. Despite my best efforts, I go too far and end up getting spat out onto the beach. Where did I go wrong?

I picture Leo storming away, infuriated by having been followed. Ashley said she was just at the top of the hill, where the path begins winding left, when Leo had vaulted into the woods, heading west. I retrace my steps slowly, picturing this playing out.

Here. A bit farther uphill than I'd expected, I find a curve that matches Ashley's description.

I step off the path into the trees. The moonlight filters gently through the leaves, creating lacy layers of darkness on the forest floor.

This is dangerous. You should never leave the path at night. The thought gallops stubbornly through my mind. Survival instincts are not easily silenced, not after so many years of surviving at all costs.

I keep track of where the path is behind me and proceed, hoping for some sign of Leo but finding none. I'm no wilderness tracker, and it's the dead of night. I'm not going to be able to tell if she crunched some sticks underfoot two days ago.

Suddenly, I'm stepping into a clearing, the light almost blue to my dark-adapted eyes. I think it's a hiking trail, but then I see the tall chain-link fence. Barbed wire loops along the top, and red-and-white caution signs declare it to be electric.

I follow it, wondering if Leo may have walked here. The electric charge buzzes lightly like a swarm of faraway bees. Something attached to one of the fence posts about seven feet off the ground catches my attention. I think it's a security camera, pointed at the fence line.

I'm gradually heading uphill, walking along the fence's cleared shoulder, and suddenly the house is in sight, peeking over the plateau above, a few windows glowing yellow.

If Leo went this way like Ashley said she did, there's no way she could have gotten meaningfully lost. The fence makes it impossible to wander too far away from the house, and they would have seen her through the cameras. I'm sure they can see me now.

With that in mind, I jog beside the fence for a while, until something ahead catches my attention, an intersection in the chain link. This fence veers right, but a different one continues straight forward.

I pull out the map and tilt it into the moonlight. My impression is confirmed: The fence turning right is the one on the map. There's no indication of a second fence continuing straight. It seems like there's a third section of the island that's not on the map. What's more, this uncharted fence looks older, and I don't see any security cameras or warning signs about electricity attached to it, though it has the requisite barbed wire strung across the top in sloppy loops.

Maybe Leo somehow got into the third part of the island. I start searching for ways she could have gotten across this barrier—an overhanging tree, a hole underneath, a broken section. My steps are faster now; I feel I'm getting warmer.

A gate stops me in my tracks. It's padlocked through a built-in hole in the latch. Jackpot. Maybe this had been left open. Maybe she got through it.

It's very low-tech, the padlock. Michael can't have anything related to the research facility over there, not with a lock that could be snapped with bolt cutters.

What's on the other side?

I look back up the hill, where the house is invisible from my current perspective. Could Leo have ended up here instead of at the house? Alone on the third part of the island, she could have fallen and hurt herself.

A new scenario plays itself out in my imagination: Leo, here on the island with Michael, searching for things to steal. Michael, catching her with her hand in a drawer. Leo running, Michael chasing, Leo hiding . . . This is the first time I've considered that she could have gotten lost on purpose.

I spend some more time investigating, searching for gaps or ways to climb over. I come up short, and stand panting, frustrated. How do you get around a barrier? Well, there are three options: over the top, through a gap, or underneath. I can't get through barbed wire, so climbing it is out. There are no gaps or breaks.

Underneath, it is.

CHAPTER TWENTY-SEVEN

LEO

FRESNO
TEN YEARS AGO

The officers were at our house every day for a while, and we were at the station more days than not. Ten days passed, and I didn't sleep more than an hour at any point. Should I tell them the truth? Should I tell them what Amanda had said she was doing that night?

She hadn't told me which club she was going to or anything about the guy she'd met. She'd mentioned he had friends in from out of town, but I argued that none of this would help the cops find her. What would they even look for? "A guy" and "his friends" in a big city?

They could show the clubs Amanda's picture, a small voice inside me pointed out, but I argued back. Who could possibly remember her? She'd have been wearing a plain black dress. She was a slim brunette with tanned skin and a pretty face. There was nothing unusual or notable about her.

And I'd have to tell my parents I'd been lying this whole time. I knew how they'd look at me.

The whole thing was my fault.

And then one day, a foursome of suited cops came to our door. The man in front was an older detective. He'd been working Amanda's case quietly behind the scenes while his team members seemed to be more out in front. We'd seen him just a few times, but each time he'd impressed me with an aura of being able to see what others couldn't. He didn't look like anything special, just an old sad-faced white man with a receding hairline and a gut. But his eyes were so . . . sharp.

I was alone in the living room, sprawled on the couch with my phone. I always had my phone in hand, charged, waiting for Amanda to call. I watched them through the window, and my scalp prickled. All of them together was not a good sign.

My mom came from the bedroom to answer the door, a glass of wine in hand. My dad was right behind her, mute and pale. This was how they were now: her with a drink, him without words.

They let the cops in. Everyone sat on the furniture. I tried to vanish into the arm of the couch.

"We don't have good news," said the lead detective, his eyes flitting among all of us. "Ma'am, do you want your daughter in the room, or would you like to excuse her?"

"Go to your room," my mom hissed, eyes huge, words like snakes.

I stood and fumbled for the hall, where I slid to the floor out of sight, arms wrapped around my knees.

"We believe we found your daughter," the man said, his voice muffled. It sounded like he was talking on the other side of a cloth divider.

My mom sobbed, a choked sound.

"We found the body of a young woman matching your daughter's description," he followed, gentle and kind. "In the woods by Shaver Lake. I'm so sorry."

A horrible pause followed, and then my dad said, "How do you know it's her?" in a voice I barely recognized.

"We'll need you to identify her," came the soft reply. "It's been long enough now that it may not be easy. We'll also be checking dental records."

My mom wailed, a sound so horrible I bit my knuckles hard enough to draw blood.

The voices pulsed into my head through the roaring in my ears. "The young lady wasn't killed in this location; she was clearly moved" and "wearing yellow," were things the man said, along with "bright red lipstick."

I sat straight up, pushed myself to standing, and lurched out of the hallway into the living room. "It's not her," I cried, banging my shin into a side table. "She was wearing black. It's not her, Mom, it's not. She doesn't wear red lipstick."

The way the officer looked at me, with pity, made me bow down and scream into the carpet.

Because it *was* her. I knew it then, and I confirmed it when I looked at my sister's ravaged body.

From the carpet, I looked up at the rows of photos neatly positioned on the mantel, on the tables, on the walls. Amanda and me, me and Amanda. Arms locked, hands clasped, her just a little bit taller always. This family wasn't real without her. I wasn't *me* without her. Hers had been the first hand I'd held. Every dentist appointment, every doctor's visit, during flu shots and setting my broken arm and my first terrifying stitches—she'd been by my side.

She was the sweet one, the one with the conscience. I was the wild, bad one, the terrible younger one, the destructive, impulsive, loudmouthed "agent of chaos"—her favorite thing to call me. I didn't deserve to live; she did. It should have been me. *I should be dead in the woods.* Not her. I ground my knuckles into my teeth, the words locked behind them. *It should have been me.*

She was gone, and it was my fault. Gone forever. Our last conversation had been a test, and I'd failed.

When I'd finally told my parents about my lie, my mother had clutched her stomach like she'd been shot. She'd fallen backward into my dad's arms, and I'd never looked them in the eyes again. I'd gone walking, out into the night, because what was the point of keeping myself safe when I deserved every horrible thing that happened to me?

Maybe I could walk away from it. If I left home, if I closed every door to my past, maybe new doors would open in front of me. After all, nothing could be worse than what I was leaving behind.

Nothing.

CHAPTER TWENTY-EIGHT

SUMMER

SUNDAY, JUNE 11

I'm standing at the window when day breaks. I watch dawn illuminate the sky behind the trees, its reflection glowing eggplant purple, then charcoal, at last bursting with striations of orange, pink, and red.

The last time I watched a sunrise with Leo, we were sitting on the hood of the Land Cruiser in Malibu. It was the morning before we went clubbing, the morning before she met Michael. We'd made coffee using the camp stove, and we were sipping it in the cool breeze, watching the dawn unfold hundreds of feet below on the Pacific. She leaned against me, shoulder to shoulder, and said, "*This is the life. This is what it's all about. Moments like these.*"

Now, without her, the early morning feels cold and empty.

I make coffee and drink it as the sun blazes to life and all the colors in the landscape are revealed. My head feels foggy and my eyes are grainy with exhaustion. *I'll sleep later,* I promise myself.

Getting antsy, I set my empty coffee cup down and check the

time. Ashley should be here by now. I called her over two hours ago.

At last, a soft knock at my door. I dash to open it. Ashley stands on the threshold, looking frightened. "It's outside, under the porch," she says. "I had to wait for everyone to be busy."

"Good." I start to close the door on her, but she puts a hand on it, stopping me.

"Don't ask me to do anything else," she whispers. "Please. I'm begging you." Her eyes are shadowed, cheeks hollow; she clearly hasn't slept.

I reject several responses and finally go with, "You should find a different job. Whatever he's paying you, it isn't worth all this."

She looks out at the hallway, then back at me. "Please. No more." She hurries away.

As promised, the shovel is tucked underneath the porch outside the west wing entrance. Before pulling it out, I look up at the eaves and corners of the porch to confirm one more time that there are no cameras.

I carry the shovel as surreptitiously as possible, tucked against my left leg. Everything looks dangerously exposed in the daylight. I make it back to the fence unseen, but, remembering the security cameras attached to the fence, I stay in the trees, not moving onto the cleared shoulder. Weaving around tree trunks and through bushes while carrying a four-foot shovel is not the most efficient way to travel, and I end up having to take little detours when the brush is too thick, so it's at least an hour before I make it to the intersection of fences.

At last, there it is: the gate. As I approach, I wonder again why there isn't any surveillance here. Whatever is on this part of the island must not be valuable. This is probably the nature preserve Julie mentioned.

Picking a spot about thirty feet away from the gate and as close to the fence as I can get, I start digging. I get into a rhythm: foot on shovel, cut through dirt, lift dirt out, set in a neat pile, repeat. I've dug many holes in my life, burying boxes of treasure around California. I can't have bank accounts since I don't have a real identity, and besides, I'm not sure I trust banks. They seem like they're run by men like Michael. How do I know they're not going to steal my money once it's in there?

Digging becomes a painful routine. Your hands hurt, then your back hurts, then your knees hurt, and then everything hurts. I should have brought water, I realize after an hour, but my hole is large now, and the ground is softer here than I'd expected, not as rocky as it would be on the drier side of the hill. I keep going.

The sun ascends and the air heats up. It's midmorning when I have an eighteen-inch hole angling down and under the fence. I have to get my upper body inside the hole and jab at the earth with the shovel to penetrate the last two feet. I could have really used a trowel to help with this part. I use my hands to claw my way through the last barrier of dirt—goodbye, manicure—and at last create a small tunnel from one side of the fence to the other. I hurl the shovel back into the woods and lay in the hole on my back, then snake myself up and out on the other side.

Dirty, panting, and soaked with sweat, I survey the forest ahead of me. It slopes slightly downhill and clearly will lead me to one of the cliffs if I head away from the fence. I wipe my filthy hands on my sweatshirt and strike out through the trees. As I move away from the fence, they shrink into a desertscape of brush and rocks, and I'm afraid I'm going to accidentally step on a rattlesnake. The sky is huge and blue, swells of hills and rock forming a landscape that would be easy to get lost in. I check behind me and realize I can't see the fence at all; it's lost in the hills. I need to mark my location, so I tie my sweatshirt to a bush.

I turn and continue pushing through the brush, cooler now in my workout tank, wary of the landscape. At any moment, I could step over a swell and find myself plummeting off a cliff.

To my left, I spot a relief in the dense brush. I head for it, wondering if it's a ravine or a stream, but when I get to it, I see it's a path. Twelve inches across, the kind of packed dirt trail you see all over California. To my left, it winds around and disappears between hills in the direction of the residence. To the right, it seems to grow wider, heading for the cliffs. I turn right.

It expands until it's three feet across and runs between rocky formations. Suddenly, the formations drop out of view, and it's rounding a clifftop. An overhang looks down onto a clear, calm cove with a small sandy beach that recedes into a tall-treed forest.

I stay on this path as it retreats from the cliffs into a forest where the trees are dense and close, and the shade is sweet and damp on my sun-soaked skin.

I round one more curve, and then I stop in my tracks.

A cabin.

It's a tiny structure, not more than one room, clearly hand-built in some former age before the island was a billionaire's playground. Except for the shriek of jays and the far-off roar of the ocean, all is quiet.

With caution, I approach. The door is locked, and the windows are shuttered from the inside.

I press my ear to the door. Silence.

They'd already have found Leo if she was hiding in here. It's too obvious a place you'd pick. Still, it's worth checking.

I pull two bobby pins out of my bun, glad I don't have to break a window. I use the keyhole to bend one into a ninety-degree angle, then pull the other pin apart with my teeth, stripping off the rubber tip. I keep tension with one hand, the other searching for the seized lock. As I'm working, I wonder about the lack of cameras and security. I don't know if I should be reassured that this cabin isn't important, isn't something Michael is hiding, or if I should be more concerned that he's keeping it off the grid.

With a click, the lock releases, and I turn the handle and swing the door open.

It's dark, as small as I'd expected, and cluttered. I step inside and push the shutter away from the dirty window for some light.

Stacked along the wall are dozens of paintings. In a corner, a roll of canvas and a pile of wooden bars are piled up neatly. By the window, a paint-stained easel sits vacant alongside a hutch overflowing with paints and brushes. The air is thick with the scent of oil paint and turpentine.

It's an art studio. Does Michael hire a painter like he hires acrobats and musicians? No wonder there's no security; there's nothing in here of interest or value.

Clarity breezes through me like a head rush. I have been perhaps too paranoid. Not everything is full of hidden malice. Sometimes, a cabin in the woods is just a painting studio. And sometimes, a headstrong woman gets lost when she goes off-trail, and Michael likely doesn't want it known that he has a girl about to die of exposure lost somewhere on his fancy island in the middle of his investors' weekend.

It infuriates me, as inevitable as it is. Of course that's what matters—his reputation. Not Leo. If she were one of his VIP guests, he'd have the entire California forestry department here combing the brush for her. But Leo's just a girl, someone to sleep with and forget. She gets drones and halfhearted searches by Alan and Javier.

Curious in spite of myself, I wonder what kind of paintings a billionaire commissions and pick one up. It's a portrait of a blonde in her twenties. She's in a fancy dress that shows off her collarbone and is sitting on a grassy plateau above an endless expanse of ocean.

It's here—the island. The backdrop is the lawn in front of the mansion. The style is just like the paintings hanging in Michael's suite of rooms. This must be the same artist.

Something occurs to me: Maybe Michael paints these himself. Maybe this is a secret little retreat for him. I could see that; he's clearly intelligent and creative. Everyone needs an outlet.

I smirk with one side of my mouth. *Let me paint you,* I picture him saying to the young woman after sex. She must have been so flattered. The painting is good, I'll give him that. It's realistic and detailed, almost photographic.

I set it aside and inspect another one. This is of a different beautiful girl, a young Black woman with long braids, seated in a chair on the lawn overlooking the ocean. Her expression is interesting; she's guarded, eyes solemn as if she doesn't enjoy being painted. I wonder if he takes pictures of them and works from those or if he makes them sit for hours while he paints.

I flip through more canvases. Some are landscapes, all clearly depicting various places around the island. Others are portraits, all similar: young women in ornate dresses, posed in various places around the mansion. One is at the base of the stairs, another in front of the fireplace, but otherwise they're all outside on the grass, in the woods, or on the beach.

How many girls have you brought here? This is what money will do—every model in Los Angeles will come to your island to fuck you. And hey, one of the girls might get lost in the wilderness; maybe someday you'll find her bones. Or maybe not. Doesn't matter, does it? There are plenty more where she came from.

I come to the end of the stack and start on the next, morbidly curious. How many times did he do this? Jesus. Some guys just keep a black book. I'm almost laughing by the time I get to the deepest stack, the ones almost buried by the other paintings. I pull one out and catalog it mentally: brunette, long hair, olive complexion, dark eyes looking serious and worried, shoulders bare in the elegant dress.

I'm about to return it to the pile when something strikes me. I take it to the window for a better look, and then I gasp.

The eyes, the eyebrows, the lips. It's Leo.

She's younger, and her face is rounder, hair longer, arms and chest fuller. She glows, cheeks pink with health and youth.

How can this possibly exist? How could Michael and Leo have known each other before this week? She would have mentioned something, wouldn't she? Or could Michael have painted this using photographs instead of her in the flesh? Perhaps he always works from photographs. The only reason Leo targeted Michael in the first place was that he liked one of her Instagram posts. I suppose it's possible that he'd used a photo from her feed as inspiration and given her a little more meat on her bones and a slightly younger face to appease his own sensibilities.

I'm dumbfounded, staring into Leo's face. She looks back at me, solemn, girlish, keeping secrets. I search the image as if staring at it long enough will answer all the questions running through my frantic brain.

Assuming Leo had never met Michael before their meet-cute at the DTLA hotel bar, I wonder how she would react to this painting. No doubt she'd be creeped out. Who wouldn't be?

Could she possibly have stumbled across this shed, this painting, sparking a conflict with Michael?

I set the painting down where I'd found it, but then I pick it back up, decisive. I'm not going to leave it here. This is evidence of a prior connection between Michael and Leo, and it could be helpful when I'm talking to the police. That said, I can't carry it around discreetly or pack it in my suitcase. It's eighteen by twenty-four. However, it's hand-stretched, and I'm sure I can pull the staples out and get the canvas off the stretcher bars. I flip it over and yank at the cloth. Some staples come out easily, but some are really stuck in there. After a few minutes of grunting and rips to the periphery of the painting, I have the floppy, stiff canvas separated from the wooden frame. I toss the frame aside and create a roll with utmost care, painted side in.

I've already been in here too long.

I peek out the door before opening it all the way. The woods are quiet and peaceful, sun shining brightly through the leaves, birds chirping. I close the door, say a quick prayer that no one discovers my intrusion, and trot back along the path, rolled canvas tucked under my arm.

My thoughts are a cluttered bookshelf. So many paintings. So many girls.

The footpath runs along the clifftop, and a faint buzzing noise makes me pause to listen. It's coming from below, from somewhere among the rock formations. I peer over the edge, down to the gentle turquoise water. You could totally jump from here. Leo loves cliff jumping, I'm reminded, and the memory of her flinging herself into space and landing like a dart in Lake Powell invites a sharp pain into my chest.

Then I see it, the whirring drone fluttering among the trees in a ravine down by the cove. There's an inlet where a small stream flows out to meet the ocean, and the drone is buzzing the adjacent treetops like a hummingbird.

I turn and run. The trail narrows, and I follow it until I get to where I'd met it in the first place, where I have to slow to a walk to make my way through the chaparral. At last, I push my way through the bushes and see I'm exactly where I expected, the tunnel thirty feet farther along the fence line.

I crawl through, protecting the painting, and push as much dirt back into the hole as I can. I drag some branches and leaves to cover the disturbed location, which will help if someone glances at this in passing from far away but won't help with the fact that the hole is still open on the interior side of the fence.

Pushing my way deeper into the forest, I find a hollow between two close-growing trees and sit down on the dead leaves that have piled up in the cool shadows. I press my face into my knees, clutching the painting like it can somehow save me.

I realize I'm hyperventilating. I want to scream Leo's name, but that won't draw her back to me. Nothing will.

I try to organize my thoughts. It's Sunday, and if I remember correctly, we're going back to L.A. around six o'clock. That puts us in L.A. by eight. My rational brain argues that the best way to find her is to return to Santa Monica, take this to the cops, and have them come search for her. This is a small island. She can be found.

And yet I can't bear to leave without her. That's what friendship is: If she falls into the fire, I follow. If one doesn't escape, neither does the other. And yet it's my only choice, isn't it?

I push myself to my feet. I feel grim, haunted, like I'm leaving her to die.

I stay inside the tree line, out of view of the cameras. It's slow going, and it's at least an hour before I'm back where I started, on the wooden walkway leading to the beach. I pause, panting, unable to hike up the stairs without catching my breath first.

At the top of the wooden footpath, heart pounding, I hide for a minute, watching the lawn for signs of people, terrified for anyone to see me with this painting. It's quiet. Everyone must either be at the research facility, in their rooms, or at the spa.

Key card in hand, ready, I run across the lawn, up the porch steps, and into the hall. It's empty. "Thank you," I whisper, maybe to the universe, maybe to no one. At my door, I fumble the key card, dropping it. I pick it up and drop the painting, which unrolls partway. Finally, I'm stumbling through the door into the soft, white silence of my suite. I shut the door behind me and curse the lack of a dead bolt.

I make a beeline for the phone and press zero. A female voice I don't recognize answers. "Hello, housekeeping, may I help you?" She sounds middle-aged and very professional.

"May I speak with Ashley, please?" My own voice is strained and vibrates with tension.

A pause. "I'm sorry, who?"

"Ashley. She works in housekeeping. She's been taking care of me this weekend."

"I'm sorry, ma'am, but I don't believe we have an Ashley here."

She must be new. I'm frustrated, but I don't want to be a Karen. "Can I speak to Javier then?"

"Certainly. One moment, please." Soft hold music thrums through the earpiece, and I clutch the painting, focusing on my breathing. I don't want Javier to hear anything amiss when he answers.

The line clicks. "This is Javier, how may I assist you?" He's smooth and calm as always.

"Hi, Javier, it's Summer. How are you?" I'm back on my game, and the words come out like maple syrup, just a little flirtatious.

"Summer, how lovely to hear from you. What can I do for you today?"

"Can you please send Ashley to my room? I'd like her to help me with something."

A pause. "I'm so sorry, and of course I'm more than happy to send someone to help you, but we don't have anyone here named Ashley."

My head spins. I must be mishearing him, or somehow I must be remembering her name wrong. "Javier, you know Ashley. We talked about her. She's got light hair, she's skinny and pale, sort of mousy."

"I'm so sorry, but we don't have anyone on staff who fits that description. Could you possibly have seen one of the guests and thought she was a staff member? Perhaps someone dressed in a white shirt and black pants? That could happen."

My temper rises. "Javier, no. Come on, you know who I'm talking about."

"I'm so sorry. Look, here are our female staff members who work in guest services. We have Matilda, who answered your call. She's tall and has dark brown hair. We have Grecia, who is petite and Latina. There's Jen, who is African American and tall. And there's Maya, who has blond hair but is heavier set. None of those remind me of your description. But I'm glad to send any of them to your room if you like."

I shake my head, trying to understand what's happening. My lips feel numb as I reply, "Never mind. I'm sorry to bother you. I must be mistaken." I hang up and stare at the painting, lying partially unrolled on the floor.

I close my eyes and return in memory to standing in front of Javier, talking to him about Ashley. Had I used her name?

Yes. A clear memory of the conversation fills my mind, and I hear myself speak the words to him. I'd told him that Ashley was great, that I would be calling on her to help me while I was here.

My eyes snap open. This can mean only one thing. Ashley's gone, and they're making it seem like she was never here.

Does Michael know she's been helping me? Did someone see her take the shovel?

A soft knock on the door shatters my train of thought. I startle, a chill flashing over my skin, and reach for the painting with shaking fingers.

CHAPTER TWENTY-NINE

LEO

FRIDAY, JUNE 9

I did a free fall through the air, a scream bottled inside my chest. The ocean rushed toward me, and then my feet sliced through the surface and I was submerged in a deep and churning darkness. The freezing cold assaulted my muscles, chilling my bones with an immediate and numbing pain.

I didn't know which way was up and which was down. It was a void. This was how I always imagined death.

Panic—my chest swelled. I needed to breathe.

Light. Above me.

I kicked hard, buoyancy pulling me up, and then I broke through. I sucked in a chestful of air and choked on salt water. The surface was choppier than it had looked from the cliff. Shivering, spitting, I told myself to hurry. There was no time. Michael could see me down here any minute.

It had been so easy to see from above, but down here, all I saw was water and foam. A swell lifted me up, and before it lowered me, I spotted the cove beach. It was close. I could make it.

Swimming freestyle for shore, I passed a few outcroppings of
rocks, and my breath started to come faster, more anxious. I was at
the limits of my exertion. I didn't swim that much for exercise,
and no amount of running could prepare you for a full-body
swimming workout. That's how I had to frame it: a workout, just
another day of training. If I thought of it this way, I wouldn't remember that I was fleeing from a man who just tried to kill me.

An inner voice offered an alternative. *Maybe he was just trying to
get me unconscious.*

Like that's better? I screamed inside my head.

My muscles burned and ached. I couldn't feel my hands or feet,
and salt water was in my sinuses and mouth, astringent and disgusting.

I could do this. I was an athlete. I could do this.

My toes touched rocks. I had done it. Stumbling out of the
waves onto the wet sand, I stayed on my hands and knees, panting,
trying to clear my head.

I wiped my hair away from my eyes. From here, I couldn't see
the tops of the cliffs. Michael could be up there.

I got shakily to my feet. My wet shorts and T-shirt clung to me,
rough and knotty. I shivered, the breeze whipping the salt water
into goosebumps.

The cove was protected on either end by cliffs. Through the
middle, a channel had been carved out by a stream weaving through
the woods. Perhaps I could follow the water and let it lead me inland. I remembered Michael saying he had visitors coming this
evening. It was probably one o'clock now. If I could find my way
to the docks, I could maybe intercept the visitors as they got off
the boats. He couldn't hurt me in front of all his guests.

Could he?

I took a few hesitant steps up the beach, onto the dry sand, and
then I faltered, looking back toward the water.

My footprints, clear as day, marked the beach behind me.

"Shit," I whispered. Through my frigid shuddering, the sylla-
ble guttered like a dying candle.

I whirled around and ran toward the forest. I searched the bank of trees until I found a fallen branch with leaves still attached, and I dragged it back down the beach toward the wet sand. Panting and cursing, I scrubbed at my footprints until the sand looked messy and disturbed but hopefully not trodden upon.

Behind the pounding waves, I heard a faint whirring. I thought it was a distant airplane, but then it rose in volume until it sounded like a large, mechanical mosquito.

I dropped the branch and loped through the hot, soft sand toward the woods, barely making it into the shelter of trees when a slip of a thing flashed through the sky above the canopy of leaves. I pressed myself into the trunk of an oak and peered up. A moment later, the object flew past again, slower this time. It was geometric, like a small helicopter trapped in a hexagonal picture frame.

A drone.

What am I going to do?

I needed to find a way past panic into action, find a way to the docks and a place to hide until Michael's guests arrived. I summoned a mental map of the island, wishing I had Summer's innate sense of direction. I'd always attributed it to a childhood spent mostly outside, away from screens and artificial light. Trying to orient myself, I decided I was southeast of the mansion, on the coast to the left of it if I were looking at a map. I needed to go inland and then bear right, cut across all that wilderness, and come out at the boat docks.

Doubtfully, I examined my bare feet. I had tough soles from all my outdoor adventures, but not hiking-across-an-island tough. Didn't matter. They would have to do.

Hiking barefoot is your open door right now, I grumbled inwardly as I picked my way upstream, staying next to the water both because the forest was most dense down here and because I worried about being too far from a water source. I needed to head uphill and try to find somewhere with a view, but the sun was changing position in the sky, getting hotter as the afternoon progressed, and I found myself increasingly disoriented.

I hummed to myself to pass the time. I found myself singing

"Bad Romance" by Lady Gaga. Never had a song been more appropriate to a situation.

At long last, I limp-climbed a final gravelly plateau. From here, I could see the Pacific, eternal and painfully blue, and the cove I'd dived into.

And then I saw small shapes cutting through the water, so tiny they could have been dolphins, but given the distance, they could be only one thing. Boats.

I checked the sun's position. It was later than I'd realized. I had taken hours to get here. I got my bearings and pointed myself in the direction of the docks. They'd be out of sight over that next rocky landform, then down through more forest. I should be able to bypass the mansion and grounds, staying out of sight all the way down that hillside until I entered the cove from the east.

I hurried as much as I could and kept one eye on the sky every time I found myself in the open, nervous about drones.

Hope was building a home inside me. I was getting close now. I should see the ground start to slope downhill soon, and then I'd be on a steep trajectory to the docks. I imagined how I'd do it, exploding out of the trees and crying out for help. I needed to time it so I was with a group of people at all times, banking on Michael not being able to kill me in full view of bystanders.

The hillside declined like I'd expected, but suddenly the forest ahead dropped out of view, and I found myself on the edge of a cliff, wheeling my arms, about to plummet a hundred feet to the rocks and ocean below.

I sat on my ass with a plunk, clutching at bare dirt. The hillside sheared off at an almost perfect right angle. Maybe, ages ago, a storm had come along and sliced part of the hillside clean off.

Far below and tucked inside the neighboring cove, the docks and their adjoining wooden walkway lay outstretched, welcoming the boats as they pulled in.

I had come out on the wrong cliff. There was no access from here. And the boats were already unloading.

"Help," I screamed. The wind swallowed my words, greedy

like it would eat me next. "Help!" I bellowed it from my gut, but my cries were like punches thrown in a dream, hapless and wasted.

My eyes pricked with hot tears as tiny ant people disembarked, the gleaming glass elevator rushing down to greet them.

I'd lost a lot in my life. Amanda, for one. When she'd been found dead, I'd cried so hard, I couldn't breathe. Alone in my bedroom, my sinuses had swollen shut, and I'd fainted, waking up hours later. Then my stable, normal parents—I'd lost them, too, to their grief and disappointment in me.

Now, watching the boats leave and chart paths across the open ocean, I felt again the loss of hope, strong enough to leave me flattened. I was barefoot with no supplies, alone in the wilderness, hunted by a man who wanted to hurt me for reasons I couldn't understand.

Not all open doors lead to freedom and adventure. Some lead to death. I should have known that all along.

CHAPTER THIRTY

SUMMER

SUNDAY, JUNE 11

The gentle knock sounds again, *tap-tap-tap*. "One second," I call. I shake off the paralysis and grab the painting, hurry to my suitcase, and tuck it inside, underneath the clothes. I jump to my feet and approach the door warily, wishing I had some kind of weapon. Again, I curse the builders of this wretched house; there's no peephole, no way to really lock yourself in. "Who is it?" I ask, a hand on the doorknob, ready to push against it if someone tries to burst inside.

"It's Julie," singsongs the familiar alto.

Relief drenches me from scalp to tailbone. I pull the door open and find Julie, clearly on her way back to her room after exercising. She's in sweat-soaked workout clothes, a towel slung over her shoulder.

"Hi," I reply, aiming for a normal tone of voice but failing miserably.

Her smile fades into an expression of concern. "Are you okay?"

"I'm fine."

She glances behind her, up at the hallway ceiling. "Let me in, they'll hear us," she says and slips past me. "Come on," she urges, guiding me into the room and pulling the door shut behind us. "What's wrong?"

All I can think to say is, "Nothing." I step away from her and catch a glimpse of myself in the mirror above the dresser. My face and arms are streaked with dirt, my bun has come half undone, and my nails are black. No wonder she's worried.

I try to come up with an excuse. Why am I so messy and dirty? Why can't I think of anything? I want to slap myself. *Get it together.*

But then I remember her words at the door, and I ask, "Why did you say they would hear us in the hallway?"

She waves that off. "I'm paranoid about cameras. Too many years married to a tech guy. Security cameras everywhere. Now, honey, please, let's get you something to settle your nerves." She opens the minifridge by the TV and withdraws a bottle of white wine. It's a screw top, and she cracks it open and grabs a pair of wineglasses from the bureau. She pours two generous servings, hands me one, pulls me to the couch, and sits beside me. "Are you going to tell me why you look like you got attacked by a bear?"

I drink deeply. The wine tastes amazing, sweet and sour and cold. I feel the breath expand to fill my chest, and I make eye contact with her, appreciating her directness. I genuinely like this woman, and her light brown eyes warm me, making me feel a little less alone.

"I didn't get attacked or anything," I reassure her. "I went jogging off the path, and I fell down a hill." The fact that I can lie tells me I'm back. I'm functioning. That's good. I take another sip of wine, then remember what she'd said. "But, Julie, I didn't see any cameras. Did you?"

She shakes her head. "Girl, they're totally hidden. Built right into the walls or something. It's the patriarchy. Hey, but seriously, you seem shaken up. Did you almost fall off a cliff?"

"Yeah, it was scary," I reply, distracted. I'm full of sudden panic, remembering my searching of the house, breaking into Michael's rooms.

Ashley helping me.

I turn on Julie, full of purpose now. "Do you remember a housekeeper named Ashley? She's pale, skinny, kind of timid?"

She nods, mid-sip. "Looks like a drowned cat. Scared of everything."

Not only does relief overwhelm me, stinging my eyes with unexpected tears, but anger flares. I'm imagining nothing. "Well, Javier suddenly doesn't remember her. He says there's no one here by that name."

Her brows do a new thing, gathering and raising, breaking through the Botox and wrinkling her forehead. "What the fuck?"

"Something weird is going on here. My friend Leo was here. I found her stuff. Michael is lying, and so is Javier. Ashley all but admitted it to me, and now she's gone." I take another deep drink and feel the cool calm of the wine running through my veins.

She puts a hand on my arm. "Summer, that's not right. You need to tell someone. The cops, probably."

"I know. I will." I laugh, bitter. "They aren't usually very helpful to people like me."

She makes an "I feel you" hum and squeezes my arm, scooting a little closer. "I'll go with you. I can corroborate or whatever. I'm married, I'm rich. I have lawyers."

We make eye contact, disbelief and gratitude warring for control of me. "Seriously?" I ask.

"Of course. Why not?"

"And you believe me?"

"Why would you lie about that? I can see wanting to blackmail Michael, or any of these guys." She flicks a hand toward the door. "But looking at you, something clearly happened out there. You're a cool cucumber, and you're shaken up. You don't want anything from anyone here. You just want your friend back. Right? And you're worried she's here, and you want to make sure she's okay."

I nod, not quite able to form words. The painting—Leo's young face, so full of trepidation—the wild hills, each one disguising somewhere she could have taken a fall, gotten lost, hidden: It's all too much.

She gathers me into a hug and rubs my back. "Hey. Hey. You're okay. I'm going to stay with you. We'll figure this out." I feel my arms winding around her, and I'm grateful for the comfort.

"Thank you," I whisper. "I thought you didn't believe in female friendships."

She chuckles, pulls back, and pushes my hair out of my eyes. I'm light-headed; I forgot how much I hate day drinking, and I haven't had any water. "Some things are better than friendship," Julie murmurs, and then her lips are on mine, soft and insistent. I find myself lying back on the couch while she climbs on top of me, breasts pressed against mine. I'm kissing her back—I hadn't realized.

Kissing is interesting. I consider the act as I close my eyes. The darkness is sweet and comforting, and I'm floating through it, wondering why I've spent so much time worrying about things I can't control.

I feel a mental jerk, a moment of panic—am I falling asleep? Something is wrong.

That voice quiets, replaced by the softness of Julie sighing in my ear. "Damn, that was too fast," she murmurs, and then I'm gone.

CHAPTER THIRTY-ONE

LEO

SATURDAY, JUNE 10

From a bank of trees behind the mansion, I watched the dressed-up guests ride on golf carts from the west wing to the main house, ostensibly for dinner. I couldn't make out their faces from here, but I could see their black tuxedos and floor-length dresses. I imagined the sparkle of diamonds on manicured hands. These were Michael's investors, I supposed.

Through the endless, hungry hours it had taken me to hike up here through woods and chaparral, to distract myself from the stabbing-burning pain in my feet, I'd worked out a plan. Michael was evil. I accepted this truth. For whatever reason—he was a billionaire with a private island, so he didn't really need a reason—he wanted to kill me. And now I needed to get off his island.

I'd watched the boats depart from my vantage point high on the cliff. I didn't think they were coming back until the weekend was over. Sunday, maybe? Who knew, maybe the guests were here for a whole week. I had passed the night in shivering fear, hidden beneath the meager shelter of a rock formation behind a cluster of bushes.

I'd cried into my hands. I was an animal being hunted. As I calmed down, I realized I wasn't trapped alone anymore. There were at least fifty people staying here. I was sure some of them were Michael's besties, willing to help him bury the bodies of young women who dared escape his strangulation attempts, but there were women here, too. I couldn't imagine that, out of at least twenty women, I couldn't find a few who would help me.

So here I was, staking them out, unwilling to get too close lest someone see me before I was ready.

At last, I saw an opportunity. A slender woman wandered alone outside the west wing, near the path that led down to the beach, aimlessly pacing back and forth, and only after a moment did I realize she was smoking. She was not just smoking but hiding it, keeping the cigarette or joint out of sight at her side, which spoke to her personality in a way I thought would help me: She was a bit rebellious, willing to do things outside the Normal Rich Person code of conduct. She was without her husband, which gave me hope that she was in the habit of hiding things from him. After all, if he knew she smoked, she could have done it out the window of their room, and she wouldn't be casting surreptitious glances over her shoulder every time she took a hit.

I wouldn't get a better chance than this.

I pushed through the trees and made my way toward her, avoiding as many twigs and rocks as I could. My feet were torn and scraped, sources of raw agony every time I took a step. Once I was twenty feet away, I smelled that she was smoking a joint, not a cigarette. *She's going to help,* I chanted inwardly.

"Hey," I hissed. "Hey!"

She turned toward me. She was a tanned brunette a little older than Summer with a Pilates-perfect body clothed in a blue cocktail dress. Her eyes widened with surprise, and she coughed out a bunch of smoke. I let her catch her breath, and then I looked both ways, confirming we were alone, and stepped onto the wooden walkway. "Hi," I whispered. "You can't tell anyone you saw me. If anyone comes along, I have to hide, and you can't tell them. Do you promise?" I was shocked by the desperation in my voice. This had sounded calmer in my head.

"Are you okay? Are you lost?" Her brown eyes were huge with concern.

I'd planned how to explain this, but the words all fell away from me now. "Someone tried to kill me, and I've been hiding. Running."

She sucked in a shocked breath. "Like, there's a murderer loose out there?" She looked behind me at the dark forest.

"No, it's . . ." I wrapped my arms around myself and cast a terrified glance toward the main house. "Someone who lives here."

She whipped around to look behind her. "One of the servants?"

"No."

She gasped, understanding. "*Michael?*" she whispered.

"Are you close with him?"

She shook her head. "My husband is a business associate."

Good. Okay. "When are you guys getting picked up? When do the boats come back?"

"Sunday. In the evening."

"And there aren't any boats here?"

"No, they all dock in L.A. It's a closed weekend."

"But what if someone needs to go back? You can't all be stuck here."

She seemed to realize she was still holding the joint. She threw it down and stepped on it. "There's a medical helicopter in L.A. they can call in case of emergency, but yeah, it's a private weekend. None of the investors want there to be any risk of information leaks." She rubbed my arm. "You look like you've been through a war. Are you barefoot?"

I held a bloodied foot out for her inspection, and she gasped. "Here, take my flip-flops." She scooted out of them and nudged them toward me. I slid my toes through the thongs with a moan of relief. I'd never been so thankful for shoes. "How can I help?" she asked. "Tell me what you need."

I gathered my thoughts, which was hard. I was shaky and light-headed from lack of food and water. "I need to stay hidden until Sunday, and then I need to sneak onto one of the boats."

She was nodding. "I have an idea. I can tell the staff that my husband and I had a fight and I want a second room to sleep in. Then you can stay there and just hide in the bathroom when they come to clean the room. You can pretend to be me, taking a shower."

I'm already shaking my head. "I'm not sure I want to stay in the house."

"You can't stay in the woods." She gestured to the darkness.

"I can," I argued.

"But they'll find you out there. You'll be safer inside."

I had no idea if she was right. I was starving, exhausted, and so woozy I couldn't think straight. "Okay," I agreed. "And I need some food. And clean clothes. Please. I'm sorry." I found myself crying, and she wrapped an arm around me.

"Don't be sorry. We're going to figure this out. Now come on, we'd better hurry. I'm already late to dinner. I came out here to pregame. I can't stand these things. I'll get you some food out of my room." She was talking fast, sifting through logistics, and I appreciated that at least one of us had her shit together. "By the way, what's your name?"

"I'm Leo," I replied.

"I'm Julie."

CHAPTER THIRTY-TWO

SUMMER

MONDAY, JUNE 12

The first thing I feel is cold.

I'm lying still, and the chill has seeped deep under my skin into my muscles and bones. In the darkness, I wonder murkily if I'm dead, if I'm somehow waking up inside my own corpse.

The thought brings a reverberation of fear like the echo of a faraway gong, and I stir. I'm on a hard, freezing surface, stretched out as though sleeping. I don't know if my eyes are open or closed.

I can't rouse any recent memories. I'm a complete blank. I blink my eyes hard, bringing the darkness into half focus. Have I gone blind? Am I really dead? My heart is pounding, erratic beats sending shivers through my arms. *Can't have a heartbeat if you're dead.*

Wake up.

I try to pull myself out of the darkness. My head is stuffy and dizzy, and I have the distinct impression of floating.

I lift hands that are attached to heavy spaghetti arms and try to rub the fog out of my eyes. I'm in a room, lying on a stone floor. I can rub my eyes all I want; there isn't much to see except a small, high window through which I can see only shadows of gray.

I haul myself into a sitting position and wait for a tsunami of dizziness to pass. I try to breathe deeply, holding on to the stone ground with uncooperative hands. I feel drugged, and the second that thought pops into my mind, I remember Julie, her hands on me, her lips on mine.

She drugged me?

"Where am I?" I hear myself whisper. Cold air swallows the words.

Shivering, I crawl toward the window. A low, oblong object beneath it turns out to be a rusty metal cot that looks like something out of one of the world wars. I crawl onto it and use the window ledge to pull myself up. My feet unsteady on the cot, I cling to the stone window frame and peer out into the half-light. What I see shocks me.

Snow.

It must be either dusk or sunrise; the sky shines charcoal and navy, sprinklings of light reflecting off the carpet and hills of snow that stretch off in every direction I can see, uninterrupted by trees or buildings. The window radiates cold, and I test it, pressing fingertips to the pane and drawing them back icy. My breath steams up the glass as I stare out at the snowscape in consternation.

Where can I possibly be? Where's Julie, the house, the island?

I search back through memory, waiting for images of transport to spring forward. I have nothing, just the suite, Julie, the wine, and then a void. It's like I've been magically time-warped from there to here.

Something was definitely in the wine. I'm steadier as I turn from the window and sink onto the cot. It squeaks in protest.

The room measures about eight by eight feet, the wall with the window made of the same wide, dark slabs of rock as the floor. The other three walls are paneled in something dark and rustic, perhaps wood. A heavy-looking white door with no knob or visible hinges faces me, its contrastingly modern presence menacing.

Am I in jail? Did Michael turn me in? I must still be slow from being drugged because the idea is ridiculous. Of course this isn't a police station. This is some kind of dungeon. If not for the door, I'd think I was in a medieval castle or something.

But the snow. It's June. How in the hell?

The answer is obvious. I've been taken somewhere far away.

For the first time, I notice what I'm wearing: black sweats and sweatshirt. I feel around and find my sports bra and underwear underneath, which means someone changed my clothes while I was unconscious but didn't take off my undergarments. I grope my body, looking for injuries. Nothing hurts, but I realize I have to pee, urgently, right now.

Desperate, I cast my gaze around. It lands on a squat thing in the darkest corner of the room. On unsteady legs, I creep cautiously toward it. It's made of darkened metal and is indeed an ancient toilet. It has a rusty chain that serves to flush the water down, and, when I lift the lid, the seat is a thin lip around a circular opening. It emits strong aromas of wet metal and watered-down sewage. Sitting on the stone floor beside it is a pile of tissues in lieu of a roll of normal toilet paper. I wonder if they think I'll put the cardboard roll to some crafty use.

I look around the room, searching for cameras. I'll never see them if they're here; the light is too low, every corner mysterious.

I have no choice. I pull the sweatshirt down to cover my crotch, drop the pants, and sit quickly on the freezing pot. The inch-thick rim digs into my butt, and humiliation burns my cheeks as I pee. I wipe with one of the tissues and pull my pants up as quick as I can, then yank on the metal chain until it flushes weakly.

Falling apart isn't an option. Crying is not going to happen. I bite my lip hard, slap my cheek, control my face.

I check the door, which takes only a moment. It's locked from the outside, no accessible hinges or mechanisms on this side. Through the quarter-inch crack that separates door from frame, I can see the striker of a dead bolt engaged in the strike plate. This means there's a knob or handle on the exterior.

I walk the perimeter and discover two vents in the floor, both about a foot wide and six inches high, protected by metal grates. They'd be impossible to unscrew without a screwdriver, and they're too small to fit a person through anyway.

Back at the window, I look for weak points and discover it's double paned, probably to create an insulated pocket of air between them in deference to the cold. I rap on it, and it rings with a dull thud much different from a normal residential window. The glass is either coated to be shatterproof or is a material I'm unfamiliar with.

Regardless, I examine the cot with shaking fingers, wondering if I could remove a leg and use it to break the window. The frame turns out to be screwed into the stone floor and soldered together at the joints.

I groan, unable to control the sound.

I turn my back to the view of snow, which is drifting down from the sky in wispy fairy flakes and spend a foggy stretch of time in a state of arctic panic. At last, I sink down onto the cot and wrap my arms around my legs. I bury my face in my knees for warmth.

Who is responsible for this? Julie? But *why*?

This can't be her doing alone. That's absurd. She's one person; how could she possibly transport me? So it's her plus other people, or at least one other. Her husband? Michael? Alan?

I turn it over and over in my mind, trying to make sense of it. What do they want from me?

Whatever the plan is, I won't be able to contact the police after all. No search and rescue team will be coming for Leo.

A crushing wave of sadness rolls over me, flattening me. I failed her. I promised myself I'd take care of her, protect her, be for her what no one had been for me, and I failed.

Curled into a ball on the cot, I shiver endlessly, the cell walls mid-night blue from reflected ambient light off the snow. I've almost never spent the night in a snowy place; it's a trade-off when you live in a vehicle.

My mind keeps returning to brainstorming ways to escape. But even if I found a way out of this cell, where would I go? Into the frozen expanse to freeze to death?

A click at the door startles me. I bolt into a sitting position, bare feet slapping the freezing floor. The door swings inward, and Javier steps through it in a beam of artificial light that stings my dark-adapted eyes. He's bundled up in a parka and boots, a cafeteria tray in his hands. The door shuts heavily behind him, leaving him in the darkness with me. I don't move, staring up at his silhouette in mute astonishment.

He brings the tray to me and sets it on the floor by my cot, then retreats to stand in front of the door. "I brought you food," he says unnecessarily. His eyes glint in the low blue light.

I spare a glance at what he's brought. It smells delicious: steaming hot soup, a cup of something warm and spiced, and a large chunk of fresh bread. There are no utensils.

Turning my eyes back up to him, I weigh my words. "Javier, what is going on?"

The way he's looking at me, with pity and a sort of fondness, unnerves me more than hostility would have. "I'm just here to make sure you eat."

"And if I don't?"

He shrugs, the movement muted by the thick, quilted parka.

"Give me your jacket and maybe I'll eat."

"I wish I could."

"Why am I here?" My voice is louder now, all my simmering anger threatening to boil over. I stand and step toward him. "Why am I in this cell? Where is this?"

"You're on another of Mr. Forrester's properties," he replies, his tone placating, voice low and calm. "Now please. Relax."

One of Michael's properties. Julie helped Michael sedate me and get me here? I still can't understand it.

I sit down again on the cot and tuck my feet underneath me. The ground is too cold to stand on for long, and besides, what's the point? I can't best Javier in a physical confrontation. I don't see a key card or anything to steal, and I can't see being able to get close enough to rummage through his pockets. Plus, I don't have a diversion or any way to distract him.

I'm helpless. A caged animal.

"You should eat," Javier advises. "I'm only supposed to bring you two meals a day."

"For how many days? How long will I be here?"

"I don't know." Again with that pitying tone.

"Where's Julie? What happened to Ashley?"

No response.

Anger flares. "Where is my friend Leo? Or did you forget she existed, too?"

He squats down so we're eye to eye. "I am allowed to tell you about that if you want to know."

I wait, heart pounding.

"We don't know her location," he says, and I start to protest when he holds a hand up. "But we know where she was last seen. On the island, there's an off-limits section that you discovered when you dug that hole under the fence. Did you run into a path? Sort of a walking trail?"

I guess I'm not surprised they found the hole, but the way he talks about it, so matter-of-fact, worries me, as if we're past any consequences for that, as if they know I was searching the island and don't care. "Yes, I saw the trail," I concede with great caution.

"That trail predates Mr. Forrester's purchase of the island. We think it's at least a hundred years old, maybe more. It winds around the cliffs in one spot."

"I remember, yes."

"We think she jumped off one of those cliffs into the ocean."

I know exactly which cliff she'd have jumped off. I'd thought about her as I'd walked by it.

He continues. "From there, she swam inland and hiked back to the residence. She ran into one of the guests, who put her up in their room. We've confirmed this with drone footage."

My heart leaps. She was at the house?

"She seems to have stayed overnight, but then something happened. She must have gotten spooked. The next footage we have is of her running from the residence, down to the beach. You've been there. It's the one where we dock the Jet Skis."

"Go on," I say, fingernails digging into my palms.

"She grabbed one of the Jet Skis and took it out to sea."

I feel my eyebrows drawing together. "Out to *sea*? Explain."

"We had a drone following her. She was clearly trying to take it back to the mainland, back to L.A." He takes a deep breath. I get the vibe he doesn't want to keep talking. I don't know if I want him to, after all. Finally, he says, "The Jet Skis can't handle the swells on the open ocean. The water was choppy. It overturned. She didn't have a life vest. She drowned, Summer."

I can't believe what I'm hearing. Leo would never take a Jet Ski into the open ocean with no life vest. That's stupid. It's suicidal.

She would have been desperate, scared.

Just like I am now.

Javier leans toward me and puts a hand on my knee. "I'm sorry."

His brown eyes are so liquid and sincere, I could slap him. A hand is pressed to my chest—my own. I don't remember putting it there. I'm frozen, eyes locked on Javier's. I want to tell him he's wrong, he's lying, but he isn't either of those things. I can hear that what he's saying is the truth.

She's gone. I'm alone.

I can't hear him anymore. I'm curling up onto the cot, closing my eyes, wrapping my arms around my knees. Whatever he wants to do to me, let him do it.

I'm not sure how long it takes him to leave. It doesn't matter. I'm alone in the dark again eventually, cold, which is exactly how Leo must have felt before the ocean swallowed her whole. That's how I feel now: gobbled up by a dark, uncaring sea.

My mother and Leo, both lost to the unknown.

The sadness is so deep, it takes my breath away. I feel my face stretched into a grimace and tears are streaming hot down my freezing cheeks, but the sobs are trapped by the clutching pain in my rib cage, locked in there. If I start, I'll never stop.

I drowse, too cold to sleep, too heavy with grief and despair to stay fully awake. In this in-between world, I remember a cold night from my childhood. My mother and I were by Mount Shasta, sleeping in a tent, and the temperature had dropped down into the thirties. Of course, we weren't prepared, and I was shivering in my sleeping bag, scared of the damp chill that was numbing my hands and feet.

I peeked out and saw that my mother was perfectly still, eyes closed, face relaxed. In the faint moonlight that filtered through the nylon, she looked dead.

Panic rushed through me. Could she have frozen to death? Was that possible?

What would happen to me if she died? I had never truly considered this before. I didn't have a father or any other relatives. Would these random friends of hers, ever changing, adopt me? Would I have to fend for myself? I had already begun picking pockets, so I imagined I had the skills I needed to secure food, but what about shelter?

"Mom?" I whispered. She didn't respond.

It occurred to me that I could see my own breath pluming from my lips, a little cloud that followed my exhalations, but not hers. Shivering violently, I extracted my arms from the sleeping bag and reached for her. A hand hovered over her chest, afraid to touch her, afraid to know for sure.

And then I lowered it to her breastbone and felt the thrum of her heartbeat in my fingertips. Relief washed through the channel that panic had carved, and I started crying.

She opened her eyes, confused and sleepy. "You okay?" she murmured.

I nodded, unable to explain.

"You cold?"

I nodded again.

"Come here." She beckoned me into her sleeping bag, and I crawled inside it. Tucked against her, I was suddenly, blissfully warm. I wrapped my arms around her slender waist and pressed my face into the soft skin of her chest, reveling in the knowledge that she was alive.

Sometimes it feels like the past and present are braided together into every moment. When I think of it like that, my mother and Leo aren't completely lost. If I squeeze my eyes shut hard enough, I can almost pretend they're here with me.

Warm at last, we drifted into sleep.

CHAPTER THIRTY-THREE

SUMMER

MONDAY, JUNE 12

When the door clicks open again later, I'm doing feeble jumping jacks by the window, trying to warm up. Outside, the snow is pirouetting in dizzy little tornadoes that remind me of leaves whirled around by the Santa Ana winds. Leo had loved the Santa Anas. "Time for fire," she'd say merrily. I always accused her of taking a dark pleasure in watching California burn.

Javier shoulders into my cell, tray in his hands. I stop jumping and stand still and wary as the door swings shut behind him.

"How you feeling?" he asks, setting the tray down by my cot.

"Freezing," I answer honestly.

"You hungry? You must be."

I weigh my words. I am hungry. Starving, actually, but it doesn't feel like something that matters, not with Leo gone. "What do you want?" I ask. "Tell me why I'm here."

"Summer, you know they don't tell me all that. I just work here." He squats down and settles into a semicomfortable position on the floor, leaning back against the door. The hard stone is probably not that cold for him; he's in a knee-length puffer jacket. I'm angry, I realize, burning with quiet rage. I want to attack this man, to scratch his eyes out.

The tray distracts me. It's soup and bread again. The soup is lentil. I can smell the distinctive, earthy aroma, mixed with fresh herbs and black pepper. My stomach lurches, growling viciously.

"You should eat," he says. "Do you want me to talk to you? Or I can keep quiet if you prefer."

He's so solicitous, so handsome, just a robot shell of a person designed to keep female prisoners in line. I feel tears well up in my eyes, remembering him delivering the news about Leo earlier with this same sincerity. Maybe it's fake. He's like me, after all, used to manipulating rich people, ingratiating himself smoothly into their world.

"Maybe the way I die is by finally eating the food. Poison. Or maybe you want me unconscious again. Maybe it's laced with whatever Julie gave me." Bitch.

"Do you want me to taste it for you?" He leans forward, tears off a piece of the bread, dunks it into the soup, and eats it. Mouth full, he says, "It's good. Hot."

Fine. I sit on the cot and pull the tray onto my lap. I pick up the cup and sniff it. Spiced apple cider? I hand it to him. "Take a sip."

He obeys, dark eyes on mine as he drinks from the cup. He hands it back. "Tasty."

If I die, I die. I drink it down, almost groaning with pleasure. For a while, I eat without pause. There are no utensils, so I soak up the lentils and broth with the soft, fresh bread, barely swallowing before preparing another bite. At last, I'm done, my stomach full, and I set the tray down on the cold floor.

"Now I wait to fall asleep or die," I tell Javier, not wanting him to think I trust him.

He smiles. "Carpe diem."

"Get me a blanket."

"You know I can't do that."

"Why? What's the point of just torturing me? What good does that do anyone?"

He chuckles, pushing himself to a standing position. He re-
trieves the tray and pushes through the door. I catch a glimpse of
a white wall, some type of corridor, and then it shuts heavily behind him.

He didn't use a key card or anything; he pressed his hand to the
door beside the lock, and then he was able to shoulder through it.
A hand or thumbprint scanner, perhaps? I remember a small black
panel on the wall beside Michael's door in the main house, and I
thought it must be a thumbprint scanner to save Michael from
having to carry a key card.

Hmm.

Another interesting thing—he'd pushed his way into and then
back out of the room. The hinges swing both ways.

My stomach, full at last, is making me woozy, but in a slow,
comfortable, non-Rohypnol sort of way. I curl onto my side, pull
my arms into my sweatshirt, and lie quietly for a long time. Eventually, I fall into a dreamless, uneasy slumber.

Something wakes me up. I can't pull myself out of sleep; I'm
muddled, and my brain murkily wonders if I was drugged after
all. I float through the anonymous dark, no idea what time it is,
snow swirling in undulating shadows behind the window.

Somewhere in the darkness, I hear a faint scream, a female
voice. It pierces through the inky black, a single, terrified note, far
away and gone before I can put my finger on it.

Did I dream it?

I raise myself half up, but sleep is a thousand little men made of
sticky, gooey tar. They're pulling me down with tiny, tacky hands,
down into the pit, and as I fall back into sleep, the screams follow
me, winding down the tunnel until we've both succumbed.

Something is wrong.

I open my eyes.

I can't focus on it, can't find the source of my sudden anxiety.

I roll onto my back, and then I remember.

Leo is dead. Swallowed up by the ocean.

I wait for the rolling wave of horror and dread, but it doesn't come. I feel okay. Everything is soft and fuzzy, happy around the edges, docile. Had someone been screaming? No, that can't be right.

The door clicks, but I don't bother getting up. My eyes track Javier; he has the usual tray. He brings it to my cot and sets it on the ground. A croissant and coffee. These thoughts register in a faded way as though I'm seeing them through a filter.

I sit up to drink the coffee, unable to help enjoying it. I eat the croissant, and as I do, a tangible peace settles over me. With it comes the utter certainty that the universe is in control in all the right ways, that we're all exactly where we're supposed to be. There's a rightness to being here, inside this cell on a snowy day in the middle of nowhere. Isn't this always where my life was headed?

But wait—didn't I hear a girl screaming? No. That was a dream. I had a nightmare, I was scared, convinced someone would burst into my cell at any moment. If anyone comes for me now, even if they want to kill me, I don't think I'll scream. I'll go easily.

A mental voice queries this. This sounds like my mom's stoned talk, not like me at all. I'm a fighter, stubborn, angry, all the things she never raised me to be. Going quietly into the night, led off by the same men I've been conning and manipulating my entire life? That's not me.

The food.

Javier is watching me closely. Maybe he can read the warring emotions written as clearly on my face as I feel them.

I need to get my head together.

Everything is fine.

Everything is *not* fine. The food is drugged. Maybe not the same stuff Julie had given me, which knocked me out completely, but something to keep me numb and docile.

"You with me, Summer? You okay?"

"I'm . . ." I stare at him dumbly, train of thought lost.

"You look like you're feeling calmer. That's perfect. Doesn't that feel better?"

He knows.

There's a noise at the door. He gets up and out of the way, and it swings open.

Michael.

My breath catches in my chest.

He's taller than I remember, or maybe it just seems that way from my place down here on the cot. The dim, snow-filtered light shines on his face, in his blue eyes. He's wearing warm clothes, a leather jacket over a thick sweater and jeans, and he's carrying an easel and a large black duffel bag.

He sets the easel and bag down, and the door swings shut behind him. He glances at me, up at the window, and back at Javier. "Let's get some heat in here so she's comfortable. It will show if she's not."

"Understood." He leaves for a moment, and then warm air hisses from the ventilation grate. He returns a moment later, pulling something out of his parka and holding it loosely at his side. I blink at it a few times, recognizing the shape, and then place it. It's a gun.

This is it, then. My whole life, I've been evading a nebulous threat, keeping to the shadows, flitting through rooms like a ghost. And now at last, here I am in the darkness. It's thick, both physical and spiritual, a deep uncleanness that goes in through the nostrils and filters into my blood.

Michael smiles. "All right. Let's get started."

CHAPTER THIRTY-FOUR

SUMMER

TUESDAY, JUNE 13

"Stay seated," he instructs me. As Javier watches, Michael unfolds the easel, screws a couple of things into place, and pulls a canvas out of the duffel bag. It's medium-size, maybe fourteen by twenty, and a strange passing thought surprises me: The other canvases in his painting shed were larger. I wonder if this means I'm less important.

I'm frozen, I realize, in a cross-legged position on the cot like I'm meditating. And I'm strangely not afraid of the gun, which seems like just another step in the staircase of life. Why isn't my heart hammering? I could be killed. This could be it.

The staircase of life? What the fuck is happening to me?

Michael is squeezing paint onto a palette. "I'll need her reclining."

Javier replies, "Leaning back against the wall?"

"That'll work."

Javier steps toward me. "Summer, you'll need to find a comfortable position leaning against the wall. Can you do that for me?"

I lean back obediently, and Javier instructs me to turn onto my side a bit. Michael nods his approval once I'm posed in what feels like a demure, old-fashioned posture, mostly reclining, one hand limp on my hip. Javier backs off and sits by the door, gun resting on his knee.

Michael gets a sheath of paintbrushes and a jar of a clear liquid I assume is turpentine out of the duffel bag. "Let's get to business, shall we?"

"What business?" I ask, but Javier shushes me, shaking his head in an advisory way.

"It's all right. I'm just blocking out the composition. She can talk as long as she doesn't move," Michael says. He has a large brush in hand and is painting with broad strokes. I think he's using brown. To me, he says, "If you're good, there will be rewards. A blanket, some soft slipper boots. How does that sound?"

"Good," I reply honestly.

I watch him as he watches me. My treacherous heart won't beat quickly, won't let me feel the fear I deserve. I'm a domesticated thing, a house cat after all.

The thought stirs something in me, and, to my surprise, I feel a tear leak out of the corner of my eye, down my cheek and along my jawline. Michael stops painting and stares at me, head cocked, eyes midnight sapphires in the snowy light. "Tell me what you're thinking about." His voice is the calm of the dead. Maybe some-day, some other woman will stumble upon his painting of me; maybe he'll hang it in his suite of rooms. I can see her—a young, wide-eyed girl, excited to be taken to a billionaire's private island.

How many paintings had been in that shed? Dozens?

I'd assumed they were paintings of women he'd seduced. Maybe the truth is darker than that. He built this cell for a purpose, and I get the feeling this isn't Javier's first time holding a woman pris-oner here.

"Tell me," Michael orders, leaning forward hungrily. "Why are you crying?"

"Leo," I whisper, apparently unable to think fast enough to lie on the medication they've given me.

"Ah." He resumes painting.

"How many other women have you painted?"

His expression turns introspective. "Hard to say."

"What will you do with me once you're done painting me?"

"I've never met a woman quite like you," he murmurs, which isn't an answer. "You're probably the most conniving I've ever encountered." His eyes flash at me, and I sense anger simmering below the calm exterior. "You stole Javier's key card. I had to watch the footage three times to see how you did it. When did you learn pickpocketing?"

I can't do anything but tell the truth. "I was about eight."

He glances at Javier. "You got taken for a little ride there."

Javier grimaces, but it seems this is all in good fun.

I force myself to focus and remember what I wanted to ask. "Where does Julie fit into this?"

Michael shrugs. "She was just being helpful." His focus is back on his painting. "You came into my house and thought you could get the best of me. Arrogant." He brushes gently, eyes studying my legs, clearly trying to get the posture correct. I'm ruminating woozily on his words. Am I arrogant? Maybe so.

He sighs. "I love painting. I don't know why people take pictures. They're always disappointing. In paintings, I can create what I want." He's engrossed, eyes flicking back and forth between me and the canvas.

"Then why do you always paint the girls looking so . . . lifeless?" I ask, the question out before I can control it.

He raises his eyebrows. "Excuse me?"

"Their facial expressions. Don't you want them to be happy little dolls? Isn't that what guys like you want?"

He bends down toward me, and a dark mania I haven't seen before creeps across his face. "I paint them exactly how I want them. I like the way their faces look. Don't ever tell me how I should paint them."

I'm spinning, and now I understand. Leo's painting—the serious look on her face.

"Javier lied," I whisper. "Leo is dead, but she didn't die in the ocean."

"No, she didn't." His eyes are alight, a fire burning from within. I'm diving in, nothing to lose, into the fire.

"This is what you do."

"Yes."

"You paint them."

"Yes."

"And then they're yours forever."

He sits back on his stool and resumes painting. "Smart girl."

With the understanding comes a rush of horror. All those girls, those women, in his painting shed. The island, surrounded by thousands of miles of open ocean, and this building, wherever it is, surrounded by endless acres of snow. So much space to disappear.

At last, I know for sure what happened to Leo, if not the details. She met her end at this man's hands, just one of many. I'll be next. It will be like Leo and I never existed. No one will look for us. No one will report us missing.

Whatever drug they've given me, it's not enough. Tears are coursing down my cheeks, hot at first, then freezing in the chilly air. I can feel all of this too strongly, imagine too many possible things he does to the girls he brings to his private rooms. I can see it—Leo, exuberant, ready to bring home the bacon, excited to pay me back. *Want to see my private island?* he'd have asked her, and she'd have said yes because she had her eyes on the prize.

I wish he'd kill me now. I don't want to be awake. I can't take another minute of what reality has become.

I look at Javier. "Do you have more coffee? More of anything?"

He meets my eyes. He knows what I'm asking. "I'm sure I can find some."

"Please."

He gets the okay from Michael in a glance. When the door closes behind him, Michael says, "You're smarter than all the rest combined."

CHAPTER THIRTY-FIVE

SUMMER

TUESDAY, JUNE 13

Leo and I are strolling on the beach. It's sunset, and the waves are spilling gently up the wet sand, the tide coming in. She's wearing a white sweater and her favorite cutoff jean shorts, and I'm so floored by her presence, I almost can't breathe. "What are you doing here?" I ask, pulling her to a stop.

She looks at me like I'm acting weird. "Same thing you're doing here . . . ?"

I take her hand to see if she's real. Her skin is cool, just the way it should be in the ocean wind. She cocks her head at me. "What's wrong?"

"Don't you remember? You've been gone. I've been searching everywhere." Tears well up and stream down my face, hot against the cool air.

She looks mystified. "But I'm fine. See?" She gestures toward the waves, the sunset, and I realize I must be in her heaven: wide-open spaces, freedom, natural beauty.

Her hair is long, flowing down her back, and she's younger, the age she was when we met. Desperate to communicate this clearly, I say, "I don't regret picking you up. I don't regret any of it. No matter what. You've brought me so much joy. You lit up my whole life."

She smiles, not even sad, just happy-go-lucky Leo. All the pain in her past is a thousand closed doors behind her. "You've been an amazing sister. The best."

I'm almost unable to speak. "I'm so sorry," I manage to whisper. "This is all my fault."

She sighs, troubled. The sun is setting orange and red, glowing her up like firelight. "You've really wandered into a dark room, haven't you?"

My reply is choked. "Took the wrong door."

"I don't want this for you." She wraps her arms around my neck for a hug. Her white sweater is soft, her body warm and real. Here I am again, just a marble in the jar. This is goodbye. I squeeze her tight, holding her close. She's too thin; I can feel her ribs, and I wish I could take care of her, feed her, love her, keep her safe, be the big sister she so desperately needs. But she's already becoming less substantial. Her warmth is fading. The jar is being shaken. This is it.

Into my ear, she whispers, "*Run.*"

My eyes snap open. I feel Leo close, hovering over me.

Run.

I'm on the cot, bundled under a fleece blanket with my feet cozy in Uggs. Above me, the window lets in wispy tendrils of faint blue light. I close my eyes, try to return to the dream, but Leo's gone, and I can't hear the ocean anymore. There's just stillness and the now-familiar damp smell of the cold stone floor.

I want to run, Leo, but I can't. I'm trapped.

It's you, she argues. *Find a way out.*

Tears sting my eyes. The dream—she's gone. I don't care if she wants me to escape the same fate she met; I don't know if I have it in me to fight for a life without her.

But if I don't, how many other girls will end up in those paintings? How can I die knowing I didn't even try?

Anyway, the door is locked, I argue back.

And then I see it: the dead bolt clicking into the strike plate, visible through the quarter inch of space between door and frame, and an idea forms.

I get up, shove aside the blanket, and approach the door. I cast a nervous look up at the corners of the room, wondering if I'm on camera. It could go either way; Michael might keep an eye on the girls he imprisons here. Maybe he watches footage of them later on, after they're dead. Maybe he likes to watch himself kill them over and over again.

But that would be evidence, a digital record of his crimes.

For sure, if there are cameras, no one will have access to them but him. I don't think he'd let even Javier observe the final act. I could be wrong, but my intuition tells me he does something private and personal with the girls, something he remembers when he looks at their portraits. *Those* are his souvenirs.

Still. I'll assume there are cameras unless I learn otherwise. I press an ear to the door, pretending I'm listening for footsteps, perhaps wondering when Javier will come with more food. What I'm really doing is getting a closer look at the lock. It's as I expected, a standard dead bolt, which is good news.

I return to the cot and wrap the blanket around my shoulders. Okay, I have the beginning of a plan for getting out of the cell itself. But even if by some miracle it works and I escape the cell, and then even more miraculously get out of whatever building I'm housed in, where will I go? There's an expanse of snow outside. I'd freeze to death.

I imagine Leo saying, *How did you get here in the first place? You didn't teleport.*

It's true. This is one of Michael's properties, which means it must be a residential, research, or commercial facility. Either way, it's going to have vehicles, a road. He's a billionaire, after all, a busy man pulled in many directions. He can't be too far out of pocket.

I remember my dream and wonder if Leo really did give this idea to me or if it came from my own subconscious. My throat closes, aching with sudden tears.

The door clicks open, and Javier steps through it. "You're awake again," he says unnecessarily.

He sets the tray in front of me. It's oatmeal and coffee, both tempting. I pick up the plastic coffee cup and pretend to sip, making sure to emit a faint slurping noise, but spit the coffee back into the cup. My whole life, I've pretended to smoke or drink when the situation warranted my staying sober. I'm always the one with a clear head in a room full of wasted people.

I clear my throat. "Javier, I don't want to be rude, but I have to go to the bathroom."

He chuckles. "No worries." He backs away, and I'm left alone. I take the coffee with me, and in the process of peeing, I do a sleight of hand for the benefit of a potential camera and dump it into the toilet. When I'm pulling my pants up, I rip the crotch panel off my dirty underwear and tuck it into the waistband of my sweats.

Step one.

I wander back to the cot and sit down with the bowl of oatmeal. I pretend to eat for a little while, then walk around with it, just a restless pacing I hope will seem natural if Michael is watching. On my third lap, I make a show of stumbling on the stone floor and spill the rest of the oatmeal. I act dismayed and confused, then mop it up as best I can with a few squares of toilet paper.

I start stretching, doing some yoga moves by the wall near the entrance. In case I'm being monitored, this should normalize my being by the door.

I'm already feeling more myself, and I could cry with gratitude just to feel clear and sane again. I make a vow: No matter what, I will fight to the end. I will not go down quietly. Whatever Michael has become accustomed to with his other victims, he will find something much tougher and worse in me.

You're smarter than all the rest combined.

The memory of the condescending words, like he'd bestowed a

gift upon me with this compliment, fills me with a deep, cold fury. I want to prove him right, but not in the way he's imagining.

Finished with sun salutations, I grab my blanket, fold it up, and use it as a cushion so I can do a few headstands. I use the wall to balance, "coincidentally" just beside the door.

As the hours pass, I keep my movements slow and mellow, pretending to nap on the cot, my mind clarifying as whatever drugs they've been giving me clear my system.

When I sense it's almost time for Javier to return with one of his trays, I start in with the yoga again and spend a long time doing slow, languid stretches with my blanket by the door. I'm coming out of downward dog when the door clicks and swings inward, pushed by Javier, who carries a tray. I make a show of stepping away from him like I'm a little afraid, and he smiles at me appreciatively. "Hello, Summer."

As the door swings shut, I catch a glimpse of a white-walled corridor. "Hi," I say. Just before the door closes, I turn to follow Javier, slip my hand out behind me and shove the piece of wadded-up fabric into the hole in the strike plate, giving it a firm tap to make sure it's solidly in there and won't fall out when the door closes. Ears strained, I wait for the sound of the dead bolt latching.

The click is softer than usual. My heart is pounding a voracious, violent beat. Javier sets my tray down in its usual spot by the cot and straightens back up. "You like yoga, I see."

I nod, trying to feign the drugged, lifeless optimism I'd felt while under the influence of whatever they gave me. "It really gives me peace. And I'm warmer now with the boots." I indicate the Uggs, my reward for being docile. "What do you think the chances are of me getting to take a bath or a shower?" I construct a hopeful expression. Someone on the verge of escape wouldn't ask her jailer to stay and chat, and she certainly wouldn't be worrying about the conditions in prison.

His smile is rueful. "I'll ask, okay?"

"Thanks, Javier." I start on sun salutations again, and he leaves. Yes, the click of the latch is softer now.

The tray contains soup and part of a baguette, as I was hoping.

Instead of eating, I peel the stiff bottom crust off the bread and begin pressing it between my thumbs, flattening and hardening it into the shape of a credit card.

That accomplished, I sling my blanket around my shoulders like a scarf, square my shoulders, and breathe deeply. Here goes nothing. I slip the bread into the crevice beside the strike plate and feel the dead bolt pull out of the now-shallow hole. I cross my fingers and give the door a push, remembering the two-way hinges.

A crack of white hallway winks at me.

My heart stutters.

Game on.

I slip through the door, and I'm in a stark white corridor that reminds me of all the spaces in Michael's world. Indiscriminately, I pick a direction and run. I imagine someone sounding the alarm, yelling that I've escaped, sending troops of armed men pounding after me. But no. It's only going to be Javier, isn't it? Michael can't have the whole world knowing what he does with the women he brings here. The thought gives me hope, which makes my feet fly faster.

The hall terminates in a heavy-looking wooden door. I have no other choices, so I turn the knob and open it fast, bracing myself for the freezing blizzard I've seen for interminable hours outside my cell window.

I stand dumbfounded.

Bright, midafternoon sunlight. Rugged terrain. Rocky hills in the distance. A gravel path leading away.

I step outside and let the door swing shut behind me. The hot yellow sun is high in the sky, beating down, and birds are chirping in the nearby oak trees. The unmistakable, briny smell of the ocean wafts past on a light, cool breeze.

I move away from the building to get a look at it, eyes stinging from the sunlight. It's a white, two-story structure the size of a house with no windows on the ground floor. Around its corner, I catch a glimpse of a rocky shoreline, a series of half-submerged wind turbines, their blades flashing in the sun, and a large, white building overlooking them from the clifftop.

That must be the research facility. I recognize its shape and location from the map.

I never left the island. There is no second property, no other
location in the snow. There's only this one place, his hunting
ground, and it all makes perfect sense now. One of the ways he
keeps women docile is by making it look like they'll die in the
snow if they escape. How long did it take him to construct his
torture room? How many years has he been using it?

"Motherfucker," I whisper, the world spinning around me.

I'm clutching the blanket, having expected to need it for pro-
tection against the cold. I hurl it aside, cursing Michael with every
cell in my body, and all-out sprint away from the building.

CHAPTER THIRTY-SIX

LEO

MONDAY, JUNE 12

The first thing I registered when I opened my eyes was softness.

I blinked, trying to clear a sticky fog out of my mind and vision. I'd been asleep for a long time; I could feel it. I spun with uncertainty, unable to place myself in space and time. I was snuggled into a nest of white bedding, and the light in the room was airy and bright. A hotel?

In a rush, I remembered Michael—the mansion—running—Julie. I sat up.

I must still be in Julie's room. I must have fallen asleep.

No. This wasn't Julie's room. It looked similar: bamboo flooring, white walls, light wood bed frame. But it was sparser than her room had been, with no furniture except the bed and, strangely, a bathtub in the corner under a window, a toilet beside it.

I pushed the covers off me, revealing a gauzy white nightgown unlike anything I'd ever owned. *Who changed my clothes?*

I traced my memory backward. I'd come out of the woods and sought help from Julie, who'd given me her shoes. She'd hidden me in her room and gone to the party. Later that night, she'd brought me food and drink, and I'd eaten ravenously. That was the last thing I remembered.

She must have drugged me. The food and drink had been laced with something. But why?

Heartbeat throbbing in my ears, I stood on shaky legs and crossed the room to the window. My head roared and spun, and I clutched the wall until I was able to reopen my eyes and focus. It was daytime, probably afternoon, and I had a view of the ocean, endless and expansively cobalt under a powder-blue sky. There was no sand, only acres of black volcanic rock, the waves thrashing against their jagged edges, spraying jets of white foam into the air. Just past the waves, a few boats floated on calmer waters, more pragmatic vessels than Michael's sleek speedboat. Past the rocks and waves, wind turbines rose out of the water, pinwheel arms steadily carving circles through the air. I'd seen these before, when I'd been joyriding around the island on Michael's speedboat. It felt like a hundred years ago.

Refocusing, I noticed the windowpane had a fine metal mesh embedded into it. I'd seen windows like this before, on liquor stores in dangerous neighborhoods. *To keep people out? Or to keep people in?*

I turned and located a door on the opposite side of the room, white on white, blending into the walls. I hurried toward it and squatted down, examining the smooth place where a handle should have been, glimpsing a dead bolt in the crack. I rapped on it and got a solid, thick sound in return; it probably had a metal core.

I banged harder. "Help," I yelled. "Help! Help! Someone!" I let out shrill, animal screams, the kind that would strike notes of alarm in anyone, the kind that should cause thundering footsteps to come running in my direction. I screamed more, harder, louder, like a chimpanzee, like a murder victim.

A noise at the door. I stumbled backward to the bed, where I sat with a soft thump. A click, the distinct sound of a lock releasing, and Michael stepped through, letting it close softly behind him.

I was shocked by his presence, though I probably shouldn't have been. He was in jeans and a soft-looking navy-blue sweater, his dark hair tousled. I tensed, waiting for him to attack, ready to fight to the death, but his expression wasn't unkind; if anything, he looked amused.

"No one can hear you," he said.

I swallowed against the rawness in my throat.

"You really gave me the runaround." He sat on the bed beside me, and I scooted away, keeping out of reach. "We were searching everywhere."

"Where am I?" My voice shook.

"You're in one of our rooms, the nicest we have. I thought you'd like having a bathtub. You'll need me to unlock it if you want a bath. We don't want you alone in here, flooding the place or . . . well." He cleared his throat. "Just let me know if you'd like to take a bath."

"Why am I wearing this?" I pulled at the stupid, frilly nightgown. "And why am I here in the first place? What do you want?"

His deep blue eyes were solemn and earnest. "I know you might not believe me, but I do care about you."

"You tried to kill me," I reminded him, my voice bitter.

He furrowed his brow. "What are you talking about?"

It was such a weird response that I gaped at him, uncomprehending.

He moved closer. I could swear he looked concerned. "Leo, tell me what's going on. Why did you run away from me? You could have died of exposure. You're lucky we found you."

"You didn't find me. That woman drugged me. You tried to strangle me. No!" I had my hands to my temples. "You're a psychopath. Something is wrong with you."

He looked sad. "Leo, I'm so sorry if you thought I was trying to hurt you. I just wanted to paint you. I didn't understand why you ran away." He reached for my hand and pressed his on top of it. "I am so, so sorry. I must have gotten carried away. I truly meant you no harm." His eyes glistened with sincerity.

In my entire life, I had never wondered if I was losing my mind. Reality was an objective thing, a place we all inhabited. But now, sitting here with him acting like I was the one who'd lost it, I wondered if the fabric of reality was starting to tear, little rips that could leave me standing in a strange wilderness, vulnerable to attack.

All at once, I was consumed by the certainty that I was prey.

After a length of time, Michael touched my shoulder. "Leo? Are you okay?"

I was stuck, remembering the painting cabin and the feel of his hands on my neck. Those hands were gentle now, and his face bore no resemblance to the mask of fury I'd seen as he'd choked me.

He'd chased me into the woods. Like a wolf hunting a rabbit, he'd grabbed for me, almost caught me, and if I hadn't outrun him, he'd have . . .

What would he have done?

I didn't understand what motivation he could possibly have had to hurt me. I'd already slept with him. I'd given him everything he might have wanted. I remembered him asking me a question, something like, *How did you know?* Understanding why he'd asked me that seemed like the key, but I sure as hell wasn't about to bring it up now while he wasn't in a strangling mood.

"Leo?" His hand tightened on my shoulder, which made me flinch, but then he started massaging the muscles. "You okay, sweetie?"

I kept my eyes away from his, afraid to meet the gaze I could feel burning the side of my face. "If nothing's wrong, why am I in this room? Why am I locked up?"

He sighed. "I'm in a tough spot. I can't have you running around scaring my researchers. I can't send you back to L.A. like this, either, selling everyone crazy stories about how Michael Forrester attacked you. So I thought we should take some time to figure out how we move forward. Sound like a plan?"

His words were like maple syrup, sticky and smooth. After a few moments spent wondering what Summer would tell me to do, I said, "Sure. Tell me what you need from me to feel safe sending me back to L.A."

"Let's just spend a little time together, make sure you're calm, get you some rest. Then we can do the heavy thinking. You were half dead from exposure when we found you. Your body needs to recover."

His mouth was crooked into a handsome smile, hair curved artfully over one blue eye. The sun was setting over the alien wind turbines, sending strange and spiky shadows across the glistening waves. Michael's face was golden in the light, and I was reminded of countless evenings spent with Summer on the beach, wrapped in blankets, drinking tea.

He edged nearer to me. "Let me ask you a question. Do you believe in fate?"

What a weird thing to ask right now. "I'm not sure," I answered truthfully.

"Take a guess."

"I . . . I guess I hope there's no fate, but I can't be sure one way or the other. At some point, I gave up on trying to find any rhyme or reason in the universe."

His fingertips reached for my cheek, and I trembled, fear ringing in my ears. They connected with the skin, gentle and delicate. He followed them with his eyes, lips parted slightly. "I never believed in fate, either," he murmured. "Not until you. But then . . . Leo, tell me how we met."

I felt a frown flicker across my brows. "We met in a hotel bar."

"Before that." He lowered his hand to my chin, which he pinched lightly between thumb and forefinger.

"What do you mean? There was no before that."

"I researched the Instagram algorithm, called their CTO personally, and I still can't figure out how your post crossed my screen."

I was so confused, I thought maybe I *was* crazy, because what he was saying made not even a lick of sense. "Michael, I don't—"

"I remember when I saw it. I was on the patio of my place in Palo Alto, drinking coffee. I don't usually flip through the posts on the Explore page, but I'd been curious about what content they'd suggest for someone like me. I was just curious," he murmured. "Such a strange thing. I'd been looking for you for so

many years. It was my mistake; I'd lost track of you when you
went off-grid. I still don't understand how the algorithm put it
together. People don't realize, the AI is constantly learning from
billions of data points, but if you ask the guys working on it, they
don't always have the answers. It's incredible and frightening, a
genuine consciousness."

"Michael, I don't—"

"Anyway. I opened up the Explore page, and there you were.
After all that time." He let out a breath. "It was a close-up of your
face, taken in light a lot like this. You were on the beach. Your hair
was messy, and you were smiling. You looked like you had all the
vitality on the planet packaged inside you."

Quietly, I said, "I remember seeing that you'd liked that post. I
clicked on your name and realized who you were. I . . ." I hesitated, not sure how much to tell him, terrified to upset him. I decided to frame the story in the most flattering way I could think
of. "I was intrigued by you. I couldn't imagine why a man like you
would even take the time to look at my picture. I wanted to meet
you."

His eyebrows shot up. "You arranged it? You found out where
I was?"

Slowly, I nodded.

He laughed, then fell back on the bed, head cradled in his hands.
A delighted, almost mischievous smile lingered, and he darted his
eyes to me. "I need to paint you," he said decisively. "That's what
needs to happen. I need to capture you as you are right now. No
more photographs." He sat up and grinned, clearly energized.

I watched him leave, feeling like I'd missed something crucial.

My eyes drifted to the window. Below, the wind turbines
reached spidery fingers out of the ocean, silhouetted black against
the red light of sunset, clawing at the air like drowning beasts.

CHAPTER THIRTY-SEVEN

SUMMER

TUESDAY, JUNE 13

The gravel path leads away from my prison in a wide arc. I imagine it will ultimately take me to the fence, the separation between the sides of the island. Sure enough, I find myself bypassing the research facility and heading straight for a black, wrought-iron fence about twelve feet high. It's formidable, but the heavy gate has a push handle and I'm able to walk through it without incident. Clearly, they're worried about people getting in, not out. The other side is outfitted with the same key card readers I'm used to seeing everywhere on this island as well as an intercom with a buzzer. I glance up as I pass through and find the expected security camera, a small black globe tucked into the wrought iron.

"*Run,*" Leo had said, and at last, I obey.

I sprint on the gravel path that heads back toward the residence, wishing I had half of Leo's running skills and a better sports bra. The trail cuts through chaparral and occasional patches of trees, and I recall the map I studied so closely in my suite just a few days ago, though it feels like another lifetime. There's not much in the way of natural cover, no way for me to conceal myself if someone comes. I'm sweating, weakened, feet slimy in the stupid, clumsy Uggs, but I keep running. I will not be imprisoned. Over my literal dead body. Leo's gone. My mom forgot me long ago. I have nothing to lose, no one to let down.

My steps are faltering. I need to rest. I step off the path and squat down in the bushes to catch my breath.

Okay. Where am I? I need to think and be organized.

The fact that no one is hot on my heels chasing me, that no alarm sounded when I broke free, tells me I was right about a couple of things. First, there are no cameras in Michael's little torture chamber, or if there are, only he has access to them. Second, Javier is his only henchman helping him with this particular project, and Javier is only one person with a host of other duties. It might be a minute before they realize I'm missing.

I wipe sweat out of my eyes and bring to mind the map of the island. This is the same path that winds along the coastline, though the ocean is out of sight right now. I've been on it a bunch of times; it's the one I ran on to throw Alan's phone over the cliff, and the one I used to connect with the beach access trail. Now that the investors' weekend is over, I'd be willing to bet there are boats at the docks if I could get to them. But that would mean following this trail right up to the residence and then out to the elevator and stairs, where I know for sure there are cameras and staff. I don't recall seeing a different way down to the marina.

A lightbulb moment—the Jet Skis. I can grab one at the beach, then take it over to the marina. It's only a cove or two away, and, thanks to Julie, I now know how to use them.

I straighten up, get back out onto the gravel path, and resume running. My head is full of static, and thoughts burst out of it like grasshoppers: I'm parched. My mouth is flaming with thirst, lips swollen and dry. I'm so hot, running in the baking afternoon sun, that if I think about it too much, I'll start feeling dizzy.

The turnoff to the beach widens on my right, and I take it, grateful that it leads me into a shady patch between trees. I follow the steps down, hurry around a curve downhill, and burst out onto the sand, ready to sprint for the Jet Skis I can see waiting at the dock, but then I notice a figure on the sand and halt in a panic.

It's a woman, stretched out on a towel, the cove's calm water sparkling peacefully behind her.

I know this figure: the black bikini barely covering round, fake breasts; the designer sunglasses, the large to-go cup at her side, probably containing cosmos. Julie.

Why is she still here?

I sprint across the sand, fury boiling over. She's glistening with sunscreen, shapely legs relaxed on her expensive towel, face free of worry under a large, floppy sun hat and designer sunglasses. She's napping while I fight for my life.

I throw myself onto her, straddle her, and grip her by the neck. She cries out, waking up with a jolt, and I start to choke her, relishing the feel of her neck beneath my palms. "Shut up or I swear to God, I will kill you with my bare hands," I tell her, and I almost don't recognize my voice for its fury and thirsty grit.

CHAPTER THIRTY-EIGHT

LEO

TUESDAY, JUNE 13

When Michael came to paint me, he brought Javier. I didn't know why I was surprised. Maybe because I'd felt like I was alone in the universe up in this room, watching the night pass an hour at a time, each ripple of the corduroy waves ticking me closer to a fate I couldn't yet imagine.

"Hello, Leo," Michael greeted me, setting down his black bag and foldable easel. To Javier, he said, "Give me a little more light."

Javier left the room, and a minute later, a light embedded in the ceiling shone down on the bed, casting a muted, golden glow on the white comforter. It was early afternoon. Michael had only visited once since last night, and then only for a few minutes, just to bring me a cup of water and a sandwich. I'd flushed both down the toilet. After what happened with Julie, no way was I eating anything they gave me.

I'd spent a lot of time reflecting on his words. If he wanted me dead, he could have killed me by now. Summer had taught me to consider people's motivations. *What does he want?* she'd whisper in my ear. If Michael wanted reassurance that I wouldn't tell anyone about the choking incident—if he wanted to see me as repentant, convinced of my own craziness, I'd give him that. Whatever it took to get back to L.A., I'd do it. Summer had to be frantic with worry. I couldn't let myself think about that for too long. It bit me like a snake, picturing her desperate concern. Would she call in a missing persons report? Unlikely. She was physically incapable of dealing with cops. Would she try to trace my phone? Contact my parents?

Oh, no. I prayed she wouldn't do that. The idea of my mother's face—my father's horrified O of a mouth—the images were too familiar, etched into my memory forever.

Now, Michael instructed Javier to sit by the door, which he did obediently, sitting casually on the floor, legs crossed. Michael turned to me. "Ready to become a work of art?"

I hesitated, wanting nothing less.

"Don't worry, you'll be beautiful. I'll make you look like you have makeup on. Now, go sit on the bed. Try to match the expression you had in the photo."

"I don't remember—"

"Just give me a three-quarter view of your face." There was a tightness in his voice. He was getting impatient with me.

I was scared not to obey, so I sank onto the bed and arranged myself. "Tuck your legs underneath you," he instructed. "Lean your weight on that back hand a little less." At last, he was satisfied. "Good. Excellent. Now hold that pose, please."

Michael arranged his easel in just the right spot to observe me, rummaged through his bag, and squeezed some paint onto a palette. He set a large jar of something clear beside him on the floor, and then he started working, the aroma of oil paint saturating the room. His expression was focused, and he was brushing onto the canvas in wide, even strokes. Breaking the silence, he said, "Let me tell you about this girl I once knew."

"All right," I murmured, trying not to move my lips too much.

"She had brown hair like you, the same golden skin. A beautiful girl. It was hard to choose her dress for the painting. She looked great in all of them."

I felt sorry for this girl and wondered where she was now. "You painted her portrait, too?"

He nodded, switching to a different brush. "I always block out the first two layers of underpainting live, and then I handle the detail work later, without the model. I have an infallible memory for faces."

His hands looked skilled, veiny and strong. I remembered how they'd felt on my body, how they'd thrilled and then terrified me.

"This girl was special," he went on. "I mean, every girl I paint is special. I wouldn't paint her if she wasn't. Not everyone deserves to be immortalized."

Something about this statement felt distasteful.

"She had a perfect body, long legs, just beautiful. She had a pretty voice, too. I asked her if she was a singer. She said no, but I always wondered if that was a lie." A frown flickered across his face. "They tend to do that."

A chill ran through me. "Lie?"

He nodded, eyes landing right on mine. "All of them."

I didn't reply.

Back to painting, he said, "I've always wondered . . . It's silly and superstitious, and I'm a scientist. Don't judge me."

"I won't," I heard myself say, the promise an autonomic response related to self-preservation.

Conspiratorially, he lowered his voice. "I've always wondered if the painting serves as a sort of talisman, if part of the person's spirit lingers. Especially when you look into their eyes. It can feel like they're right there with you."

It *was* a superstitious thought, and I was honestly shocked to hear him speak it aloud in front of Javier. But Javier sat unmoving, face neutral and unimpressed. Maybe he'd heard this type of thing before. Careful not to sound critical, I asked, "Do you feel like it takes part of them away? And then they live their lives missing part of their soul?"

Michael's mouth tweaked at the edges. "Sure," he said. "Let's go with that."

A quiet minute passed between us before I asked, "So why did you want to tell me about this girl?"

"She reminds me of you. Or at least, I thought she did. You're different now that I've gotten to know you. Darker. More layers. More life experience. You've seen things. You've lost all your innocence."

I couldn't argue with any of that, but I didn't like to hear him say it. "Is that why you put me in this nightgown? To make me look more innocent for the painting?"

"I thought it was an interesting contrast, yes."

What a dick. He hadn't complained about my lack of innocence when he was fucking me on his stupid boat.

I was invested now, and I needed to know what had happened to this girl he'd known. "Do you still keep in touch with her?"

"No." He examined me clinically for a moment, then fiddled with something on the canvas. "No, I don't keep in touch with any of the girls I've painted."

Javier shifted his weight, moving something under his blazer. I noticed a bulge there, and when he settled into a more comfortable position, I caught a glimpse of a holster. He had a gun.

Maybe I shouldn't have been surprised. After all, Michael was a billionaire. His bodyguards would be armed. But here? Now? Against me? I was almost naked, helpless, and trapped.

"This girl was a good listener. You are, too, Leoneli. That's one of your best qualities. I get the feeling you don't judge."

I returned my eyes to him. He was watching me intensely.

"I . . . You're right, I guess. I'm not very judgmental." Usually. Right now, I was full of judgment.

"I want to tell you so many things." His face was earnest. "Javier, go. Bring me the painting."

Noiseless as a cat, Javier hopped to his feet and slipped through the door, clicking it open with a key card. Michael got up from the easel and came to kneel in front of me. My heart was thundering, head swimming with anxiety.

He took one of my hands like he was going to propose and kissed it. "I want you to know this has never happened to me before."

My body had turned to ice at some point. I hadn't noticed it happening. I was a statue.

He sat on the bed beside me, bigger than me, encroaching on my space. A hand went to my shoulder, played with the hair that hung tangled and unwashed. "She had long hair. I assume you used to have long hair, too. When I saw your photo on Instagram, the first thing I thought was, 'What happened to her long hair?' You shouldn't have cut it. Why did you cut it?" I could barely breathe, let alone answer. He studied my face and sighed. "You're afraid. Don't be. I want to tell you this story. Don't ruin it."

"Sorry," I managed, not sure what else to say.

He frowned, pouty.

"She had long hair," I prompted.

His face cleared. "She did. Long and brown. Pretty." He ran his hand through mine. "She was younger than you. Beautiful. She'd lived a sheltered life. The things I told her should have shocked her, but they didn't. I could see she was an angel, someone you could confess anything to. She had something special. I spent so long trying to replicate that experience, looking for a way to live it over again." He gesticulated. "Imagine. I clicked 'like' on your photo as a private little joke to myself. What were the odds? And then when we met I was terrified. Did you know? How did you find me? I realize now, the universe is just like that sometimes. Magic exists. Synchronicity. Or maybe it's just the AI." This made him bark out a boyish laugh.

I was lost in a maze, trying to understand why he was jumping back and forth from some girl he'd painted years ago to finding my photo on Instagram and us meeting. The door clicked, and Javier entered carrying a canvas. It was the same size as the one he was painting of me, the back of it facing me so I couldn't see the image.

"I just restretched it," Michael told me. "And then I gave it a fresh coat of varnish. Javier, bring it here." Javier handed it over, then backed out of the room, shutting the door behind him.

Michael turned the painting so we were looking at it together. The young woman pictured was posed on a bench on a sloping lawn overlooking the ocean. Her hands were folded in her lap, hair arranged in brown waves over one shoulder. But her face was all I could see. The expression—the way she seemed to look right at you—the way she glowed with serenity.

She was so much like me, my body froze, every muscle, every bone. Those cheeks, just a little rounder than mine. The breasts a little fuller. The mouth not as broad, the eyes more serious. *Born with the soul of an old lady,* I'd said a million times.

It was Amanda. In the yellow dress I remembered too well.

CHAPTER THIRTY-NINE

SUMMER

TUESDAY, JUNE 13

Julie thrashes to no avail, hat flying, but I'm pinning her down and guess what, bitch, I go to the gym, too. Her sunglasses fall off, revealing panicked brown eyes that are wide with fear.

"Stop fighting and I'll let you breathe," I say, panting between clenched teeth. She obeys, and I loosen my grip just enough to let her gulp in a breath. "Why are you still here? Where is Steve?"

"He's working," she hisses, barely able to get the words out. She yanks at my hands, manicured nails digging into my wrists.

I squeeze again, and she turns red, gulping and thrashing. "Stop fighting me or I'll choke you out," I order, putting my weight on her windpipe. "I have been on the road my entire life and you don't even *know* what I'm capable of. Do not fucking test me, Julie, because I could kill you right now and not feel an ounce of guilt." She goes limp, and we look into each other's eyes. I ease up on her neck, and her chest rises and falls.

"Why are *you* still here?" she asks.

I want to reach back and slap her until she cries. "I'm here because you drugged me and turned me over to that fucking psychopath. Why the hell do you think?"

"No, you were supposed to be airlifted back to L.A. with your friend," she replies, confused and frantic.

I frown. "With my friend? Do you mean with Leo? What do you know about Leo?" She inclines her chin, a refusal to answer, and I squeeze hard to remind her who's in charge.

Her words come out fast and whiny. "None of this is my fault. When you're dealing with—"

"*Tell me about Leo.*"

She looks frustrated, inconvenienced. "She was lost in the woods for a couple of days, and then she came crawling out and got caught, and they helicoptered her back to L.A. with you, or at least I thought they did. None of this is any of my business!"

I turn this over and over, considering the timeline. "What exactly did they tell you?"

She swallows, eyes darting left and right, and a tear rolls into her hair. "Michael told Steve he had a girl here who got drunk and wandered off. He said he just, you know, brought her here for some fun, but she turned out to be kind of unbalanced, off her psych meds, a one-night stand gone wrong. So they were looking for her, pretending it was a dog they were searching for. Then she came out of the woods as I was smoking before dinner, and she *was* totally off her rocker. I set her up in my room, and Michael was worried she would run again if he came to get her. We were worried about the liability, she was talking crazy—she had it in her head that he wanted to kill her—she was not a normal person, she was a mess—"

I try to follow the thread. "What did you do, Julie?"

"I gave her some food that was laced with a sedative so they could medevac her off the island. I swear, that's all I did."

"And did you *see* them medevac her off the island?"

She hesitates. "Well, no, but I'm sure they did it when we were at dinner so the investors couldn't—"

"You can't hide a fucking helicopter!" I'm screaming. I suck in a breath, worried I'm going to pass out. I'm dying of thirst. "You drugged me, too. What was the justification for that?"

Her reply is quiet. "You conned your way in. You were trying to steal trade secrets. They found my bracelet in your suitcase, Summer!" She squeals this out, a self-righteous note in her frightened voice.

"And what about Ashley?" I demand. "How do you explain that? She suddenly didn't exist?"

"You're so paranoid," she wails. "She just went home to see her family. No one told you she didn't exist. You're inventing stuff to support these ridiculous conspiracy theories you and your friend are obsessed with!"

I laugh bitterly. "You're either the dumbest person I've ever met, or you're as evil as he is."

"He's not evil," she protests. "He's protecting his—"

"Say another word and I will hit you," I warn her.

"He *isn't*. I don't know what's happening, but you have to understand. Michael is a nice person. He's done *so much* good. He's one of the most impactful men fighting climate change on Earth. Steve's known him for twenty years."

"He kills girls, Julie. I literally just escaped from his girl-killing torture chamber. Why do you think I look like this?"

"That can't be true," she protests. "I don't know why you and your friend think that. Have you tried just . . . talking to him?"

I realize this is a preview of what it will be like if I survive and call the cops about this. My anger is evaporating, replaced with a trembling despair.

I look at the trees, picturing Leo stumbling out of the woods, begging Julie for help, only to be dismissed as a "crazy" date gone wrong, a girl "off her meds." That's all Leo and I are to people like this. We're not even completely human. All a man like Michael has to do is make one derisive comment, and there won't be a single person on this earth who will believe a word I say.

Julie takes a huge gulp of air into her lungs and lets out a horror-movie scream that scares the shit out of me. I clap my hands over her mouth and she bites. I curse her and backhand her across the face, and we wrestle for a minute until I have her wrists under my knees and my hands on her neck again. "Would you fucking *stop*," I pant, and she cries like a child, open-mouthed sobbing that infuriates me.

The ringing in my ears triggers a sudden memory—the voice I'd heard while in my cell. I'd been drugged and half asleep, but I'd heard a woman screaming. She'd sounded like she was being tortured.

Leo?

It hadn't occurred to me that he could have been keeping her in a cell just like he was keeping me. If she was caught on Saturday, that was only a few days ago. Hope swells up, demanding and warm. My eyes drift to the Jet Skis, and I remember my plan to find a boat. I can't do that now. I can't leave this island if there's any chance Leo is still alive.

So it's going back in, then, instead of trying to break free.

I refocus on Julie's face. My brain is spinning up, gears turning, plans forming. "How did you get here from the house?"

"Golf cart. It's by the path up there, tucked into the trees in the shade."

"And what's Steve working on? Why are you still here? Shouldn't you have gone home with the rest of the assholes?"

"Steve and Michael have a venture they're looking into," she answers haughtily, which is pretty rich in her situation. "They wanted some time to discuss it privately."

I spot her clothes, folded into a pile a few feet away by her thermos. "It must be hard for Michael to balance all this. Killing girls, running companies, saving the world. Hopefully he'll have energy left over for Steve. He's a busy guy." She starts to argue, but I silence her with a look. "I'm going to release you, and you're not going to run or scream or do anything stupid. Because if you do, I'll tell them you're in this with me. You're a spy for the enemy. I'm a really good liar, Julie. I can ruin your life."

She actually smiles. "You have zero social capital."

"I don't need it. I'll tell Michael that you and I knew each other years ago, that we had a pact to catch a rich guy. You met Steve, and I coached Leo on how to catch Michael. You helped us, giving us information about where we could find him."

"Please." Her tone is mocking. "I've known Michael for years. There's no way—"

"You think he trusts you? Think about what you're saying. You're one of the *wives,* Julie. From their perspective, all you want is to find a rich man and screw him out of all his money." She's not fighting me at all anymore. She's thinking fast; her eyes flit back and forth, a frown fighting to break through the Botox. I've stuck the dagger in; now I just have to twist it. I lower my voice, keeping it strong and confident. "I can spin a hell of a story, Julie. Do you want to test me?"

She meets my eyes, a decisive strength in the way she clenches her jaw. "What do you want?"

"I'm going to put on your clothes and take your golf cart. You're going to stay here and sunbathe in your bikini. You never saw me. I never saw you. I'm going to get one of the boats and go back to L.A., and I'll be out of your hair for good. How does that sound?"

Her lips are a thin and unflattering line across her sculpted face. "That sounds amazing."

I get up and pull off my sweats and Uggs. In my underwear and sports bra, I examine the clothes and shoes she'd brought to the beach, a bodycon minidress and a pair of gold thong sandals. I pull the dress on and slide my feet into the shoes. "Give me your hat and glasses," I command, and she hands them up to me. She's gathered her knees to her chest and is watching me with pouty eyes. I smooth my hair into some semblance of order and pull the hat on, then set the sunglasses in place. "Do you have lipstick or anything?" I ask.

"No, I didn't bring my bag."

Fine. This will have to do. "Keys are in the cart?" I check.

She nods. "Please just go before anyone sees you here," she says, and I start to walk away, wishing I could hurt her half as much as she's hurt me.

But then my conscience nudges me to a stop. I turn and look down at her, a pretty body on the sand. "These guys get tired of their pets, Julie, don't forget. You've seen and heard a lot. Don't ever think they won't get rid of you in a heartbeat. You're still just a woman like the rest of us."

I don't give her a chance to reply. I leave her there to think things over. Maybe there's a little part of her that can still be redeemed.

Probably not.

CHAPTER FORTY

LEO

TUESDAY, JUNE 13

The painting sat drying in the afternoon sunlight. He had turned it to face me and set Amanda's beside it, two same-size canvases side by side on the easel, both of us posed on the same bench on the same grassy hill overlooking the ocean, our hair fluttering in fake ocean breezes, our faces peaceful, skin glowing honey-smooth. Mine wasn't finished yet. The shapes were blurry, missing the final layers of paint. Michael said the detail work took forever and he never did it with a model present, but always later, after the underpainting had a chance to dry. The effect was that of a rain-soaked window, the images beyond it hazy and indistinct, while Amanda was rendered in full, photographic detail, eyes piercing from across the room.

My heart was beating in shivers, each a series of earthquakes running through my bones as I waited for him to start talking again, to explain why he had this painting of Amanda in the yellow dress, that horrible yellow dress in which she'd been found dead. "Later," he told me, and then, "Soon."

He finished arranging the portraits and set a series of tea light candles on the floor in front of the easel, lit them one by one, and then came back to sit beside me, shoulder to shoulder, conspiratorially, two friends in an art gallery.

"I'm going to hang these in my front hallway," he said, like this was a major compliment. "I'm going to take all the other girls down from there. They'll detract from this. It's perfection. This is called a diptych. Did you know that? Two paintings always displayed as a pair. Two halves of one work of art."

Now what? I wondered. What was his plan?

Like he read my mind, he turned to face me, drawing a knee up onto the bed. "Leo. Look at me."

I obeyed, worried he could see the terror in my eyes.

His were hungry, and he struck me as younger than his years, energized from within. "I need to tell you so many things." He leaned in and kissed my cheek, lingering on it, lips moist on my skin. "Lie back so I can look at you."

I did not want him on top of me, but he was already pressing me backward, and I was no match for him. He climbed on top of me and settled in, leaning his weight on his elbow, looking down into my eyes and stroking my hair back from my forehead. "Michael, I feel claustrophobic," I said, trying to keep my voice calm. He rolled slightly so he was beside me, one leg between mine in a way I didn't like at all.

"Better?" he murmured. I recognized the hunger behind his eyes. I'd seen it many times now. But there was a new flavor, something sharper, more urgent, that I couldn't identify. Without waiting for me to respond, he said, "I want to tell you about Amanda."

"Tell me," I whispered. This was a descent into the depths, but I had to do it. I needed to know.

"I met her at Stanford. I was there giving a lecture. I invited her out to a club with me and my friends. But, of course, it was just me." He grinned, roguish. "I can be tricky." His hair spilled down over his eyes, and he pushed it back. "It was Friday night, and she was wearing a short black dress. You looked so much like her when

I met you, Leo. I thought I was seeing a ghost. She talked about you a lot and said you looked alike, and of course I had seen your selfies, but that didn't prepare me for how *much* you looked like her in person."

I felt a tear roll into my hair. Amanda felt close at hand, memories of her seeping out from behind the doors I'd shut on them.

"We got along so well," Michael went on dreamily. "I was working on desalination techniques for third world countries, patenting technology. It was an exciting time. And *she* was exciting. So fresh and clean, not a part of the city at all." He touched my cheek. "I wish I had known you then. You must have been even better, before all this."

Before what? Before adulthood? I gripped the sheet beneath me.

"We had a great night. She was perfect." He sighed, peppermint breath tickling my face. "I could have had so much more time with her. But she said she had to go. She was insistent. We were at my place in Palo Alto. I wanted her to stay." A frown flickers across his brow. "I wish we could have had longer together. I didn't have a chance to tell her everything." He touched my shoulder, the strap of the nightgown, my collarbone, my throat. "I told her some of the things I needed to. Most of them."

I could barely breathe let alone speak. He was so close, I could feel the buttons on his shirt, the buckle on his belt, the folds in his jeans against my side, where he'd pressed himself tight against me. "What did you need to tell her?"

"There's a price. Do you understand?" His voice vibrated with intensity, but its volume was lowering, becoming a deep, throbbing murmur. "You can't understand the pressure I'm under. You see the net worth, but every single one of those dollars weighs pounds and pounds. I'm responsible for . . . so much. Every day, I go out, I fix things that can't be fixed, I work on a scale you can't imagine. It takes and it takes and it *takes*. It's unbearable." He put his hand on my forehead like he was taking my temperature. "Sometimes, I feel like I'm being eaten alive. Consumed."

I wanted to scream. *I* was being consumed by *him*.

"Amanda understood. She was compassionate. She listened to me. She held me. Like this." He rested his head on my chest and wrapped his arms around me. My own arms were splayed out on either side, but I forced myself to put one of them on his back. He sighed, relaxing into the embrace. "She was a saint. A gift. She took that weight from me; she listened. I want you to know, I appreciated her. I worshipped her. I'd painted girls before, but painting her was the first time I thought about the idea of the painting capturing pieces of someone's soul. Hers was the first one I felt I'd captured."

A long, horrible silence settled down upon us. I felt more tears well up and stream down my temples, into my hair and ears, as I stared straight up at the ceiling. I had never been able to imagine exactly what had happened to Amanda, what her last hours had been like. I'd imagined she had been assaulted, of course; what else was there for a beautiful girl her age? The cause of death had been strangulation, and I'd had vivid and horrible nightmares for years. I'd thrown myself into every drug I could lay my hands on, trying to escape them. I'd heard my careless words, *Can't take your V card to graduation,* and I contemplated ending my own life just to free myself from the mental pictures and my own thoughtless joke playing relentlessly on repeat. This is what I could never share with Summer—my own culpability.

But now, a new picture was forming: Amanda, swept up into Michael's world. He would have been in his thirties, no gray in his hair, with even more swagger and charisma. She was an introverted Fresno girl away from home for the first time. She would have felt so special to have been chosen by this man.

Hadn't I also felt special?

"What happened then?" I made myself ask, needing to bear witness, descending deeper.

His voice was just above a whisper. "She could have stayed with me longer, but she said she needed to go."

"She was supposed to be home for brunch," I managed, my

voice breaking, picturing her still trying to be good, trying not to disappoint us. I'd told her not to be late, and she'd promised to get there on time. Now I understood; she had tried.

"So my time with her had to end early. It was too bad. It always felt unfinished. Now I know why. It was one half of the diptych. You are the second half."

The room was quiet, just warm afternoon sunlight and him, his words humming through my head.

I squeezed my eyes shut. "Tell me how your time together ended."

He lifted himself back up onto an elbow and kissed my cheek. "That's private, honey."

"Was she in pain?"

"No more pain than anyone else in this world. Do you know what the world is like? What it's like to stand in the gap for an entire dying, swarming, sweltering world? Billions of people?" His lips stretched tight across his teeth in a grimace. "I need this, Leo. I need it. I need you to hear me. See me. Feel me. Know me. I need you to *see.*"

His belt buckle dug into my hip, blue jeans rough against my bare legs. I hated that I wasn't wearing underwear, hated the intimacy of this moment. Inside my head, I was screaming, thrashing, scratching his eyes out.

Like an apparition, I felt Summer close to me. If she were here, she'd have some wisdom to share, some tips about flipping the balance of power. *I have no weapon,* I'd yell at her if she started going on about how the world has everything you need.

You have everything in front of you, she'd argue. *What you need is always there if you're willing to reach out and take it.*

Again, he pressed against me, and I opened my eyes to a familiar heat in his. He wanted me to complete his ritual. It was confession, then sex, and then . . . I didn't want to name the third part.

My mind named it in spite of me: death.

CHAPTER FORTY-ONE

SUMMER

TUESDAY, JUNE 13

I pull the golf cart up to the gate, aware I'm on camera. *Smile,* I think, trying to control the energy I'm exuding. The facility is quiet and serene, creepy wind turbines spinning slowly in the ocean at its back. Behind its farthest corner peeks a white structure—the prison I'd escaped.

I imagine Michael's thought process right now. They're probably searching for me on the residential side of the island; no way will they expect me to come back to my prison. Most likely, they'll head straight for the boats, imagining I'd make a beeline to them. If he doesn't know I'm missing yet, he's either in with Leo, assuming she's still alive, or he's in the research facility, or he's across the island at the residence. Hell, maybe he's in his creepy painting shed finishing my portrait. I might get lucky; I might find the cell building empty, and my biggest obstacle will be finding a way in.

I press the buzzer on the intercom and lift my chin, imitating Julie's haughty posture. It takes a minute for someone to answer. "Hello?" says an unfamiliar male voice.

I summon my best Julie impression. "This is Julie Lodstrom. Please open the gate."

A pause. "Ma'am, I'm sorry, but I don't have you on the list for today."

I cough out a Karen laugh. "Excuse me?"

He begins to repeat himself. "I'm sorry, ma'am, but—"

I lean forward so my voice will be louder through the speaker. "My husband is Steve Lodstrom, and he funds your salary. So unless you'd like him to reevaluate his contributions to this project, you will let me come in and join my husband, as I was asked to do. What is your name?"

"I'm sorry," he stammers. "I didn't—one second." I count to three, and the gate buzzes and swings gently inward.

Somehow, despite everything, I've still got it.

I drive forward and to the right, hurrying behind the building that had served as my jail. I tuck the cart into the corner and power it off, then look for something to use as a lock pick. I settle on the key ring, which could feasibly be unspooled into a long poking tool, and a Bic pen from a clipboard with a paper titled "Charging Log."

I discard the hat and sunglasses and face the building, squaring my shoulders. If Leo is in there, this will all be worth it. If she's not, well . . . my life is anchorless now. I don't want to die, but I don't want to live in a world without her. As strong as that feeling is, the idea of Michael getting what he wants from me is so repugnant, I almost turn and run.

I cut through rocks and dirt to the path, then follow it to a set of steps that lead to the wooden door from which I'd escaped, a keypad beside it. I duck to examine the doorknob. With keypad locks, there's often a manual backup. Whether it's on this side of the door or not is another story.

Suddenly, the door swings open, knocking me down the steps onto my ass. Javier explodes over the threshold, a lantern-eyed expression of contempt where his calm smile usually sits. He raises his gun, aims it at me, and fires.

CHAPTER FORTY-TWO

LEO

TUESDAY, JUNE 13

I was frozen in Michael's rattlesnake eyes. They searched me end-lessly as though he was hoping I'd spill buckets of tears from which he could slake his thirst.

"Leoneli," he murmured, leaning down to kiss my neck, my collarbone. I seized up, terrified he'd bite me, and he reacted hun-grily to my fear. He must have been able to smell it. He pressed into me, belt buckle and crotch rubbing my leg, jeans rough, the stupid flimsy nightgown riding up.

Get into the driver's seat, Summer would say. *Control his attention.*

How? I cried frantically at the imaginary Summer who wasn't there, who would never be there again.

And then I knew.

The belt.

Where terror had taken hold, rage bloomed, a volcanic flower. This man had stolen my sister, had used her like a tissue to cry into, and had thrown her away, petulantly angry that she'd wanted to leave early.

I whispered, "Michael," and pulled his face toward me, kissing him on the lips. He kissed me back, a little rough, not in complete control. I stayed timid, girlish, making little moaning noises like I was afraid of the things he was making me feel. His hands roamed my hips, my back, tangled in my hair, and I let mine run down his arms, which reminded me how much stronger than me he was, a terrifying truth in this moment. At last, my heart thundering with nerves, I moved them to his belt, where I quickly explored the buckle with fingertips accustomed to thievery. It had a simple, rectangular frame and a single prong.

I unbuckled it, squeaking with undisguised anxiety when this heated him up, drawing groans and thrusts. I pressed into him, making sure he was distracted by the way our bodies rubbed against each other, and I slid the belt free. I did it in a single gliding motion while his hands moved onto my breasts, his lips back onto mine. My breath was coming fast now, but that was fine. He would want it that way, and symptoms of fear were a fair substitute for lust.

The belt slid through my hands behind his back, tight in my fists.

Control the attention, Summer reminded me.

I let him push the nightgown down, exposing my breasts, and as he made voracious, lustful noises and buried his face in my chest, I lightning-fast slid the belt around his neck and pulled it tight.

He roared, bucking off me. I clung fast as he reared onto his knees and tried to get his hands under the belt. Unmasked fury lit his face like fire. "Bitch," he sputtered, and my hand faltered, sliding down the leather strap, giving him enough air to hiss out a series of curses. He punched me in the diaphragm, but I'd followed him up and was on my knees in front of him, clinging to the belt, and there wasn't enough distance between us for him to get much power into the punch. Still, I found myself grunting, panicked, the wind knocked out of me. He grabbed at my hair, pulled, yanking some out from the roots. Pain flared and burned, and I cried out, but I clung to the belt.

He got his hands under the belt. It was no good. He was going to get it off. I needed only ten or twenty seconds of cutting off oxygen to his brain for him to go unconscious. I'd have to use the belt buckle as leverage to get it tight enough, but I couldn't thread it through while grappling with him like this. He was going to get one good punch in, and I'd be done.

Summer's instructions through the panic: *Control his attention. Be unexpected.*

He lunged forward, hands on my throat, wanting to out-choke me. His nails raked my skin, lips flared in a snarl. I rolled, releasing one hand from the belt, and he fell forward onto his face. How long had passed? Five seconds? It felt like hours.

The instant he fell, I was moving to regain control of the belt, and then I was behind him, grabbing the lost end of the leather.

I had one second while he got his hands and knees underneath him. *It's enough,* Summer would say. *It takes only a second to pick a pocket.*

I put the end of the leather through the open square frame of the buckle and cinched it tight. It dug into his throat. I got a knee between his shoulder blades and yanked with all my strength.

He made a wet, choking noise and thrashed wildly, but I had all my weight digging into his neck, into the space between his shoulders, all my strength in the belt, pulling it so tight, I thought it might rip his head off. He sagged, fighting clumsily with fists on the rumpled comforter, and then he went still.

He was unconscious.

I remembered what I'd done in the painting cabin, feigning a blackout and slumping to the floor. I clung on another ten seconds, taut, vibrating with terror.

He had to be out now.

I held on to the belt with one numb hand. With the other, clumsy and shaking, I checked his pockets and found the key card.

I got up and covered my breasts with the nightgown. I turned and faced the portraits, my breathing hard and fast.

How dare he paint Amanda and me in these stupid fucking

dresses? Who did he think he was? Our images were not his to possess. A piece of her soul was not going to be stuck in this cursed painting. Over my dead body.

I picked up the paintings and threw them onto the bed beside Michael's limp form. I felt my face set into grim, hateful lines. He'd think I was ugly if he could see me now.

I stooped, got one of the tea lights, and carried it to the bed with maximum caution, cupping a hand around the flame.

"You can burn in hell," I whispered.

I squatted by the corner of the bedspread and aimed the flame at the cloth. It caught quickly, a sharp orange lick of fire flickering to life and spreading like delicate lightning.

CHAPTER FORTY-THREE

SUMMER

TUESDAY, JUNE 13

I flinch away from the gun, throwing myself off the gravel path, instinct from a lifetime of tight corners saving me. Javier roars in frustration as the bullet cuts through the earth. He recalibrates and aims again, door propped open against his shoulder.

Mind racing—trapped—ears ringing—I hold a hand out to him, a supplicating gesture. "Javier, wait. There's something you need to know. We're all in danger." It's bullshit. I'm making it up as I go along.

He frowns, gun aimed straight at me. "What?"

I'm grasping for straws. "It's Julie. She's called the police. They're on their way."

He looks confused. "Julie? How?"

"She has a cell phone, one that actually works on the island. It looked like—" I scramble for the memory of Alan's phone. "It was like a chunkier Android. She said she stole it from Alan. She told the cops there are murders happening here, that they should send the FBI. They're on their way. I heard them say it; I heard the whole phone call."

I watch him calculate. He's wondering what the odds are that I'm telling the truth, and if so, whether he should continue with this shooting-Summer plan. I lift my hands in a gesture of sur-render, the Bic pen tucked behind my palm, out of sight, and get slowly to my feet. "I can show you where she is," I tell him, pointing around the side of the building. My voice quivers as I throw lie after lie into the mix. "She's around the corner, she has a golf cart, that's how I got back in. She told the cops to meet her at the research facility. I guess she thinks there's a helipad over here. They should be here fast. They have the LAPD helicopter. They told her half an hour max, and that was at least twenty min-utes ago."

Visible through the open door behind him, a figure steps into the hallway, slim, barefoot, a gauzy white nightgown shimmering around her. Her collar-length brown hair is tangled, huge eyes fixed on the back of Javier's head. The expression on her face is wild and furious, like she's here from the afterlife to seek ven-geance.

Leo.

In a paralyzed moment that seems to last several minutes, I'm certain it's her ghost. The filmy white cloth, the bed head—I can't understand. But then she spots me. Our eyes lock, and she jolts with shock, a hand clapping to her mouth, and I see the life in her. This is Leo, and she is *alive*.

I tear my eyes from her and return them to Javier. "I'll show you where Julie is parked. You can ask her yourself."

Behind Javier, Leo darts to the nearest door. She lifts a small object—a key card—to the panel beside it, and the door clicks. She presses in, and the door swings shut behind her.

Javier spins, searching for the source of the noise. "Who's there?" He turns to face me, gun aimed at my face. "Get inside. Come here. I'll kill you if you try to run."

I make a show of reluctance—as though I have any intention of staying outside when Leo's in this building—and take tiny steps toward him. He frowns at my outfit. "Where did you get those clothes?"

"Julie gave them to me." It reaffirms the story I told him.

He scowls. "I told Michael not to trust her."

"She is very untrustworthy," I agree with no irony at all.

He pulls me into the air-conditioned, white-walled corridor, gun digging in my back, and holds me in front of him as he advances slowly down the hallway. "Hello?" he calls.

A door clicks behind us, and he spins, gun following. It's all I'm going to get. I grip the pen in my palm, whip around, and stab it into the side of his neck.

A small trickle of blood runs into his collar—the pen is nowhere near sharp enough. He cries out and thrashes with his gun hand, shooting off a useless round into the wall and dislodging the pen from his neck, sending it flying. Arms and legs flail, and I'm inside his grip, trying to wrestle the gun out of his hand. He curses, punching my back. I focus my energy on the gun hand, getting my fingers into his fist. He tries to spin away, loses his balance, and we go crashing to the ground, him on top.

A bare foot stomps his hand, grinding the knuckles into the hard floor. He shrieks in pain and the gun clatters away. He grabs me by the throat, uses me to pull himself up. Pain shoots through my windpipe, and the look he gives me is free of all his usual calm. He's feral, muscles in his neck bulging where his blood stains his shirt red in a spreading semicircle. He straightens into a standing position, ready to confront the person who'd trampled him.

He faces Leo, who stands with legs spread in a practiced shooting stance, Javier's gun in both hands. Her hair is tangled, spaghetti-strapped nightgown falling off one bony shoulder, and her eyes burn with rage and cold hate. She squeezes off two shots, and I remember in a flash that her father was a proud gun owner. She'd gone shooting with him since she was a kid. The bullets take Javier in the chest, and he jolts back, then topples to the floor.

Behind her, from the stairwell she'd come from, smoke drifts in.

"Shit. Leo." I point, almost unable to get words out. "Fire."

"I know. I set it."

Javier makes a spluttering sound and reaches up for her, hands like claws. She glances down at him, face pitiless, and fires once more. He goes still.

I close the distance between us and pull her into a hug. She wraps her arms around me, and we stay there for five long seconds, just breathing. The feel of her ribs expanding to make room for air, the life within her, is a miracle. After so much searching, so much grief, this moment feels eternal. When I pull back, I'm crying, and so is she.

"What are you doing here?" she asks. "How did you get onto the island?"

"I followed you. I got one of Michael's friends to invite me."

"Oh my god, Summer." She wipes her eyes with a shaking hand. "How did you know I'd be here?"

I shake my head. "Later. Where's Michael? Do you know?"

"Upstairs. Dead." She swallows, grimacing like she's fighting nausea.

Something bangs upstairs and a new plume of smoke, thick and black, blooms into the hall. "Outside," I command. "Gotta go."

"We can steal a boat to get home," she says. "I saw some on the water by the facility."

"I was thinking the same thing." It feels amazing to be reunited, to be thinking with two brains instead of one.

Hand in hand, we hurry toward the glass door, passing the door that led to my cell and another across the hall.

The second door flies open, and a man steps into the hallway. He's burned, shirt blackened, hair singed along the left side of his scalp. His face is red, blue eyes blood-veined and ferocious with rage. At his side, he clutches a leather belt like a whip.

"You—little—bitch," he says, stepping toward us, eyes on Leo like I'm not even here. "You burned my paintings. They're ruined. You worthless *whore*."

She raises the gun and holds her ground, aiming for his heart. She says nothing, but the set of her jaw and the gleam in her eyes would be a terrifying sight to confront across a loaded gun. She pulls the trigger, and the gun clicks. It's empty.

"Shit," she whispers.

His burned face twists into a smirk. "That's the universe. She says you're mine. My next open door."

He storms forward and grabs her, lightning-fast. She cries out as he slams her up against the wall, smoke curling around them, a scene from hell. His hands on her throat, he squeezes, letting out a moan.

Absolutely not. I pick up the gun, grip it by the barrel, reel back, and hammer it on the back of his skull with all my strength. He cries out, stumbles, and I hit him again before he can recover.

Coughing, Leo snatches the belt from his hand, wraps it around his neck from behind, and yanks it tight. He yelps and chokes on the cry. I hurry to help her, holding the belt with her, doubling her grip strength. He falls to his knees, and she gets a foot between his shoulder blades, pressing him forward while pulling the leather back. I get a foot on him, too, and help her pull.

His neck snaps, head lolling in an unnatural direction. We release him, and he topples to the ground, where he rests motionless on his stomach.

Something crashes on the floor above us, and a new cloud of smoke pours into the corridor.

"Come on," I say, grabbing her hand, and we flee, out the glass door into the afternoon light.

CHAPTER FORTY-FOUR

LEO

TUESDAY, JUNE 13

The small boat rocked, barely a match for the darkening waves. Ahead, a fuzzy black line at the horizon was the California coast. We had no idea where in Southern California we would end up, but as long as we hit the mainland, that would be good enough for us.

I turned to look back. The island was disappearing, swallowed up by the Pacific as the sun sank all the way into the west and the earth turned away from us, but a pillar of smoke wound its way up, up, up, into the distant clouds, marking the island's spot.

This was a humble research vessel, nothing as powerful as the small speedboat Michael had let me drive, but I controlled it easily. I'd been in boats many times before. So had Summer. She sat at my side, cheeks drawn from dehydration, tangled hair windborne. Her face carried a grim expression full of dark emotion, one I hadn't seen before. I wondered if I looked different, too.

Sensing my attention, she met my eyes and put a hand over mine. Even her skin felt dry. I flipped mine palm-up and squeezed it, gratitude welling up inside me. Of all the doors I'd ever walked through, deciding to do life with her was by far my best choice.

"What is it?" she asked.

"I can't believe you followed me to the island, that you . . ." I choked up and couldn't finish the sentence.

She squeezed my hand harder. "We're a team. I'll never leave you behind." She hesitated. "I have to ask. Your sister. I heard from the police that she . . . She didn't really die in a car accident, did she?"

I shook my head, unable to meet her eyes. "She was murdered. By Michael, it turns out." Even now, after all the emotional exhaustion of the last day, tears sprang to my eyes, and I burned with shame remembering my last phone call with Amanda.

"By *Michael*?"

I took a shuddering breath and nodded. "He showed me her painting. That yellow dress. We always wondered why she was found in it."

Summer sat straight up. "That was *Amanda*? I saw that painting. I thought it was you."

I felt the sad smile claim my features. "We looked a lot alike. My mom used to dress us up as twins. But when people got to know us, they said our personalities were so different, we stopped looking alike after a while."

"How can it be that Michael killed her and then you met up with him a decade later?"

My mouth bent into a grim shape. "He wanted to collect the pair. All those years."

"Jesus." She let out a breath, and I felt like she clutched my hand with desperation now, taking comfort instead of giving it. "Why didn't you ever tell me she'd been murdered?" she asked. "I tell you everything. Why lie about that?"

I closed my eyes briefly. When I reopened them, the horizon was blurry. "What happened to her was my fault. I was . . . hiding from it. When I left home, I slammed that door shut. I couldn't open it again."

She smacked my hand. "Hey. Look at me." I obeyed, meeting

her brown eyes with my own. "It *wasn't* your fault." She said it firmly. "Michael killed her. No one else."

"I'm sorry I kept it from you," I managed, though my throat felt like it was closing. "I guess that's me. When the truth is too hard, I just run away."

Summer was decisive now. "She was your big sister. There's no right way to handle that. You did what you had to do to survive the loss."

And then I really remembered Amanda. For once, I let that door swing wide open, and I imagined she was sitting here between us. Her long brown hair would have floated around her in the wind. Her skin would have glowed in the orange sunset light. She'd loved boats and had constantly wanted to explore different lakes and rivers. Anything outdoors was her jam: camping, hiking, paddle boarding, rafting, archery. We had that in common. We were different, but we loved the same things, including each other.

I couldn't run from Amanda, no matter how hard I tried. I'd been wrong to think I could lock her behind a door. She was everywhere. She was the world and everything in it.

"I'll miss her every day for the rest of my life," I heard myself say.

"You will," Summer agreed, wrapping her arm around me. We leaned our heads together and watched the dark shoreline approach.

"I still can't believe you followed me to that fucking island," I said, unable to express my gratitude. "What were you thinking?"

She choked out a laugh. "Couldn't let you have all the fun." We were silent awhile, and then she added, "I was feeling insecure. I thought you were leaving me. I thought this was you telling me you were tired of, you know, the Land Cruiser, California . . . you wanted more."

I looked at her in surprise. Summer feeling insecure—it wasn't something I ever expected, not really. She seemed so certain of who she was and her place in the world. "I lost one sister, and the universe gave me another." I held her hand, and we sat like that, heavy with loss, and with gratitude.

A wave knocked the boat sideways, and a spray of salt water drew a shriek out of us. The sound was gleeful, reminiscent of summer days and free, open-air nights. Michael's hungry lips, devouring me, and his sterile, white-walled rooms were separated from us by the freezing weight of the Pacific. And yet they echoed, all the terror tattooed invisibly inside my skin.

CHAPTER FORTY-FIVE

SUMMER

YOSEMITE
THURSDAY, JUNE 22

Gently, so as not to send smoke billowing into my face, I set a fresh log on the fire. It accepts the wood with liquid-hot arms, and the flames grow higher, brighter. Sitting back on my heels, I watch a flurry of sparks float up into the night sky. The smell of smoke saturates my hair, my sweatshirt, my skin, and it's nice to be a little bit feral again. Campfire is the smell of my childhood and of countless nights with Leo.

"Feels so good," Leo says. She's tucked into a camp chair and wrapped in a blanket, a book and reading light in hand. She's not just talking about the warmth of the fire, a welcome thing in the mountains even when the days are hot. She means the freedom.

"I was thinking the same thing." I pull my chair beside hers and tuck my hands into the pockets of my hoodie. We're at the northern end of Yosemite, and this campground is a little more private than a lot of the more popular ones that are easier to access. Still, it's tourist season, and we're just two out of a million campers. Our nearest neighbors are an overwhelmed couple with three children and a retired couple towing a trailer with their Ford F250. We've been here six nights, and so far no one's paid us any mind.

Still. I worry.

I get my phone out, search for "Michael Forrester," set the criteria for "last 24 hours," and sift through articles. All the new articles contain regurgitated information about his death—so far considered accidental, in a fire at his research facility—and speculation about his estate and the future of the Tenet Holdings corporation, of which he was the founder and CEO. This is expounded upon in tech publications and blogs, where I've learned over the last few days that the board has been in closed meetings, no doubt figuring out their next steps.

"What are you looking at?" Leo asks. I look up from the screen and find her watching me with curiosity. "I can feel your stress," she explains.

"I'm fine." I force a smile. "Want to play cards?"

"You don't have to do that."

"Do what?"

She closes her book. "I'm okay. Really. I'm ready to crawl out of my hole a little bit."

She barely spoke, slept, or ate the first three days after the island. She's fully traumatized from her time with Michael, waking up screaming in the night, unable to be in confined spaces for more than an hour or two at a time. I've been keeping all my worries to myself, focusing on her recovery.

I smile at her, grateful that she's alive and here with me pouring into my chest. "No need to rush it. I'm glad you're starting to feel a little more human, but you can take all the time you need. We're off-grid. We're safe."

She puts a cool, soft hand on my arm. "I appreciate you taking care of me. You're the best. I just needed some time. *Need* some time. I know I'm not all the way . . . I don't want to say 'better.' I don't think I'll ever be 'better.' I haven't been 'better' since before Amanda died. But I'm here." She looks into the fire with haunted eyes that go sparkly orange with reflected light. It makes me shiver. "So tell me what you're stressing about."

I scoot my chair closer so I can lower my voice. "I keep checking the news. Waiting for the story that says they're looking for
two women who were with Michael on the island the day he
died."

She shudders and gets up, hurrying off toward the Land Cruiser.
I think I've gone too far and sent her into a trauma spiral, but she
grabs a bottle of red wine and two glasses from the food drawer
and returns to me. I accept a glass appreciatively as she sinks into
her chair; this is the first time she's been the one to get us something to eat or drink since we've been here. She offers me part of
her blanket, and we drape it over our laps, feet propped on the
rocks surrounding the firepit. The wine is delicious, dark and rich.
I've noticed certain things taste better after escaping the island.

Leo takes a sip and sighs, the sound contented. "Let's talk about
it. Go."

"You sure?" I search her face for confirmation.

"I'm sure."

I collect my thoughts. "All right. Here's what I keep thinking
about." I tick them off on my fingers. "Javier had my phone because staff members collected them all when I first arrived with
the other guests. I left my suitcase in my room. And I had your
phone and wallet in it with my stuff. That's physical evidence link-
ing us to the island. Who knows where they put those things?
Someone could run across them, especially if the cops do a real
search of the island. They have to be investigating it as a homicide;
Javier was shot to death. The news says it's looking like an accident, but the cops never release all the info about their investiga-
tions to the press, do they?"

She's nodding. "And how many people saw us there? All the
servants saw me, and you were seen by all the guests and staff there
over the weekend."

"So many people," I agree. "But as far as those I'm most worried about, it's Steve and Julie—and Alan. And what happened to
Ashley? If she's alive, she could also identify us." It hits me with a
pang of responsibility and guilt. I'd dragged Ashley into the mess.
If anything happened to her, it was my fault. I'd searched online,

but I could find nothing to match someone named Ashley on Michael's island.

Leo sips her wine and says, "Michael was going to kill us. So maybe he had Javier destroy all our stuff. Maybe nothing will ever get traced back to us."

"But what about Julie? I can't see a single reason she'd cover for us. Can you?"

"Maybe because she'd also be complicit," she guesses. "Then we'd tell people she drugged us, she was helping him."

"It'd be our word against hers. And who do you think they'd believe?"

"I just hate that he's being remembered this way. They're making him sound like this amazing philanthropist, this guy who saved lives fighting climate change. I can't stand it."

We return to gazing at the flames. They've died down a bit, and the light flickering over our legs is more orange than yellow.

"You don't have a name," Leo murmurs. "If they're going to link those deaths to one of us, it's going to be me. If that happens, I want you to let me go to jail. I don't want you to do anything stupid like turn yourself in. Nothing like that."

"Leo," I protest.

"No." She slashes a hand through the air. "I shot Javier. I killed Michael."

"You only shot Javier because of me," I argue. "And we both killed Michael."

"*I* killed him, and I'm glad to go to prison for that. He took Amanda's life, and I took his. If they nail me for that, I'll go public. I'll tell everyone what he did. Every single person will know what he was."

They won't, though, I argue silently. No two women can topple the reputation of a man like Michael. We could have photographic evidence of his crimes, and he'd still go down in history as a great humanitarian.

I put a hand on Leo's knee. She lays her palm on my knuckles, and we watch the fire as it sends sparks up to be extinguished by the dark. At least we're together. On the island, that was all I wanted. Now that we've escaped, I have a new desire: I want her to be free and stay free. We need to put distance between ourselves and what happened.

"Leo?" I ask, and she shakes herself to attention like she'd sunk so deep into thought, she'd forgotten I was here. Examining her deep brown eyes, trying to decipher the liquid sparks playing over her irises, I say, "What do you think about leaving California for a while?" Her eyebrows shoot up, and I shrug. "Could be smart. You know?"

She straightens, shoulders squaring, and her face tilts up to follow the sparks and their journey away from the fire that birthed them. "Away from California," she muses, and I know by the way she savors the words that the next chapter has already begun, the page flipping forward to a new and uncharted adventure.

CHAPTER FORTY-SIX

SUMMER

LAX
THREE MONTHS LATER

Leo points the phone at my face. "Summer is on her first flight ever!" She turns the phone so she's looking into the camera. "She's terrified. She won't tell you, but she is peeing her pants."

"I am not." I laugh, in control on the outside, scared as shit on the inside. We're tucked into our seats—I have the window—and people are weaving through the aisle beside us, chattering happily as they board. We're all fine with being hurtled through space inside this steel cylinder, apparently.

She points the phone at me again. "What does it feel like?"

I consider this. "It's small in here."

"And this is first class. You haven't even done regular people seats yet."

I tap a fingernail against the shade that covers the weird little oval window. "Everything is very plasticky." I examine the seat pouch in front of me. "What are all these pamphlets?"

She cackles. She's probably recording this for TikTok or whatever, on the #vanlife account she's grown to a million followers.

She's transitioned from sugar baby antics to influencer antics, and I can't say I hate it, though I don't love being perceived and recorded this much.

I flip through a trifold brochure. "Jesus," I say, scrutinizing a photo of someone taking the seat apart and turning it into a life raft. "How are we supposed to do all this while the plane is crashing into the ocean?" I shove the brochure back into the seat pocket. "Well, now I'm terrified."

"Okay, okay, I'll leave you alone." She stops the video. "But seriously. How does it feel? You're free. You have an identity. You're legit."

I pull my passport out of my purse and we look at it together. There's my picture, and there's my full name: Summer Hayes. It's still so weird to have a last name.

I am officially a person. While I agree with my mom that it's stupid that we need a document to prove our existence, the fact that I can buy things in my own name comes with overwhelming feelings of warmth and belonging. I'm real, as legitimate as anyone else. I was born somewhere, and when I die, they will be able to create a death certificate. I'm embarrassed by how much it means to me that I'll be allowed to be buried in a cemetery, that if I go missing, someone can report it to the cops.

With the guidance of an attorney, I'd submitted a DNA sample to two different ancestry databases. It had turned up some third cousins, and from following a chain of public records, we'd found my mother. Janelle Hayes, born to William and Esther Hayes in a suburb of Chicago. Her parents had died when she was in high school, and she'd run away, only surfacing in the public record twice since then. Once was in 1992 when she got a speeding ticket outside San Francisco. The second time was only seven years ago when she was pulled over for driving under the influence. She'd been in Seattle. So she's probably still around, off the grid but living her life. And perhaps the jar will shake someday, and we'll run into each other. Or maybe not.

In the months since the island, Leo and I have lived on pins and needles, waiting to be connected to the accidental death of Michael Forrester. But we never were, and the news of his tragic, untimely demise lasted only two news cycles. People all over the world mourned the loss to clean energy advocacy, and his estate passed to charity. Someone took over his company, and the world moved on.

Only one news story from a couple of weeks ago haunts me. I have it saved on my phone and return to it every few days. The headline reads, "Wife of Venture Capitalist Dies in Home Invasion." The article describes a late-night burglary of a Palo Alto mansion that cost a wealthy couple a considerable amount of valuables and ended with the wife, Julie Lodstrom, dying from a gunshot wound to the head. Her grieving husband, Steve Lodstrom, gave interviews to various newspapers about the rise of gang violence and the decline of society and civilization and whatever other talking points I can't make sense of.

I think about Julie a lot. I wonder if there's anything else I could have said to her. I should be angry with her, but I'm not. I'm sad for her.

"You good?" Leo asks, and she lets the in-public mask slip, revealing worried eyes and the seasoned, wary eyebrows that have become her new normal.

"I'm okay. Don't worry."

She nods, and the darkness passes like a shadow, leaving her bright again.

An older man in a gray suit approaches the seats in front of us. He removes his blazer and tosses it onto the seat. "Good afternoon, ladies. You taking a vacation? Looks like we're neighbors."

"We're doing a little traveling, yeah," Leo replies, adjusting her position so her legs are hidden under her purse. His eyes travel over her figure anyway, then mine. He gives me a wink and settles himself into his seat. Leo and I exchange a meaningful look.

I whisper, "Don't look at me."

She holds her hands up in protest. "I wasn't." I've set my thievery aside for the most part after legitimizing my identity, afraid of getting caught now that I have a real name to which the cops could attach my crimes. We've been living off Leo's sponsorships, getting comped accommodations as long as we make videos about them, and all kinds of other free stuff along the way, including this flight. Now we're going international for the first time, something Leo's been dreaming of as long as I've known her.

This is not how she pictured it, though. Between us, an unspoken reservoir ripples ominously. Nothing is as either of us had ever planned.

Relaxing back in the seat, she toys with her seatbelt. "There are seasons for things. Right now, it's time for adventure, expanding our reach, being visible." She turns her phone over and over between her fingertips.

The engines hum. Everyone is in their seat now. The flight attendant makes announcements, and I close my eyes and grip the armrests. "Oh god," I mutter.

The man in front of us turns in his seat, cranes his neck so he's looking at me, and grins at us. "You girls ready for takeoff?" Seeing me, he raises his eyebrows. "Uh-oh. A bit scared of flying, honey? Don't worry, you'll be fine. Safer than driving on the freeway."

I hate this man and want to relieve him of his credit cards, but I forget about him as we speed up. We're going to launch. It's happening.

And then we're off the ground. The moment registers in my stomach, a weightless lurch, and then the sudden increase in altitude goes to my head, where a balloon of air seems to be expanding, ready to pop.

"Remember," Leo tells me, having to speak up above the roar of wind. She makes a show of pinching her nostrils, and I remember I'm supposed to clear the pressure out of my ears. I do, and they pop, which gives me instant, blissful relief.

Below, LAX has disappeared. We're looping over the ocean, and the Pacific is a wide, huge blue sphere to the horizon—much like the view from the island.

"What do you think?" Leo asks, looking over my shoulder.

"It's amazing," I reply. We watch as the ocean is left behind, replaced by the desert, which blooms forever in an expanse of warmth. The plane is stabilizing, and the flight attendant announces we've reached cruising altitude. I ask Leo where the restroom is, and she points to a tiny door in the front. Getting up and over Leo reminds me of the balance required on a boat or a bus, and I hold on to the seat as I step into the aisle.

The bathroom is hilarious and ridiculous. Is this a joke? Can they really expect you to do your business this way? I've felt more comfortable peeing in the woods. I make it happen, though, poking at all the little icons until I get my hands washed.

Claustrophobia and panic well up inside me, prompted by the closeness of the space. It happens sometimes since the island. I take a minute and breathe, hands on the sink to steady myself. I'm not trapped. I'm here by choice. I look up into my own brown eyes in the mirror. Michael is dead and gone. Leo and I are together. We're safe.

Or rather, we're as safe as we can be given the circumstances. We'd unanimously agreed it was time to clear out of California for the foreseeable future, especially now given Julie's fate. Leo's obsession with social media goes beyond making us a living on sponsorships; she's making sure we're visible, that we can't easily disappear. She's building us an audience if we ever need to go public. It's insurance.

Back in the cabin, our annoying neighbor is turned around on his knees in his seat, chatting with Leo. She's being nice enough, but I can tell she's getting close to snapping. She's less patient with men like this since the island, and I can't say I blame her. My eyes do an analysis of him as I approach. The lump in his back pocket is his wallet. It's even sticking partway out. Behind his back, I make a hand gesture to Leo to indicate she should keep him talking. She flicks her eyes at me in surprise, but she obeys, brightening her smile and showing a little more leg.

In my signature move, I lift his wallet, remove some cash, and have it back in his pocket before he notices a thing.

Still got it.

I fold the cash into the comfortable little hollow between thumb and forefinger. "Hello there," I purr as I slide into my seat.

Leo is looking at me with lightbulb eyes. I wind my arm through hers and tell the man I'm sorry, but we actually do have a lot of work we need to get done on the plane.

He has work to do, too. He gets out his laptop, humming happily, probably thinking he's got fun times ahead of him with us. While his back is turned, I count the money I'd taken from his wallet. Three hundred twenty-four dollars. Not bad.

Leo grins at me. I extract a hundred-dollar bill from the pile and mouth the words "finder's fee" as I slide it into my bra strap. She dissolves into silent laughter and divides the rest of the cash between her purse and my carry-on bag.

We settle in and start to discuss our trip. Our destination is Athens, where we'll visit a boutique hotel that wants to pay us to post photos to our Instagram account. From Athens, we'll head to Italy, where Leo has a few friends we can stay with. We'll be there for a week or so, and then we're not sure.

It doesn't matter. Home is a person, not a place, and everything we need is here, no matter where we go.

ACKNOWLEDGMENTS

This was a rare project and one I'm so grateful to have had the opportunity to publish. Summer has lived rent-free in my head for years and has survived my attempts to put her into a few different stories. When I matched her up with Leo, I knew I had found her home. I hope readers enjoy spending time with these two women as much as I have. I will miss them constantly.

This book is a love letter to California, my beloved home. All my life, I have roamed its mountains and shores, and I could keep exploring it for another century without slaking my thirst. Please indulge me a moment to thank my parents, who individually inspired this love of my home state. From camping in Gaviota to hiking in Sequoia to endless hours spent exploring Golden Gate and Griffith parks, they each shared their restless love of adventure and are probably responsible for the setting of this book.

What a pleasure it has been to work with such an incredible team on this book. Jenny Chen, I have admired your work for years, and partnering with you is an absolute dream. You are kind and direct, brilliant and creative. Mae Martinez, thank you for all your invaluable feedback; what a privilege it has been to have both of your eagle eyes on this manuscript. To my super agent, Lauren Spieller, we did another book! I'm so proud and grateful to be on this journey with you. Thank you for all the work you have done and continue to do for my dark little stories.

My writer support system has kept me going through many long drafts of this book spanning different seasons of life. Layne Fargo and Halley Sutton, thank you for always bouncing ideas around with me. I don't know where I'd be without our plotting sessions. Mike Chen and Diana Urban, thank you so much for all the wisdom and friendship over the years. Aiden Thomas, thank you for being the best person to call with good news. There are too many valued writer buddies to name here, but let me say— thank you all, for your hilarious jokes, your spotless commentary, and your friendship. Just a few additional writer friends whose wisdom and kindness have kept me going through writing this book: J. T. Ellison, Amina Akhtar, Hannah Mary McKinnon, Kimberly Belle, Wanda Morris, Emily Carpenter, and Jennifer Hillier. Karma Brown, your kindness in connecting me with Adam, and his kindness in return, is something I will never forget. The writing community has been a gift; it's my theory that people who plunder their darkest imaginations in the name of art exorcise their demons in the process, making them some of the best friends you could ask for.

And to my family, thank you for tolerating this Wednesday Addams wannabe through another publishing cycle fraught with angst, distraction, erratic excitement, and rants about esoteric topics. I love you more than I can say.

ABOUT THE AUTHOR

WENDY HEARD is the author of suspense and thrillers for adults and teens, including *You Can Trust Me, The Kill Club, She's Too Pretty to Burn,* and *Dead End Girls.* Wendy has spent most of her life in Los Angeles, California, which is on fire more than she would honestly prefer, and can often be found haunting local hiking trails and bookstores. She loves all things vintage and has a collection of thrillers and adventure books from the '80s. You can hear more from Wendy through her newsletter.

www.wendyheard.com
Instagram and Twitter: @wendydheard

ABOUT THE TYPE

This book was set in Bembo, a typeface based on an old-style Roman face that was used for Cardinal Pietro Bembo's tract *De Aetna* in 1495. Bembo was cut by Francesco Griffo (1450–1518) in the early sixteenth century for Italian Renaissance printer and publisher Aldus Manutius (1449–1515). The Lanston Monotype Machine Company of Philadelphia brought the well-proportioned letterforms of Bembo to the United States in the 1930s.